Kaleidoscope Hearts

Claire Contreras

Kaleidoscope Hearts
Published by Claire Contreras, 2015

Cover Design by Okay Creations
Photographer: Perrywinkle Photographer
Formatting by: Champagne Formats
Edited by Tracey Buckalew

ISBN-13: 978-0986416705
ISBN-10: 0986416703

"and she always had a way
with her brokenness. She would take her pieces
and make them beautiful."

-R.M. Drake

Prologue

THE FIRST BOY I fell in love with used to regale me with stories about kings and queens and war and peace, and how he hoped to one day be somebody's knight in shining armor. I lived vicariously through his late night adventures, watching the way he swung his hands animatedly as he told his stories, and loving the way his green eyes twinkled when I laughed at his jokes.

He taught me what it feels like to be touched and thoroughly kissed. Later, he taught me the pain one feels at the loss of someone that you've grown attached to. The one thing he forgot to teach me was how to deal with the way my chest squeezed after he broke the ghost of what heart I had left. I'd always wondered if it had been a missed lesson. Now I wonder if maybe he'd been trying to figure it out for himself, or if he just never felt anything at all.

Chapter 1

THEY SAY THE best way to move on is to let go. As if letting go is the easy part. As if trying to dim or erase three years of memories, good and bad, is something you can do in one day. I know it's not, because in a couple of weeks, it will be one year, and the memory of him is as potent as if he was still here. His San Francisco Giants sandals are still in front of the sink, right where he left them. The smell of him lingers on some of his shirts—the ones I still haven't gotten around to wearing to bed. His presence is powerful even in his absence. As I walk around the house making sure everything is out of sight, I know that for me, this is a huge step in the letting go process.

I'm in the kitchen taping up the last of the boxes, when I hear the jingle of keys followed by heels on the hardwood. Another sound I'll miss, I'm sure, once I leave this place.

"Estelle?" she calls out in a soft melodic voice.

"Kitchen!" I wipe my hands over my jeans and make my way over to her.

"Hey. You got a lot done last night," she says, smiling sadly, her eyes glistening as she looks around the nearly empty space. She has the same wild curly hair and expressive caramel eyes her son had. Seeing her makes my heart hurt all over again. I shrug and bite the inside of my cheek so that I won't cry. Anything not to cry over this again, especially since I haven't in so long. When Felicia pulls me into her arms, I let out a slow breath and try not to completely lose it. I try to be strong for her and Phillip. Wyatt was their only child and, as hard as his loss is on me, I can only imagine the emptiness they must feel. We usually don't cry when we get together—not even when she comes over here—but selling this place is more than just saying goodbye to a house. It's leaving Christmas mornings and Thanksgiving dinners behind. It's saying, "Wyatt, we love you, but life goes on." And it does, which is one of the reasons I feel guilty. Life goes on, but why does it have to go on without him?

"It's going to be fine," I say, wiping my wet cheeks as I pull away from her.

"It is. It is. Wyatt wouldn't want us to break down over a house."

"No, he would definitely think we're dumb for mourning a structure," I say with a small laugh. If it were up to Wyatt, people would live in tents and bathe in rainwater.

"Yeah, and he would have cut the electricity on this place two months ago since you've been eating takeout anyway," she adds.

We shake our heads, new tears forming as the laughter dies and silence settles around us.

"Are you sure you don't want to stay with Phillip and me?" she asks, as we walk from room to room, making sure nothing is left out. The realtor is going to start showing the house tomorrow, and it needs to be perfect for potential buyers.

"No. Victor would be highly offended if I didn't take him up on his offer. He would probably start bringing up my not wanting to go to the same college as him, not liking the same football team, and the fact that I never paid up and did his laundry for a year that time in high school. I think that's why he's so eager to have me move in with him, actually."

3

Felicia's shoulders shake as she laughs. "Well, tell him I said hello, and invite him to dinner with us on Sunday. We'd love to have him over!"

"Sure," I say, my smile disappearing as I notice the sandals on the floor.

"You want me to take those, or do you want to keep them?"

"I . . ." I pause to take a shaky breath. "Will you take them?" I don't think I can bear to look at them every day in a new place. I'm already keeping all of Wyatt's t-shirts, and it's not like the sandals fit me—they're like five sizes too big for my feet—but they're his favorite. Were. They *were* his favorite. That's something my therapist had me work on—speaking of Wyatt in the past tense. Sometimes I cringe when I do it, but I've gotten better. For a while, I was living this false reality where Wyatt was away on a business trip or something. He loved to travel alone and let the different cultures inspire his paintings. After a month, I started accepting that he wasn't coming back. After three, at the request of my therapist, I started putting his things in boxes so that I wouldn't have the constant reminder.

Putting them away didn't do much. The house was a reminder, and our art studio couldn't be packed up either. It was something I had to learn to live with . . . being without him. After six months, I was able to walk in and out of both places without having my heart squeeze in my chest every time. And now, a year later, I think I'm ready to move on. If Wyatt's sudden death taught me anything, it was that life is short, and we need to live it to the fullest. It's something I understand, but still struggle to follow through with some days.

"Honey, everything he left behind is yours, you know that," Felicia says. I don't even realize that I'm still crying, until I taste the salt of tears on my lips. I try to thank her, but the words stay lodged in my throat under the boulder that's settled there.

After one last look around, we hug, and I promise to see her on Sunday. I glance over a shoulder as I walk to the car, letting my heart squeeze one last time before I get in and drive away. The memories . . . the comfort . . . the past . . . all become a distant picture in the rearview mirror as I head to my brother's house. I'm running through a mental checklist of things I have to do, when a ringing phone cuts into my thoughts.

"Hey, how'd it go?" Mia asks in greeting.

"It was okay. A little sad, but not terrible."

"Sorry I couldn't be there. Did Felicia come to pick up some of his things? How is she doing these days?"

"Good. She looks good."

"Are we still going out tomorrow night?" Mia asks slowly, treading water.

"As long as we stick to one bar, I'll go. I'm not in the mood for bar hopping and doing the college girl thing you like to do."

Mia never shed her wild side persona when we graduated and started living our "grown-up lives." As much as I love hanging out with her, replenishing my liver with an insane amount of water after drowning it in alcohol the night before isn't something I can do every week, like she does.

"Okay, no bar hopping. I have a brunch date on Saturday morning anyway and can't afford to look like crap, so we'll take it easy."

"A date?" I ask with a frown, as I pull into my brother's driveway.

"Blind date. His name is Todd. He's a curator at The Pelican. Maria seems to think we'd be perrrfect together," she says, rolling her R's exaggeratedly to imitate her Italian author friend.

"Hmm . . . I don't think I've heard of a Todd," I say.

Mia and I have known each other for as long as I can remember. Our mothers were best friends growing up and later, married men who were also best friends. Much to our mothers' dismay, we realized early on that history wouldn't repeat itself when Mia kept going for the bad boys, while I stuck to the quiet types.

"Damn. I was hoping you had. Don't you know everybody in the art world? Todd Stern?" she says, a hopeful note on her voice.

I laugh because it's not far from the truth. Wyatt and I opened up Paint it Back—a gallery-slash-art studio—a couple of years ago, and between our artist and gallery owner friends, and Mia's connections in the photography world, we pretty much did know everybody. Well, obviously not everybody.

"Nope. Rob doesn't know him?"

"I'm not going to ask him! You know my brother has a big mouth. He'll go and tell my mom, and they'll start planning a wedding over a guy I haven't even seen yet."

I laugh, knowing she's right. "Well, I've never heard of the guy."

"Maria said he just moved here from San Fran, so I figured you would know him. New guy in town and all that jazz."

"This isn't really like high school, Mia."

"Actually, it's exactly like high school, which leads me to believe that if we haven't heard anything about him thus far, he's probably ugly."

"You're probably right," I agree with a laugh.

"Shit. Stefano is here for his shoot. Let me know if you need me to come by Vic's later. Love you!"

She hangs up in the midst of my goodbye, so I put my phone away and switch off the ignition. I do a quick face check in the rearview mirror to make sure my mascara is still intact and run a couple fingers through my wavy brown hair, picking it up into a quick ponytail. The only sound, as I walk up to the house with the last of my clothes in the bag in my hand, is that of the gravel crunching below my flats, and the waves from the beach just steps away.

Anticipation buzzes through me as I crouch down and flip the welcome mat to get the spare key out and open the door. I call out my brother's name as I walk through the door and past the living room, assuming that his car is parked in the garage. I get no response. I head upstairs toward the spare rooms. His master bedroom is downstairs, which is convenient for a twenty-eight-year-old single male, since the kitchen and living room (complete with a ginormous television) are only a few feet away from his door. When I step into the room, I'm taken aback by what I see. Not only did he make my bed with the new sheets I bought and left here the other day, but he also painted my room a soft shade of gray that I love.

I leave my bag on the bed and head to the balcony right outside the room. The balconies are one of my favorite features of this house, and what I went crazy over when he was thinking of buying it. There's one in each upstairs bedroom, and they both face the beach behind the house. As I'm stepping out onto the balcony, the phone chimes with a text message from Vic, telling me he'll be here in a couple of minutes. As I'm responding, I walk into the back of an easel that wasn't there when I last visited. Walking around it, I read the huge letters in Vic's handwriting that say: "Welcome Home, Chicken" and below, a drawing of a chicken that only a five-year-old would be proud of. I erupt in laughter and snap a picture of it, sending it to Mia and my mom, since they're the only ones who would get it. My brother started calling me that when I was five and afraid of the dark—like most five-year-olds are—and for some reason, the name stuck. Probably because every time he called me that growing up, it was in the form of a challenge he knew I wouldn't back down from.

I turn the page of the large sketchbook and leave it on a blank page before turning my attention to the ocean. My eyes take in the different shades of blues that twinkle in the sunlight—the cerulean, aqua, and midnight blue. It's a view that can't be ignored. It's one that reminds me of how small I am in the grand scheme of things. How small we all are. I'm not sure how long I stand there, just staring. Just breathing. Just enjoying the taste of salt on my tongue that I seem to get from the smell alone. A hand lands on my shoulder and I jump, snapping me out of my meditation.

"Holy crap, Victor!" I say, pressing both hands to my heart.

"You like your present?" he asks with a laugh as he pulls me into a hug.

"Yeah, you asshole," I say, smiling as I slap his chest playfully.

"Asshole? I get you the best present ever, and you call me an asshole? It was the terrible drawing of the chicken, wasn't it?"

"You know I hate that nickname." I groan and step into the house, trailing behind him as he walks downstairs. "Where's the food? I'm starving."

"It should be here soon. Let me go change," he says. "I have to go back to work soon."

"You're going back?"

"The case I'm working on is a fucking mess. The guy's wife is trying to take everything he has in the divorce. I don't know when these athletes will learn that they need a goddamn prenup."

"Oh," I cringe slightly. It's something Wyatt and I discussed when we got engaged—and had a huge disagreement over—every time it was brought up. You would never think an artist would care about that, but Wyatt was successful and wealthy. By the time he turned thirty-three, he'd been selling to a very wealthy group of people for years. That same group of people talked him into thinking that marriage without a pre-nup was grounds for a messy separation.

A knock on the door has me pivoting on my heel. I'm in a daze as I walk over to answer it, thinking, in hindsight, about how stupid the disagreement had been. We weren't even married when Wyatt died, and his parents insist on me keeping everything. They're older—much older than my parents will be when I reach Wyatt's age of death—and they're wealthy in their own right. The way they see it, they're not going to do anything with that money, and it rightfully belongs to me since I was half-owner of Paint it Back when he died. But alas, that's in the past. I don't want to think about it more than I already have—this is my fresh start.

The thought brings a smile to my face, which stays put as I swing the door open, quickly transforming into a full gape at the man standing there in a pair of green scrubs and a white doctor's coat. He's looking down, trying to wipe scum off his sneakers, his sandy brown hair covering most of his face. I can only make out his strong jaw and the bottom half of his full lips, but I recognize him immediately. When he finally looks up, his green eyes soak me in as they travel up my body until they reach my own. He smiles that slow, uneven grin that always made my breath fall short.

"Bean," I whisper, making his lips twist even higher, revealing twin dimples.

"Hey, Elle," he says. I clutch the doorknob a little tighter. I haven't seen him for so long, I'd forgotten the sound of his voice. "Food's here."

My eyes drop to the bags in his hands, and I step backward, opening the door a little wider. "Oh! Yeah. I wasn't expecting you."

"It's been a while," he says, stopping in front of me as he comes in. I back up to the door and stop breathing completely when he dips his face into mine and lets his lips brush lightly against my cheek. I do everything in my power not to breathe in the familiar scent of him that used to make my head swim. "It's good to see you again," he says, as he pulls away. The way he says it and the twinkle in his eyes make my heart drop to my stomach. How is it possible that he still manages to do that to me? Even after Wyatt. I hate him for it.

"It's good to see you too," I whisper and follow behind him after closing the door.

It is so *not* good to see him, though. Over the years, I've learned a lot about Oliver Hart, but the only one worth remembering, is that he's bad for my health.

Chapter 2

"**YOU LOOK FAB**," Mia says when I step into view at the bar she picked for our weekly happy hour. "As do you, my lady," I reply with a small bow that makes her snicker. She's wearing a Victorian-style dress with a bustier that makes her boobs look like they're going to pop out the top. Her long, blonde hair is curled loosely and pulled back in two sections at the front.

"You're silly. I talked my parents and Rob into a family Halloween shoot so that I can showcase them around the studio next month, and I didn't have time to change before coming over here." She turns to the waitress. "Two lemon drops, please."

"What in the world are you dressed up as? Queen Victoria?" I ask, looking under the table to see what the rest of her outfit looks like. When I straighten again, she's looking at me like I'm crazy, and I realize she has no idea who Queen Victoria is.

"No! I'm Cersei Lannister."

"Ooohhh . . ." I say, taking a sip of the drink the waitress places in front of me.

"Rob dressed as Jamie."

"What?" I ask, sputtering half of the gulp back into my cup.

The bubbled laughter that escapes her lips soon turns into full hysteria. "I swear," she says, gasping for air. "You should have seen my mom's face!"

Robert is Mia's brother. Twin brother. And . . . clearly, neither are normal.

"You guys are sick. What did they say?" I ask, laughing with her.

"Mom doesn't know what the hell Game of Thrones is. Dad was horrified when he figured it out. He didn't want my mom to send out the Halloween cards she said she was going to make, but it was the first time we'd taken Halloween pictures since Rob and I were, like, eight. Anyway, she dressed up as Mary Poppins and Dad was Bert."

"Aww that's cute . . . you two are so, so weird though," I mutter. "Tell me about this Todd guy. Did you find out anything?"

"His last name is Stern—"

"He sounds like a lawyer or something," I interrupt.

Mia rolls her eyes. "He's an accountant."

"I thought he was a curator?"

"I don't know what Maria was thinking. I swear, sometimes I think it's a language barrier thing."

"What is?" I ask, trying not to laugh.

"This is the fifth guy she's tried to set me up with, and he's a freaking accountant! Do I look like I would date an accountant?"

"Well, no, but you don't have the greatest taste in guys, so maybe this is a good thing."

"Anywayyyyy," she says, dragging it out before finishing off her drink and signaling for two more. "How was your first night at Vic's?"

I let out a long sigh . . . my first night at Vic's. Heartbreaking, lonely, weird, sad, happy, weird . . .

"It was fine." I shrug.

Mia places her hand over mine to stop me from drawing lines of water on the table, beckoning my attention. "It's okay to not be okay, Elle."

"I am okay, though," I answer with a frown.

"You don't need to be strong for every single person, you know? You're allowed to break down. The love of your life died, you're in the process of selling your house together, and you moved in with your brother. It's a lot to take in. It's okay to not be okay. It's okay to take a break from work if you need it."

"It's been a year. And I already took a break from work," I remind her. After Wyatt died, I took two months off work, but that meant being home all the time. I even went to live with my parents for a couple of weeks to get away from the house. I couldn't take the memories and being there without him, but you can't turn your back on your struggles and expect them to disappear on their own. It just doesn't happen. So, I went home and dealt with the fact that he wasn't coming back. I went to see a therapist and got to a good place, but not staying in the house any more feels like . . . it's really over.

"Sometimes I feel like a bitch for selling the house," I say, finally. "I feel like I'm erasing him from my life or something."

Mia squeezes my hand. "Oh, honey, nobody thinks you're trying to do that. You need to move on. You're young, you're smart, you're talented as hell, and you're fun. You can't stop living because of a ghost."

My eyes cut to hers. "I haven't stopped living. I just don't want to move on like that. If I find someone, I find someone—if I don't, I don't." Mia has tried to set me up on two blind dates in the past couple of months. Even Felicia tried to talk me into going on one, but I wasn't ready. I still don't think I am, despite what everybody thinks. Even my own mom is driving me up the wall about the dating thing, as if some man is going to magically take the pain away.

"Elle . . ."

"I'm just saying that I don't care to date right now. Besides, I don't need a guy. I love being alone."

"Elle . . ."

"I'm serious, I do. And now I come to Vic's house thinking that this is going to be like summer camp or something, and freaking Oliver comes over my first fifteen minutes there, so really it's exactly like—"

"You saw Oliver?" Mia shouts, effectively shutting me (and a couple of people around us) up.

I nod, taking a sip of my drink.

"What happened? Oh. My. God. What happened when he saw you there? Did he know you would be there? Did you know he was here? Victor didn't even warn you? Holy shit!" Mia says, practically squealing.

"This is why I didn't want to bring it up."

She shoots me a look. "Spill. Right now. I want to hear every single detail of what happened. Is he still hot as fuck?"

"What do you think?" I say, letting out a short laugh.

"I think he's aging like fine wine. Does he still have the long hair? His hair was so hot," she says, fanning herself with her hand.

"His hair was so hot? Yeah, it's still long. Not as long, but long enough," I say before I realize the way that sounds—not because of the actual words—but because of mental images of me threading my fingers through it.

"Well, the whole package was hot. What was it like though—seeing him again?" she asks.

"For him, I guess like old times. For me, I don't know. It was . . ."

"Like old times pre-Oliver or post-Oliver?" she asks in another interruption.

"Easy on the questions, Columbo."

"You can't tell me something like that and then hold back. Just humor me!" Mia whines.

"Fine. Seeing him was . . . uncomfortable. I felt like I was

13

being ambushed, even though he was just standing there with food in his hands. He brought sandwiches and sushi."

Mia searches my face. "So he knew you'd be there."

I shrug. Obviously, he knew I'd be there if he brought enough food for me to sit and eat with them, but I don't know how far in advance he knew I'd be there. It's not like sushi is difficult to find in Santa Barbara, but still. Victor and Oliver don't really care for sushi. It's my favorite food. I can eat it all the time and anytime.

"I didn't question it," I tell her quietly. "We didn't really talk about much other than his residency and my sculptures."

"He asked about the hearts?" Mia asks in a whisper.

I nod.

"Did you tell him why you make them?"

"Of course not," I say, scoffing. "I'm not that brave."

We share a small, pathetic, commiserative smile before she drops the subject. "So, what are you up to this weekend?"

I start telling her what the rest of my weekend looks like, and we ease into a conversation about that instead. Anything to get away from the topic of Oliver Hart.

Chapter 3

I START PACING the studio, placing blank canvases on each easel, as I make my way around the room. Saturday night is Ladies Night here, and tonight I have a group of bachelorettes coming over as the first stop of their party. The maid of honor already came by earlier with wine she'd wanted me to chill for them, and a CD of music she wants to play. Aside from doing a presentation in the beginning of the party, I don't get involved with anything. They usually pay to have fun and talk shit with their friends. The last thing they want is for me to tell them what strokes to use on their creative masterpieces.

At seven o'clock, I go to the bathroom and check my make-up. I feel good. I'm wearing a red shirt with black bows on the sleeves, black pumps and ripped skinny jeans that I couldn't even dream of fitting my ass into this time last year. At the sound of footsteps, I pull myself away from the mirror and into the open space, walking toward the front of the gallery with a smile on my face, as I make ready to meet and greet. I stop dead in my tracks when I find Oliver standing in the room, looking at one of Wyatt's paintings.

He's not in his scrubs today, so I guess he has the day off. He's wearing jeans that hug his narrow hips perfectly and a blue button-down shirt. He's thrown on a charcoal gray suit jacket over it, and he looks totally GQ, as Mia would say. I guess he's on his way to the group date Vic mentioned. He'd said they were going to a sports bar tonight, which for them is code for: We're taking out the girls we're currently fucking so they don't accuse us of only wanting sex, and, let's do this as a group at a sports bar so they know we're not serious.

"Hey. What are you doing here?"

Oliver gives me a onceover when he turns to face me. "You look better every time I see you. How is that possible?"

I don't let myself react the way I know he wants me to. Instead, I focus on the painting he's looking at. The one with the dark eye with butterfly wings for eyelashes. The one that watches the way Oliver is looking at me, and eavesdropping while he flirts.

"I was in the area and wanted to stop by to see the place. I hope that's okay," he says, as he walks toward me.

"You've never wanted to see it before," I say, keeping my voice quiet, but the words scream inside of me. He's never made an effort to come see the studio—not even after I sent him an invitation for the grand opening of the gallery portion a few years back.

Oliver's gaze pins me with something serious and intense—something that makes my insides rock—but I push back against the current. I push back against everything that draws me to him like a magnet as he takes one last stride and stands directly in front of me.

"I should have," he says, his voice a low purr that begs for me to close my eyes. I don't give in, though. I turn my face to look away—back to the eye that's still staring at us, judging. I swallow before I speak again, to make sure my voice sounds steadier than I feel.

"Why'd you come now?"

"Are you almost done here?" he asks, looking around.

"Actually, I'm just getting started. I have a bachelorette

party—" I'm not even finished speaking before I spot a blonde in a short black dress pulling the door open. Her five friends follow closely behind her, all wearing black except for one wearing a short white dress and a tiara. I smile at them. "There they are now."

"Hi!" Gia, the maid of honor I've been in contact with, smiles and greets me.

"Oh my God, does this come with eye candy?" one of the girls says. "Is he our muse for the night?"

Oliver chuckles and flashes them a smile that makes all but one blush ridiculously. On principle, I assume she's not into men, because that smile makes every female swoon.

"Unfortunately for you, he's not. This is my friend Oliver, and he's on his way to a date," I say, meeting his amused eyes. "You girls can go on to the next room, and I'll be with you shortly. Gia, your stuff is on the table."

"Thank you so much," she gushes as she walks past. All the girls follow, but their eyes never leave Oliver. I'm about to ask him to stand here as an exhibit one of these days. Maybe that'll get me the movement I've been lacking around here.

"So . . ." I say, turning to him again.

"I came by to see if you wanted to join us tonight," he says, dropping his voice an octave as he reaches out and twirls a loose curl around his fingers.

"Why would I do that?" I ask quietly, taking a step back so he has to drop the strand of hair he's holding.

"Because you need a night out," he says, as his eyes flicker from my eyes to my lips.

I take one more step back, suddenly needing more than just a little distance between us. "I had one yesterday."

"Not with me."

The memory of the last time he said those words to me floods my brain, and he smirks like he has front row seats to the show inside my head, where he has the lead role.

"I have to go. They're waiting."

Oliver nods, stuffing his hands in his pockets. He does this thing where he looks down at his feet and lifts his head just slightly so that he's looking at me through his lashes. It's sexy and alluring and makes me feel uncomfortable about the way my heart stirs at the sight. I look back at Wyatt's painting again in an effort to squash that feeling, but it doesn't leave. It stays there, marinating in my core between the slice of yearning and the dash of guilt that sit there.

"Maybe another time," he says, his gaze still on mine.

"Maybe."

"The place is really beautiful, Elle. You've done a good job."

"Thanks. It was mostly Wyatt's doing, though," I respond. Oliver's smile drops. I watch his Adam's apple bob as he swallows his pride and nods.

"You both did a great job," he says. "Did Vic give you my number like I asked him to?"

"I haven't really seen much of him," I say, which is a lie. I saw my brother this morning and last night, and he didn't mention Oliver's number either time.

"I thought maybe he gave it to you, and you just hadn't used it."

"Why would I use it?" I ask, looking back when I hear the girls erupt in laughter from inside the studio.

"It would be nice if you did for a change," he says, shrugging.

My mouth drops. "It would be nice if I did?" I repeat.

We stare at each other in silence, me waiting for him to correct himself, him waiting for me to challenge him about what he said. Neither of us bites. We both know this is too much to cover in just a couple of minutes, and personally, I'd rather not cover it at all. I remember the bachelorette party I have waiting for me in the other room, and clear my throat.

"Okay, well, I'm sure I'll see you around. Have fun on your date tonight." I give him a small awkward wave as I pivot to walk in the other direction.

"Would you be interested in coming by the pediatrics unit in the hospital once or twice a week?" He smiles when I turn back around and raise an eyebrow, urging him to continue. "I was thinking maybe you could paint with the kids or something. I know you like that sort of stuff," he suggests. Visiting the hospital would mean being somehow connected to Oliver again. As if he senses the doubt in my thoughts, he soldiers on, "I'm busy finishing up my residency, so I wouldn't be able to help much, but I have a friend that can help you iron out details."

"Sure. Give me a call and let me know what day is good for me to drop by." I turn one last time as a grin splits my face, and walk into the room full of overly excited, buzzed girls. Then it hits me: Oliver put this smile on my face. Memories of all the previous times he put a smile on my face bombard me all at once, and suddenly, as I look around the room at the happy women before me who are celebrating life and love, I feel like crying. But I don't. Oliver doesn't have the right to make me cry. Not anymore.

Chapter 4

O
N SUNDAY MORNING, I wake up to the sounds of metal clanging and groggily get out of bed to find the source of commotion.

"What are you doing?" I ask over a yawn.

"Shit! You scared me. I still haven't gotten used to having you around," Vic says as he bends to pick up a pan off of the floor.

"At least you're wearing clothes," I say, glancing at his white and blue basketball shorts. "What are you doing?" I repeat.

He sighs. "Okay, this is awkward." He lowers his voice to a whisper. "There's someone in my room, and I'm trying to make breakfast."

I cover my mouth to keep from laughing at the thought of Vic making any kind of food worth eating, and peek my head around the wall, looking toward his room.

"And I'm not sure if she'll be dressed," he adds.

My eyes widen. "Maybe you should tell her I'm here."

"Yeah, I'm thinking I'll have to . . . you're kind of cock blocking what I had planned," he says, looking around the kitchen.

I cover my ears. "Don't speak. I'm going to shower and go have breakfast with Mia."

Vic's eyes light up in laughter. "You don't have to."

"Shh! Don't speak."

I go upstairs and pick out my clothes before going into the bathroom and getting ready as fast as humanly possible. It hadn't really occurred to me what sharing a place with my brother would be like. I switch on my phone as I slip out of the house, thinking about the desperate email I'm going to write my real estate agent, and I see two new text messages from an unknown number.

This is my number- Oliver

I program it into my phone before I read the next one.

Jen wants to know if Tuesday is a good day for you to swing by the hospital. She was able to get you an empty room that you can use for art.

After looking at my calendar for the week, I'm able to move some things around—not that I have much going on these days. I respond.

Tuesday is great. Tell her to give you a time and where I should go when I get there.

I don't expect a response from him because it's only nine o'clock, and most childless humans our age are asleep at this time, but my phone buzzes as I'm pulling into the coffee shop I frequent.

I'll ask her. Will I see you later?

I try to remember if I'm missing something, but can't think of anything.

See me?

21

At Vic's.

Didn't know you were coming over.

Football Sunday.

I frown over this, realizing how long it's been since I joined them on football Sunday.

Vic keeps forgetting I'm living with him temporarily.

Uh-oh . . .

Let's just say I got dressed and out of the house a lot earlier than I hoped to on a Sunday.

LOL. Sorry. Where are you now?

About to have breakfast.

Want to come over? You can sleep here.

I freeze and stare at the screen, expecting the words to switch up on me and say something else.

Not with me, by the way.

I start typing out a message, but delete it when his next one comes through.

Okay, this is awkward. If you don't respond, I'm going to call you.

The phone vibrates in my hand a moment later, and I pick up, clearing my throat.

"I didn't mean for it to come out like that," he says. His voice. God I love his voice. It's deep and rich, and always sounds like he just woke up.

"It's fine. I'm fine, though. Thank you."

"I don't think we've ever spoken on the phone," he says.

"No, I don't think we have," I respond, not adding the gazillion other things that seep into my thoughts—*because you're an asshole, because you left, because I'm your best friend's little sister, because you couldn't have a relationship if your life depended on it . . .*

"Well, now we have. Okay, I just wanted to make sure you didn't take that the wrong way. I mean, unless you want to, and that would be totally fine by me too." I groan at the smile in his voice.

"Oliver . . ."

His chuckle jumps through the speaker and ricochets through my body. I hate what he does to me. "I'm just playing, Elle. Anyway, are you making bean dip tonight?"

"Do you want me to make bean dip tonight?"

"Is the Pope Catholic?"

"If you ask nicely, I'll make you some bean dip, Oliver. If you're going to be a sarcastic asshole, I'm hanging up on you."

He exhales. "Estelle Reuben, my favorite person in the entire world, would you please make me some bean dip? With extra guacamole."

I smile at his words, even though I shouldn't. *I shouldn't.* He's dangerous, I remind myself. This is what he does to you. Every. Single. Time.

"Okay."

I hear a door slam wherever he is, followed by rustling and then more rustling, finishing up with a heavy sigh. "There's an empty spot on my bed for sleeping, in case you're tired."

"Thanks for the offer, but I'll see you later."

I hang up at the sound of his laughter and put my phone away, as I turn my attention to the now-cold egg sandwich that I'd ordered for myself. Once I'm finished eating, I take the short walk to my studio and lock the door behind me. Glancing around at the paintings on the white walls, I wonder if I should rearrange them. A lot of them are Wyatt's, but most of them are local artists' work that I've fallen in love with through the years. Some of mine are also there, but I don't display those in the front part of the gallery. The front of the gallery is reserved for items I have for sale, and the only creations of mine I sell are my kaleidoscope hearts.

I went to school to become an art teacher, but was unsure about it. When I told Wyatt I wanted to be an art teacher but couldn't see myself in such a demanding field, he presented me with the idea for Paint it Back. He said this way my creativity would stay alive, and if I wanted, I could start a program for kids. Through the studio, we were able to start a summer program where older kids come over after their day camp and work on paintings. It started as a way to get them off the streets and focusing their energy on something else, but once school started, they kept setting up appointments to come by in small groups.

I'm setting white sheets over the easels for my Monday afternoon class, when my phone rings.

"Elle," my brother says brightly, as if he hadn't practically kicked me out a couple of hours ago. "I forgot to tell you, some people are coming over later."

"Oh, yeah?"

"Yeah, around twelve. You think you can make some of your bean dip?"

It takes everything in me not to growl at his request. "Sure. How many people?"

"Hmmm . . . me, Bean, Jenson, and Bobby . . . that's it."

"So only four people are eating?" I ask.

"Yeah, four."

I blink rapidly, wondering if he's going to include me in there at all.

"Well, five, if you want to stick around," he says, clearing his throat as he corrects himself.

"Who's Bobby? That guy you work with?"

"Yeah, he's the new guy. You'll like him, he's cool."

"Cool like you, I'm sure," I mutter. My brother and his friends are undercover comic book nerds in the guise of jocks. He's had the same group of friends since he was in grade school, and it's not often he brings another one into the close-knit group they have. I imagine that Bobby must fit the same description as the rest of them.

"You can tell Mia if you want," he adds, as a selling point.

"Mia and Jenson in the same room? No, thank you."

Vic laughs. "She's not over it?"

"Over him leaving her to be with his ex-girlfriend? I doubt it." I raise a brow as I take new brushes out of their package and put them in the silver canisters that sit beside each easel.

"He's a dick," Vic says. "Then again, she's not very bright. I would never have let you date one of my friends."

I put down the supplies in my hand and brace myself on the edge of the counter. "And why is that, exactly?"

He laughs a deep, rich laugh that would have made me smile under other circumstances. "Come on, Elle. You know them."

His words make me cringe. I do know them. I know them well.

"Anyway, I'll see you later. They get here at twelve for the pre-show so . . ."

"Yeah, I got it, Vic. Your dip will be ready before kick-off. Did that girl leave already?"

"Yeah, she left. I invited her over for dinner on Wednesday. Oliver and Jenson are also coming over with some . . . female friends, so you'll meet her then."

I make a mental note to disappear on Wednesday night, and tell Vic I'll see him later. Walking back to the gallery section, I notice one of my kaleidoscope hearts is crooked in its holding place, so I tilt it back upright. A magazine that covered an event we held here once had described my hearts as "heartbreaking, poignant, beautiful pieces." This specific one is on display, but not for sale. It was one of the first ones I made, and Wyatt refused to get rid of it. I used a lot of purples for this particular piece, and every time the sun peeks in here, speckled beams of purple light bounce off the walls.

"If anybody comes in here trying to buy it, you tell them I'll match their price and double it," he'd said to me with a grin.

Tears begin to well in my eyes as I stand there, looking at the way the light reflects off of it, and thinking of Wyatt. I wipe my eyes, take a breath, and walk out, locking the door behind me. I make it back to Vic's and hear him in the shower. I pop open a bottle of wine while I work on the dip, pouring the mashed beans at the bottom, the avocado in the middle, and sour cream on top. Once I'm done making a large bowl of that, I take out the Crock-pot I bought my brother three Christmases ago that he clearly hasn't used, and begin to set up some meatballs. Taking one last sip of wine, I walk to my room and throw myself into the bed.

Chapter 5

I DON'T KNOW how long I sleep, but boisterous shouts coming from the living room downstairs wake me from my nap. I blink rapidly, trying to clear my eyes, as I drag myself out of bed and walk to the bathroom. My reflection is a mess, so I brush my elbow-length hair, and put drops in my eyes until the pink clears and they're back to bright hazel. After applying some make-up, I readjust my black *Elvis is King* shirt so that the loose part at the top falls off my left shoulder, and brush off my fashionably torn jeans before heading down to the living room. It isn't until I'm already there that I realize I'm still wearing my Darth Vader slippers. It's too late to turn around though, since I've already been spotted.

"Hey, Elle," Jenson calls out, making all heads turn my way.

"Hey, Jenson. Did you move back?"

"Nope, but I'll be around a lot for the next couple of months," he says.

"Cool. Hey guys," I say, looking around the room and waving at Oliver, Vic and some blonde guy I've never met.

"Hey," they all say unanimously.

"Elle, this is Bobby. Bobby, this is my sister, Estelle," Vic says, not taking his eyes off the television.

Bobby stands and offers me his hand, which I take. He's actually pretty good looking in a preppy, boy-next-door kind of way, which makes me smile because I was wrong—he's not like all of my brother's friends. He's not tall and athletic like Vic and Oliver. He doesn't have the bad boy thing going that Jenson has, but he flashes a huge Colgate smile as he shakes my hand, and I am treated to the charming vibe that they all share. It's one that makes women do a double take, regardless of what a man looks like.

"When you said little sister, I was picturing a teenager with braces," Bobby says as his eyes travel down my body.

I drop my hand from his. "I'm sure that's what he sees when he describes me."

"That's definitely not how I would describe you."

At the hint of flirting in his tone, I look over his shoulder to look at Vic's reaction, but instead my eyes land on Oliver's. It kills me that I can't tell what he's thinking. He doesn't look upset or jealous, or even curious; he's just staring.

"I'm not sure I want to know how anybody would describe me," I respond.

Before he can say anything else, I step away and walk to the kitchen to get the stuff I made and place it on the table, somehow managing to dodge the beer bottles that cover it.

"She's beautiful, and she cooks?" Bobby says, reaching for a chip. "I think I might keep her."

"Yeah, right," Jenson says, slightly bothered. My brother's friends have this thing. They think they're all supposed to protect me from outsiders, as if the danger lies beyond their lair. I think my engagement with Wyatt threw them over the edge since none of them saw it coming.

"You're not going to give Bobby the whole spiel about staying away from your sister?"

My eyes find Oliver's again, and I smile when he pats the

space beside him. My body stirs, wanting to move toward him, but my brain zaps sense into me. I take a seat beside Victor instead.

"Drop it," Vic says in response to Jenson's comment.

"When we were young, we all got this huge lecture about it," Jenson explains. I lean forward to get a better look at him while he tells the story, since I've never heard this before. "When we were little, we didn't care because Elle was totally like our own baby sister . . . but then she grew up, and any time any of us would make a comment about it, Vic was all *don't look at her, don't touch her. If I find out you did, I'll break your arms, and you'll never be able to come over to my house again.*"

"For the record, I would have gladly gotten my arms broken," Bobby volunteers with a smile, as his blue eyes flick to mine.

"It wasn't the arm breaking that was the issue; it was the ban from the house! He had the best parents! We practically lived in that house." Jenson says, laughing and taking a swig from his beer, which he raises toward me. "And I had a good throwing arm, so I couldn't risk it for a girl. Sorry, Elle."

"Trust me, I'm not sorry." I sit back and stretch my legs while they chuckle.

"Elle knows to stay away from you idiots. None of you are good for her," Vic says, taking a handful of chips and going for the dip.

My eyes find Oliver in time to see him wince slightly at Vic's words. Our gazes stick, and a million things run through my mind—*was that the cause of what happened? Did Vic's approval mean more than mine?* They're questions I know the answers to. They're thoughts that shadowed me for years, despite my attempts to sidestep them.

"Serious question," Jenson says, jolting my attention back to him. "Growing up, who would you say was most your type?"

I try not to laugh at the question and the face my brother

makes. Victor has always been a guy's guy—the one everyone wants to take to a game and hang out with at a bar. Junior, Jenson and Oliver are all pretty similar in that sense. Out of the four, Junior is the only one married with a family, while the other three are forever bachelors. Or so it seems. Jenson is the epitome of what you don't take home to your parents. He's good looking and has the whole tall, dark, and handsome thing going, but he also has that dangerous edge to him with his motorcycle, tattoos and bad boy persona.

I look at Oliver, who has always had this easy way about him, from the lazy smile to the disheveled, sandy brown hair that makes you want to run your fingers through it. He has a way of looking at you that makes you feel like you're the only female in the room. And those dimples . . . God, those dimples. All my friends wanted to date the unattainable Oliver. He has that magnetism that powerful men have. Even when we were young, charisma oozed out of him in bucketfuls.

"Yeah, Elle," Oliver says, giving me a slow, sexy grin as his eyes bounce from my mouth to my eyes. "Who was most your type?"

I shoot him a look before tearing my eyes away from his and toward Jenson, who's watching me with amusement.

"Honestly? Jenson," I say, shrugging.

"Boom!" Jenson yells. "I always fucking knew it! So you would have hooked up with me?"

"I didn't say that. I only said you were most my type," I say, laughing. I don't mention that he was pretty much every teenage girl's type at the time.

"And this is exactly why I had to threaten them," Vic says, looking at Bobby, who's shaking his head in amusement.

My eyes fix on the Cowboys-Forty-Niners game on TV, and I jump slightly when I feel a tap on my foot.

"Really?" Oliver mouths, placing both hands over his heart as if he's wounded. I smile and shake my head. "I like your shoes," he says, flashing that half-grin of his.

"I know you do," I respond with a wink, then mentally kick myself for winking at him. We're still looking at each other when Bobby speaks up, and this time Oliver's eyes narrow at the question.

"So has the ban been lifted? Am I free to ask her out on a date?"

"I don't date," I respond, dropping my eyes from Oliver's.

"Impossible. A girl like you definitely dates," Bobby says.

"A girl like me." I let out a scoffed chuckle. I'm about to leave it at that, but then think better of it and soldier on. "Even if I was interested in dating, I wouldn't date one of my brother's friends. All of you are trouble with a capital T. Didn't you hear the speech?"

"Trouble with a capital T?" Jenson asks.

"Do we really want to go there right now?" I say, glaring at him until he catches my drift, and his laughter fades away.

"No, you're right. You're right. Vic was right." Jenson concedes.

"Let's drop the *dating my sister conversation* and watch the game," Vic says, giving each of the guys a long, pointed look. After a couple of seconds of being elbowed by him every time he moves to get food, I get up and sit beside Oliver on the loveseat.

"Ah . . . you did miss me, after all," he says, as soon as I get comfortable.

"Well, for starters, I couldn't think with your eyes burning holes into the side of my face, and you were my second choice for most my type, so . . ." I shrug and flash him a smile. We look at each other for a long moment before his eyes drop to my mouth and finally away from me to the television. Another touchdown is scored, another kick is made, and a long string of curse words is thrown out by each of them. Just as I'm contemplating making an exit, Oliver shifts beside me.

"I seem to recall a different order of hierarchy," he whispers huskily in my ear, making me shiver.

"Of course you do," I whisper back, unwilling to acknowledge the way my heart is playing Double Dutch in my chest.

"It's true." He moves closer so that his arm is pressed up against mine.

"You have your memories; I have mine."

Oliver's expression changes from playful to serious. "Yeah, I guess so." He exhales. "So, you ready for Tuesday?"

"I am. I'm excited to see the space and get the ball rolling. Thank you for asking me," I say, hoping he understands how much something like this means to me.

"I couldn't think of a better person for the job." He bumps my foot again and my heart vibrates at the touch.

"Stop playing footsies with me," I whisper.

"Or what?" he whispers back, cocking his head in a way that makes his hair fall over his left eye and bounce over his lashes every time he blinks.

"Or Darth Vader will be forced to draw his light saber."

His chuckle vibrates the couch and into me. "Trust me; he doesn't want to compete with mine."

When the double connotation hits me, my mouth drops open, and he laughs.

"Some things never change," I say.

His eyes darken. "Sometimes they get better."

I look away and sit there for a couple more minutes before I go back to my room, using the excuse that I need to see Mia before I go to Wyatt's parents' for dinner. After I say my goodbyes, I keep thinking about Oliver's words. I swear, the man haunts me more than my dead fiancé. It's unnerving.

Chapter 6

I USED TO be that girl who was optimistic about everything, but then life slapped me in the face and forced me to become a realist. I'm not cynical or anything, but I've been through enough not to see the world through rose-colored lenses. The day started off normal enough—my mom called to try to set me up with this guy, Derek. She's been trying to set me up with him since I was, like, six. This time, I said yes. The shrieks of happiness that permeated through the phone lines were intense, to say the least. It was as though she was channeling her inner hyena. I recall it all went downhill from there.

The gallery was spotless when I got here, just the way I like it. Now, it looks like ten groups of toddlers tore through it. It all started when Finlay, a thirteen-year-old boy, asked Veronica out on a date. Finlay's best friend, Brett, had apparently wanted to ask her out, so when he overheard the conversation and she said yes, he lost it. LOST. IT. In my studio! He threw his paintbrush at Finlay, splashes of the blue he was using to paint an ocean went everywhere, and that started a paint fight, which resulted in me calling their parents to pick them up.

So here I am, an hour after I wanted to be here, wiping paint off every surface in the room. My one salvation is that the room is an enclosed space separate from the art outside, because if they'd gotten any of this mess on one of the local artists' work, or worse—Wyatt's—I would have died. My ass hits the floor when I get tired of bending over, and I look around once more. The canvases they are painting on are still on their designated easels, and I take a moment to look at the one Fin was working on. It's a gloomy day in his world. The gray sky makes the water below it hit the rocks angrily. The dark blue brush strokes on the ocean almost make me feel like I can hear the waves, and I decide I want to see the real thing. My studio isn't far from the beach, and I don't enjoy it as often as I could. I gather everything I need for the hospital meeting into one box and set it aside, next to the door. As I'm locking up, I see the splashes of paint on my arm from the paint fight. Damn kids.

The temperature usually drops around sundown and, like clockwork, when the sun begins to set, I feel a cool gust of wind hit me. I pull my light jacket closed, as I stroll toward the water.

I stop at the light a block away and listen for the waves, feeling lighter already. Aside from the other galleries in the area, the ocean was a huge selling point for us when we got the place. If I close my eyes and think hard enough, I can picture Wyatt running toward the beach with his board under one arm, his wet suit practically falling off his body. The memory makes me smile, even though it makes my heart squeeze in my chest. When I first came back to the studio, that was my first thought. Not the gallery, not the painting he was working on that I have put away in the back room, not our daily breakfast together, or the way he would smile when I walked in a room—but remembering the way he ran toward that water.

Surfing was quite possibly the only thing he had in common with my brother. When I first got together with Wyatt, my mom joked that I purposely brought home the artiest man I could find. Forget the fact that he was highly successful, older, and made the effort to wear a suit to their house the first time they met. My mom saw him beneath it all. Not in a bad way.

She grew to accept Wyatt, as did my dad. Vic never really did, but didn't say otherwise. I think they all saw him as an extension of me. I was already kind of an outsider in their world anyway. I hated going to those pretentious parties and galas my parents attend annually. My dad's an orthodontist, and my mom's an English professor, so everybody assumed their kids would follow in their footsteps. Well, Vic became an attorney, and I became a painter. They're supportive of me, though. They love my work and cheer me on, so even though I know I'm the black sheep in some ways, I'm never made to feel like one.

When I reach the sand, I take a really deep breath and close my eyes, relishing the moment. *Every second counts. Live in this moment. This is life. This is what matters.* It's a simple thought, but it's so easy to forget. The ocean is there as a constant reminder though. The big waves crashing against the rocks are as cleansing as they are dangerous. I take a seat in the sand and watch the surfers, young and old, and let the sounds wash over me. Instead of drowning out my pent-up sorrow, it cuts me in half. The anniversary of Wyatt's death was a couple of days ago. It came and went without much remembrance, other than from me and his parents, via the phone call we had to check up on each other.

A little over a year ago, I was on this very beach for a completely different reason. I saw ambulances drive through the sand and followed them because curiosity got the best of me. God. What would I have done if I hadn't followed them? How would I have found out? I wore a frown as I walked closer to the water, recalling the small crowd of people—mostly surfers—watching the paramedics work on someone. It was like I was having an out-of-body experience as I reached them. It felt like something was pulling me closer to the chaos, but I instinctively knew I wouldn't want to see what was going on once I reached it, so I walked slowly. I caught a glimpse of the man on the ground and thought, "Holy shit, that looks like . . . but . . ." and glanced down at my phone in a panic. I looked in every direction—toward the gallery, the beach, and the little colorful wooden shack that sold drinks—all the while my heart pounded in my chest.

My feet drove me forward, closer to the paramedics . . . closer to the body. And then I saw him. Really saw him. His long, blonde hair fanned over the sand, his brown eyes were closed, and his wet suit was pulled down to reveal a thin torso. My vision began to blur, walls that weren't there, beginning to close in around me. I felt like I was fading. Like I was there, but not really, because I wasn't supposed to be looking at what I thought I was seeing. My knees began to buckle when I finally reached him and saw just how white his lips were and how pale his face was.

"Wyatt?" I heard myself say, but the shriek belonged to someone else . . . someone in a panic . . . someone who felt like she was losing the love of her life, and that person couldn't have been me. "What happened? He's my fiancé. What happened? Wyatt!" I screamed over and over as panic rushed through me.

One of the paramedics held my arms, as I watched them work on him. CPR . . . pumping his stomach over and over . . . Finally, they brought out that machine I'd seen a million times in movies—the one that "clears" and zaps people when they're dead and need to be revived. When I saw that machine, I fell to my knees with a scream. I clutched the warm sand below me as the paramedic tried to calm me down.

"Why isn't he waking up?" I sobbed. "Why aren't you letting me go to him?"

"I need you to stay calm—"

My pleas died out with a howl and the sound of the tide crashing behind us.

"He was just surfing," somebody behind us said.

"He was taking too long to come up after his last wipe out," another added.

"I called nine-one-one when I noticed he wasn't coming up," a third one said. "I hope he pulls through!"

The paramedic helped me get up as they put Wyatt on a stretcher, and I let her walk me into the back of the ambulance. I sat there beside Wyatt's feet, staring at his face. "Will he be okay?" I asked, half sobbed, half shrieked. Nobody answered. They just kept on tapping him, breathing into his mouth, and pumping his stomach. They pronounced him dead on arrival when we got to the hospital, before they even wheeled him in. I knew he was gone before he even made it onto the ambulance, but it hurt so much more to hear them verbalize it. For days, I felt lost. He was only thirty-five and an excellent swimmer. The only thing I could think about was that those brown eyes would never look at me again. Those hands would never paint again. Those lips would never smile again. And coming back to this beach now, always brings back the memories.

The autopsy said he'd had a heart attack while he was in the water and that there wasn't enough water in his lungs for him to have drowned. The only thing I kept thinking was—he was only thirty-five.

I no longer cry when I come here. It's not filled with bad memories anymore because I know Wyatt loved this place as much as he loved the gallery. Today, though . . . today I cry. Today I let myself remember the look on his smiling face when we had breakfast in the morning. I close my eyes and take a breath, hoping to smell dry paint and gloss on him and hug myself tight at the memory of being in his arms at night. I let those thoughts break me open and hope that, even from a distance, the waves can wash away my pain. Tomorrow I'll be okay, but today I let myself bleed, and that's okay too.

Chapter 7

THE THING ABOUT life is that you never know when it will show you something that touches you so deeply that you can't help but be grateful for everything . . . even the bad. That's how I feel when wheelchairs holding kids pass by me as I walk down the halls of the hospital with the box of supplies in my hand. I round the corner on my way to Jen's office and stop dead in my tracks when I see Oliver leaving a room, still talking to whomever is inside. Apparently, his residency keeps him in the hospital for endless hours, because every time Vic mentions his name, he's here. I'm still standing there when he closes the door and walks toward me. Those green scrubs and that doctor's coat really do nothing to diminish his good looks. If anything, it makes him look even better, but it's that confident stride of his and the lopsided smile on his face that makes my heart thunder.

"You're early," he says, stopping in front of me.

I frown. "No, I'm not. I'm on time."

Oliver grins. "On time is early for you. You're always fashionably late."

"I *used* to always be fashionably late. Now I'm on time."

"I'm impressed," he says, his green eyes playful, as they

scan my face. My hands full with the box I'm carrying, I'm forced to blow out a breath to get a strand of hair out of my face. Oliver chuckles, grabbing the hair and tucking it behind my ear. It's a simple motion, but somehow he makes it feel intimate. His eyes are on mine, his hand still behind my ear, when he steps closer. I've never been happier to be holding a box in my life, because the way he's looking at me makes my heart trip, and I'm not sure what I would do with my hands if they were free.

"What?" I ask, my voice a whisper.

"You're so grown up," he says, dropping his voice to match my whisper. It ignites little butterflies in my stomach to take flight.

"You make it sound like you're so much older than me."

Growing up, Oliver loved reminding me that he was older. Sometimes he would say it in a lighthearted tone—other times it sounded like a curse—though the curse was only when it was paired with, *you're Vic's baby sister.* And then one time he said . . .

He smiles softly. "I'm old enough to know better."

My mouth pops open, and I take a step back so he's forced to drop his hand. *That.* He said that.

Oliver clears his throat, as he seems to recall the same memory.

"I have to go. I don't want to be irresponsibly late," I say, rushing off before he can stop me.

What is he doing?

What am *I* doing?

I stop in front of a sign that reads: Jennifer Darcia, Assistant Coordinator, and I knock on the door. She calls for me to enter and I do, bumping the door with my hip to close it. I place the box down on one of the empty chairs in front of her desk and smile.

"Hi. I'm Estelle," I say, letting out a heavy sigh.

"Take a seat. I'm Jen," she replies.

We shake hands, and I sit down in the chair beside the one that holds the box. She looks like everything I picture as being Oliver's taste—blonde hair, bright blue eyes, nice smile, and big boobs. The only thing that throws me off is that she's older. I'm pretty sure she has ten years on me, which would give his little statement a whole new meaning. Maybe that's his deal—he's into older women, and I'm too young for him.

"Thank you so much for doing this for us," she starts. "I'm always looking for new things to keep the kids entertained, but lately the clown shows and movies aren't cutting it. I just want them to do something different, or at least *with* someone different, you know? If they have to be here, they might as well have a chance to interact with people other than the ones giving them their medicines." Her eyebrows draw together as she speaks, and I can tell she's passionate about the kids. I decide I like Jen.

"I'll do my best to keep them happy," I say with a reassuring smile.

"Thank you." She pauses. "Oliver says you two go way back."

I startle at the sudden change of subject. "Yeah, he's my brother's best friend."

"I believe the term he used to describe you was his 'favorite person, ever,'" she says. She's smiling, and I get the impression she wants me to tell her something private about Oliver, but the thing is, her statement floors me to the point of speech loss.

"He said that?"

Jen nods. "He did."

"That's . . . interesting." *Considering everything,* I want to add, but don't.

"Let me show you your new work space. You said you are available three times a week, correct?" she says, standing up.

"I'm available upon request, kind of like a clown minus the face paint—unless you need me to face paint—but I can't promise you the stuff I work with will come off easily."

She laughs and puts her hands up. "No, thank you. I don't

want to be held responsible for that disaster."

Jen takes me to the next wing and shows me where to go and who to speak to, before heading back to her office. As I walk the hallways, I take in the outdated murals that adorn the walls. The only contrast to the blue that covers the walls are the fish that swim in all different directions. Looking at it makes me feel like I'm suffocating. Who would paint a fish tank on the walls of a children's hospital? For a place that's supposed to be comforting to the children and parents that have to see this every day, this is unacceptable. I'm shaking my head in disgust when a laugh snaps me out of the moment.

"I take it you don't approve?" Oliver says, appearing beside me.

"Don't you have a job to do?" I ask, dishing out my annoyance at what happened earlier and at the hideous hallway in front of us. I move to brush past him, and I bump his arm slightly.

"I'm sorry," he says, making me stop dead in my tracks. I don't turn around. "I'm sorry about earlier," he continues. "It's just . . . seeing you and then you . . . I just . . . shit." He laughs.

I turn and face him. "It's okay. Apologies have never been your strong suit, after all."

He cringes, and this time I walk away for good.

Chapter 8

EVERYBODY HAS A different definition of *moving on.* For me, selling the house I shared with Wyatt is a way for me to move on with my life. For my mom, moving on means dating. So here I am, sitting across from Derek, who's actually a really nice guy. He's been attentive, holding the door open for me, waiting for me to take a seat before he does, and asking me about my day while listening intently. He's not bad looking either. He's in shape and has a good sense of style, but for some reason, I'm not really here with him. I keep zoning out as he talks about his job as an architect.

"I'm not boring you, am I?" he asks in a polite tone.

"No, not at all. Sorry! It's just," I sigh, "this is a little weird for me."

"I understand. My mom was telling me about, you know," he says, waving his hand in my direction.

"Yeah. I'm okay talking about it. It's just weird to be out with another guy." I offer him a small smile.

"It's your first date since you lost him," he says with an understanding smile.

"Yeah."

"Are you still . . . how do I say this . . . it sounds weird to say *hung up on him* because it's not like it's your ex-boyfriend and he's moved on . . . " he says, letting his words hang.

"No, I'm okay. I mean, I'm okay with everything, really. It's just I'm sitting here thinking about what will happen next— will you try to hold my hand or kiss me good night, or I don't know," I shrug and laugh as I look away from him. "I think I just made this weirder."

Derek laughs. "What if we just take this one step at a time? No holding hands if you don't want that, and no kiss if you don't want that. I mean, we haven't even gotten our entrees yet."

"You're right," I say, smiling and feeling a little bit less uncomfortable. It is just dinner. I have the bad habit of jumping ahead of myself in every aspect of my life. Sometimes I need to learn to rein in some of my anxiety and just breathe. I start to tell Derek about the hospital and the kids I worked with the other day. I tell him how much it opened my eyes to the things I have and take for granted. Dinner goes by quickly after that, and when we reach my brother's house, the sun has gone down.

"Looks like you have company tonight," Derek comments, as his headlights flash over the cars outside.

"Yeah, Victor loves having people over. It's a shame he can't remember to turn the porch light on," I say, making him chuckle.

"I'll walk you up and make sure you don't trip."

We reach the door and stand there awkwardly, not knowing what the right thing to do is.

"So . . . kiss or no kiss?" he asks. I can't see his face, but the smile in his voice makes me feel comfortable.

I take a moment to think about it. I haven't had a pair of lips on me since Wyatt, but I can't say I'm not curious to know what it would be like to kiss someone else. Kissing Wyatt always felt easy. It felt comfortable, familiar. Taking a deep breath, I lean forward. Derek's hands hold the upper part of my arms, and his lips press to mine. A moment later, the light turns on and the front door opens. My eyes pop open, and Derek and I jerk apart from one another like we've been caught doing a lot more than just kissing. It feels like ninth grade all over again. Our heads snap to Oliver, who's holding the door open, arms crossed over his black t-shirt. His green eyes bounce from me to Derek and back again.

"Sorry. I didn't know you were out here," he says, though he doesn't look sorry at all.

"A gentleman walks his date to the door," Derek says, smiling at me.

I return his smile. "Thanks for the date."

"It was my pleasure. I'll give you a call tomorrow. Maybe we can do it again soon?"

I glance at Oliver who's brazenly watching our conversation, and I glare at him before looking back at Derek. "Sure. Call me."

I wait until he's halfway to his car before I face Oliver again, narrowing my eyes. "Well? Weren't you leaving?"

"No, I just heard a noise outside and came to check it out."

His eyes are glinting with mischief, and it fuels my anger. I move to brush past him, but he grabs my arm and leans into my ear, his whispered growl making me burn from the inside out.

"When do I get to take you on a date?" he asks.

My heart begins to beat frantically, and I tear my arm away. "Never."

I hear him chuckling behind me as I run up the stairs like a scared little girl, and I realize I *am* scared. I'm fucking terrified of having Oliver in my life because the last time I let him in, I barely made it out with my heart intact. I wonder if he even knows it.

Chapter 9

BEING ON THE phone with my realtor all morning made me realize something: You can try to steer your life in a certain direction all you want, but ultimately, the wind is in charge of your sail. It's a sucky realization. I spend the rest of my morning painting the ocean from the balcony in my room, and then gather my stuff and head to the hospital. When I get there, I walk to Jen's office and knock once, even though her door is slightly parted.

"Come in!" she calls, so I peek my head in. Unlike most of the people in the hospital, Jen wears slacks and a blouse to work—at least that's what she's worn every time I've seen her. She looks up and smiles at me as she continues to wipe a stain on her white blouse. "Sorry. Damn coffee."

"That's what happens when you wear a white shirt," I say, as she laughs.

"Every single time. You would think I'd learn."

I look down at my own white shirt and shrug. "I'm a painter, so I can get away with it. Anyway, I came by to ask you a question."

"Of course. Take a seat." She signals to the chairs in front of her, and I plop down in the nearest one.

"I know this is probably impossible to do, but I have to ask—is there any way I can repaint the halls in the pediatrics wing?"

Jen's brown eyebrows pull into a thoughtful frown.

"I totally understand if it's not a possibility, but I had to ask."

"No, no, we actually have to move some patients to another wing temporarily to get some new equipment in, so I guess if you could take advantage of those days, it would be doable. I need to run it by my boss first, though."

I nearly squeal in delight. "The rooms will be vacant?"

Jen searches my face and smiles. "What do you have in mind?"

"Well," I start, wringing my hands together. I'm starting to feel like I'm taking advantage of this opportunity, even though I would be the one paying for all of it and spending my time here. "I would fund this one hundred percent. I don't want you to think I want to be compensated, but if I can get some of my friends in here, I think we could do something really nice."

She's quiet for a beat, pulling her sandy blonde hair into a ponytail. "So you would pay for the paint and compensate whoever helps you?"

"Yes, of course," I respond quickly.

Jen is quiet again, searching my face for a little longer than I'm comfortable with, but I stare back, holding my hands on my lap as I wait for her answer.

"You really want to do this," she says finally. "Why?"

A rushed breath tumbles out of my lips and my shoulders sag a little. "Do I need a reason?"

"I suppose not," she says with a shrug. "But not many people would do something like this pro bono."

"I'm not many people," I respond with a smile. "I can speak to your boss myself if you'd like."

She shakes her head. "I'll call him right now. I doubt he'll have a problem with this. He's been saying for years that wing needs a facelift. I'll text you as soon as I have an answer."

"Thank you so much. I look forward to hearing from you."

I stand and head to the door.

"Estelle," she calls out, her words bringing me back into her office. I turn, and she gives me a small smile. "The world needs more people like you."

Her words make me smile proudly. My life may be chaotic and sticky, but most days I go to bed feeling comforted by the thought that maybe I made a difference in one person's life. It's nice to have somebody else recognize it. I thank her and head to the pediatrics wing before I make a fool of myself and start crying or something. When I get there, the first person I spot is Oliver. He's got his back turned to me, leaning his hip on the counter of the nurses' station.

I can't hear what he's saying, but judging from the giggles of the two nurses he's talking to, you would think it's a Jim Carey-worthy joke. I'm sure it's not. Oliver isn't a funny joke teller—though he tries—but the female species never seems to mind. Myself included, once upon a time. I cover the urge to roll my eyes with a huge smile and move along, passing the station with a small wave and a smile as I say good afternoon. I don't stay long enough to look at Oliver's face, but I catch his movement as he straightens and pushes himself away from the counter.

I scan the room I was assigned to, my eyes bouncing from easel to easel and to the containers beside them. Taking a large stack of white paper, I clip one to each board on the easels and look up when I hear the door open. Gemma, a plump, red-haired nurse, walks in pushing a wheelchair. I met the kids the other day when I was here, so I recognize the young boy as Johnny, a thirteen-year-old with cerebral palsy. I greet him and then Danny, Mae, and Mike—all in their early teens—all cancer patients.

"You guys ready?" I ask with a smile.

They each bob their heads, but none say anything. Of

course, all but Johnny are on their phones. I sigh, knowing what's to come. This is something I deal with every time a new set of teenagers comes in for the after school program at the studio. Through this, I've come to realize that teenagers are a lot like new shoes—uncomfortable and a bitch to break in—but once you do, you don't regret a single blister they caused.

"Do you want to do the boring, sappy introductions or do you just want to start painting the shit out of these canvases?" I ask, gaining the attention of all of them at once. Their eyes widen as if they can't believe I just said that.

Mike tucks his phone into his pocket and finally, for the first time, looks at me. He's not shy about it either, he lets his gray eyes wander my body as if I'm some girl he's about to hit on.

"Do I get to paint you?" he asks. I shake my head and laugh. He's definitely ballsy. Mae does not seem impressed by his comment and rolls her eyes, putting her phone in her back pocket and crossing her hands over her chest.

"Okay," I start. "First of all, we're not painting people. Secondly, I can see you're going to be trouble," I say, pointing at Mike with a raised brow. "And I'm going to let it slide because I kind of like trouble . . . as long as you do not start hitting on me." My back is turned toward the door, so I don't know what other kids come in once I start talking, but I soldier on with my little speech even though I know I'll probably have to repeat myself various times.

"That's actually one of my rules. Yes, I have rules," I say when Mike groans. "Rule number one: No hitting on your teacher. Rule number two: Keep your hands to yourself," I look between Mike and Mae and am glad I said it when I catch her blush. "Rule number three: Respect everybody's creativity. We all draw differently, and let's be honest—not all of us draw well, me included. Please don't bash each other's paintings, or sculptures, or whatever else we do in here. And lastly, the art room is Vegas. In this room, we talk about anything and everything you want. We scream and throw paint at our canvas and nobody gets to judge us. Got it?"

All of them nod their heads slowly.

"I have a question," Mae says, sitting in one of the stools set up in front of an easel. She adjusts the machine she's carting around so that it's out of the way and then looks at my expectant face. "You said you're not a good drawer, but you're a painter. Is there a difference?"

I smile at her question. "Huge difference. I'm best at making things with my hands. I usually use broken glass to make small sculptures."

"Broken glass?" Mike asks, wide-eyed.

"Yup."

"What do you make?" Danny asks.

"Hearts."

"You make hearts out of broken glass?" Mae asks in a gasp.

I nod and turn around, my hands flying to my chest when I see Oliver leaning on the wall beside the door with his arms crossed over his chest. His green eyes light up in amusement as his mouth turns into a full-blown grin at the look on my face.

"What are you doing here?" I ask, still holding my thumping heart.

"All of my patients are in here right now." He drops his arms and shrugs as he slips his hands into the pockets of his white coat.

"Oh," I respond, blinking away from him and turning back to the kids. "Anyway, let me show you what I'm talking about." I walk over to the box I brought over the other day, which is on the table beside Oliver. My arm brushes the front of his body as I reach across him, and I hear him intake a breath, which makes me do the same. I need to get a fucking grip around this guy. I grab the small box and walk to the other side of the room so I'm facing the group and can see who walks in. Gemma comes in and tells Oliver something quietly. I watch him nod before she walks out.

"Bathroom break," he mouths in explanation when he catches me looking. I nod and open the box, carefully taking out the glass heart and the stand it's on before placing it on the table.

"Oh my God," Mae says, her blue eyes widening as they take it in. "You made that?"

"I did," I say, smiling proudly. My eyes flicker to Oliver, who has a smile on his face. It makes my heart skip a beat, because it's not the gorgeous one he uses to impress women. Instead, it's a warm, comforting one. This one, he only offers when he agrees with something you said, or is proud of something you did. I turn my attention back to the heart and pick it up. It's what we call a 3-D heart, since it's not flat and has a circumference.

"That's legit," Mike says.

"It is really nice," Danny agrees.

"Thank you. This is my specialty. Most artists have one thing that they're known for. Warhol used blotted ink to create his signature Campbell's soup and Marilyn Monroe images. Romero Britto uses eccentric colors, so when you look at one of his sculptures or paintings there's no question as to who made it. Even if they were to make something different, you would have a hint letting you know that it's theirs. My thing is hearts. I paint them . . . sculpt them . . . but this right here is my kaleidoscope heart. It's my specialty."

"Ohhh," Mae says, as if what she's been looking at just dawned on her. She reaches for it, but thinks better of it and drops her hands.

"Take it," I say.

"No, I don't want to break it. It's too pretty."

"Take it. You're keeping it anyway. You might as well get used to holding it."

Mae's eyes widen. "I can keep this?"

"Of course."

"But what if it breaks?" she asks, hesitantly lifting the

heart from its stand. She turns it over and over, creating little rainbows of color throughout the room as the light bounces off of the glass.

"Well," I say, raising my eyes to Oliver, who's watching me intently. "It's a heart. They always break at some point. Sooner or later someone will come along and shatter it anyway—might as well be you." I pause, my heart beating wildly in my chest as Oliver's gaze turns serious, and I find myself mesmerized by it, and trying to back my way out of its intensity. "Besides," I continue, looking at Mae again. "I know the girl who made it. If it breaks, I can get you a new one." I wink and clap my hands together. "Now let's talk about paint!"

Oliver's eyes burn holes into me for the next hour, but I refuse to look at him again. The kids paint different things: Mae a heart, Mike the LA Lakers logo, Danny a fish. They all get comfortable with the brush and the canvas in front of them. I make my way around the room, helping them perfect their strokes and learn how to control the weight of their hands. When the time comes for them to go back to their rooms, they thank me, and each says they are looking forward to their next session. I feel relieved and warm inside, which lasts all of three minutes before Oliver pushes himself away from the wall and walks to where I am busying myself cleaning up the room.

"Shattering hearts," he comments, his teeth grinding. "It's fitting."

"They're not shattering hearts, they're kaleidoscope hearts," I correct him.

"What's the difference? You make them with broken pieces."

I inch forward, standing close enough to feel his warm breath on my face, when I tilt my head to glare at him, my hands making tight balls at my sides.

"The difference is that it's already broken, but I use the pieces to rebuild it. The difference is that the heart has a second chance, and maybe it'll get broken again, but it's already shattered, so maybe the fall won't be as bad."

His eyes search my face as if he's looking for another answer. We stare at each other for a long time—long enough for my breath to quicken and my heart to begin to burn. Long enough for him to cup the back of my neck with his nimble fingers and pull my face to his abruptly, smashing his lips to mine. My resolve leaves me quickly, as my hands thread through his hair. I pull, begging him to come closer, as our tongues dance around each other in a passionate tango. He groans deeply into my mouth, and I feel it travel down my body to my pelvis, where it simmers. I can't remember the last time I was kissed like this. I feel like I'm floating and drowning at the same time, taking a breath and being submerged with the next.

When we pull away, we're both breathing heavily, and my face feels flushed. For a beat longer, I look at him—at his disheveled dark hair and the five o'clock shadow he rocks like nobody's business. My gaze wanders over his plump lips and slightly crooked nose, to the shallow dimple on his chin and the intense green eyes that cast me under a spell so long ago. When the reality of our shared kiss catches up to me, it hits me quickly, like a foul ball out of nowhere, and I back away from him.

"That shouldn't have happened," I say, rushing past him before he can react. He doesn't come after me, and that's just as well, because even if a part of me wished he did, I didn't expect him to. He never does.

Chapter 10

Past

Oliver

THERE'S A LOT to be said about evolution and the way beauty sometimes blossoms from the most unlikely ducklings. That's how I felt about Estelle when I went home for summer break that year. I had just finished dropping off Jenson and Junior's drunken asses and had parked in front of Vic's house. He wasn't in much better shape than they were. I'd given up drinking that year after learning what it did to your liver. The guys had given me shit about it all night, taking bets as to how long my drinking hiatus would last, as I nursed the same beer I'd gotten hours before. While they were busy getting wasted and hitting on a few questionable girls that would, for sure, make them cringe tomorrow morning, I'd been making mental plans with Trish as her face bobbed between my legs. She was not a questionable hook up. She was a model, and practically every man's Playboy fantasy come to life.

I sighed and hoisted Vic up, knowing he wouldn't make

it to his room without my help. It was annoying that I had to babysit three guys who normally knew how to handle their liquor, but that night, they'd all acted like the sloppy sorority girls we made fun of at keggers. I opened the door, Vic gave me a slurred thank you, and I watched as he walked to his room.

Shaking my head, I turned back around, locked the door, and put the keys inside one of the flowerpots his mom had outside. I trotted down the steps smiling at the thought of Trish—her big tits, firm ass, and the way she sucked my dick, still fresh in my mind. As I reached the edge of the house, I stopped and realized I would have to walk home. It was fine since my mom's house was only a few blocks down, but I still contemplated whether or not to go back into the house and stay the night. The brief sounds of crying caught my attention. For a moment, I thought nothing of it—it could have been anything. It was dark out, and way past the hours that any normal human being went to bed. But then, as I pushed my long hair back after a gust of wind tossed it into my face, I heard it again and stopped walking.

I looked around and realized it was coming from Vic's house. I froze for a moment, hoping it wasn't Mrs. Reuben. The last time I tried to comfort a friend's crying mother, she came on to me, and I had to get the hell out of Dodge. Begrudgingly, I looked up and saw a small figure sitting on the roof of the house. The sight almost knocked me on my ass, partially because I was craning my head so hard to look up, but mostly because I could have sworn it was Estelle—except it couldn't be. The girl sitting up there wasn't a girl. But then it hit me—*when was the last time I saw Elle?* I squinted, trying to get a closer look, but couldn't. I walked to the back of the house and climbed the oak tree I'd climbed a million times before for different reasons, and stepped onto the roof. She was sitting down, head bent, her long, wavy hair falling over her shoulders and blocking her face.

When I sat down beside her, she jumped and faced me with

a yelp, surprise and fear on her otherwise grief-stricken face. I'd known Estelle since I was thirteen and I'd never, ever seen her look like this. Not even when she didn't get the leading role in the Nutcracker, a performance she'd rehearsed for months before the tryouts. Immediately, I assumed a break up was the reason for her tears, and my blood began to boil at the thought of some loser doing this to her.

"What's wrong?" I asked as she wiped her tears and shook her head. Her face was no longer wet, save for the dip over the top of her lips. I'd never noticed how full they were before then. I'd never noticed how rosy and defined her cheekbones were, or the way her eyebrows turned into a slight frown when she looked at me. I'd never paid attention to how ridiculously alluring her eyes were. The different shades made them look like the marbles I used to collect when I was a kid. My gaze drifted down to her neck, where I noticed her swallow, and then over her tits, which were now full—not like the last time I'd seen her in a bathing suit when she was still flat chested. Jesus Christ, this girl was hot.

The clearing of her throat made my eyes snap back to hers, putting an end to their voyeuristic journey down her now grown-up body.

"You're so grown up," I said before I could stop myself, cringing at the voice I said it in, all needy and husky and—fuck my life—desperate. I expected her to roll her eyes, the way she normally did when I said anything to her, but this girl—this freaking girl—looked at me and smiled the sexiest smile I'd ever seen. And I had just been at a party full of hot girls smiling, but Elle's was slow and sensual when she wasn't trying to make it be. It was just her smile, the one I'd been seeing for as long as I could remember. Putting that smile on this grown-up version of her should be downright illegal.

"Are you hitting on me?" she asked, using a sultry voice that surprised the hell out of me.

"That depends," I said, inching to sit closer to her, somehow completely forgetting that I was at my best friend's house, and this was his little sister. The thought of Vic finding us crossed my mind, but I pushed it down. In that moment, under a sky full of stars with a sad Estelle, all I could think about was making her smile.

"What does it depend on?" she whispered.

"Whether or not it's working," I whispered back, lifting my hand and running it down her back—a motion I shouldn't have done, because now I knew Elle wasn't wearing a bra under the oversized sweater she had on, and that knowledge woke up everything in my lower region.

She shook her head softly, her eyes flickering between my eyes and mouth like she was actually thinking about my lips on hers. I shouldn't have liked that thought as much as I did.

"It's not," she said finally.

"Why were you crying?" I asked, gathering her hair and pushing it behind an ear so that I could get a better look at her. The wiggle of one of her outstretched legs caught my attention, and I realized she was wearing a knee brace.

"What the hell happened?"

"I blew out my knee in dance practice the other day for the fourth time, and when I went to the doctor today—thinking they would tell me my brace would come off in a couple of weeks like the last time—he said I have a torn ACL and can't dance anymore," she said in a hoarse whisper. As she looked away, I saw new tears begin to gather in her eyes. "Ever. My Julliard dreams are gone, just like that. Not that I had a real chance of getting in, but now the possibility is ruined."

I had no words for that. The only things Estelle did with her life were dancing and painting, but dance was her passion. It was her light. You could see the way it made her feel and how much she loved it with every move she made.

"You still have a year of school, Elle. Don't rule it out. Like you said, it's happened before," I said, cupping her face and wiping a stray tear with the pad of my thumb. She looked at me again and shook her head, but didn't move away.

"Not like this, Bean," she whispered, licking the tears off of her lips. "This time it's over for me. I just know it."

I pulled her face to my chest and held her there, letting her cry all over my shirt, because that was all I could do.

"I'm so sorry, Chicken," I whispered, as I pressed a kiss to the top of her head. It would have been considered a brotherly thing to do if I hadn't closed my eyes and smelled her hair, picturing it draped over my pillow.

She leaned away from my chest, wiped her face, and looked up at me. Her eyelashes stayed stuck together as she blinked. "Why are you here, anyway? Aren't you supposed to be at one of those crazy parties you're always talking about?"

"I was. I came to drop off Vic and heard you crying."

She nodded once, averting her eyes for a beat before looking at me again. "So, I'm so grown up," she said, repeating my words and smiling with a twinkle in her eyes that made my chest squeeze and my jeans tighten.

"You are."

She leaned her face closer so we were breathing on each other. If either of us leaned in a centimeter, our lips would be touching, and God, how I wanted that to happen.

"What are you thinking about?" she asked in a whisper.

"Things I shouldn't be thinking about," I whispered back, my eyes on her mouth again, wondering how it would feel.

"Like what?" she asked, her breath falling over my lips.

I closed my eyes and leaned back just a little bit. "Like things a nineteen-year-old shouldn't think about a sixteen-year-old."

"You act like you're so much older than me." We were both still whispering, trying to keep, whatever this crazy thing was, a secret. I was sure the crackling in the air between us would alert everybody in the general vicinity of this house that something was going on.

"I'm old enough to know better," I responded, tilting my

face and leaning into hers, letting my lips brush hers lightly, then dragging them until I reached the edge of her mouth. I dropped a kiss there.

"I always wondered what that would feel like," she said, releasing a long breath as my lips grazed over hers.

"You've never kissed a guy before?" I asked, rearing back. What the fuck was wrong with the guys in her school? I hadn't even kissed her. Not really, anyway.

Elle laughed quietly. She looked at me like I'd grown two heads. "I meant what kissing *you* would feel like." She smiled bashfully and looked down at the space between us where our hands touched.

"You've thought about it?" I asked, smiling, wishing her confession didn't make me as happy as it did.

"Often," she said, trying to smother a smile of her own.

I sighed heavily, ran a hand through my hair, and looked back at her open window. I needed to change the subject. I couldn't think about her dreaming of kissing me, or the way I suddenly wanted to do so much more than that with her. "I can't believe you got out here with that cast. Let me help you get back in."

I offered her my hands and helped her up, looking away into the distance and paying attention to the sound of the ocean behind us—anything not to look down at her. Our hands were still connected, and I could feel her gaze on mine. I knew if I looked down, I would kiss her—full-on kiss her—and plunge my tongue in her mouth while I suck that plump bottom lip. I knew it. I wanted to so damn bad. But I couldn't. That wouldn't be fair to her or Vic.

"Ready?" I asked with a heavy sigh, as I pulled her hands in the direction of her window. I watched as she climbed in without turning back to me. When I said goodnight and started to walk away, she called my name. I walked back and dipped my head, holding on to the edge of the window.

"Will you come back tomorrow?" she asked, her eyes wide

and hopeful.

I looked up at the sky, hoping something would tell me what a bad idea that was, then I let out a breath and looked at her again. "I can't think of anything else I'd rather do." And the thing is, it was true. For that month, I went back every night after the guys and I went out, and then I told Elle all about our adventures. Most of my stories were filled with warnings of what girls shouldn't do at parties, so despite the attraction I felt, I was offering my older brother knowledge. Estelle made it difficult to stay away from her, so I kept going back nightly. I loved our easy conversations about everything and anything. I loved the way she thought my jokes were shitty and the way her eyes brightened when I finally said a good one. But some nights, she would lean into me and ask me if I would kiss her when she was eighteen and what I'd do if she was a stranger in one of my college classes. Those questions made it hard for me to think straight. I tried to dodge them by smiling and laughing. I never told her that if she was a stranger in one of those classes, I'd be on her like white on rice. I never said that if she was eighteen, I would break my rule and face the consequences. I did, however, tell her that I usually dated older women because they were less complicated and didn't expect as much. I was way too busy focusing on school and the college experience to be tied down. She always gave me a small frown when I dropped those little hints, like she wanted to challenge me and change my aversion to a real relationship. I kind of wished she had taken up that challenge, just to see how hard she'd try, even though I knew the outcome would be the same.

Chapter 11

Present

"YOU DID WHAT?" Mia asks in a bewildered tone that makes me bury my face in my hands.

"I know," I say in a smothered mumble.

"Look at me! I want to see how you really feel about this whole thing, because let me just say, I am shocked."

I drop my hands and look at her, really trying to school my features and not start laughing at the expression on her face.

"Oh my God. You liked it. I thought he kiss attacked you and you were pissed off, but you obviously liked it! Are you insane, Elle?"

I frown.

"No, really," she continues. "I'm all for you moving on with your life, *but Bean?* There are a million other guys out there."

"I know. I know." I let out a frustrated growl. I can't believe I freaking kissed him. "At least I walked out on him this time."

"I guess," she whispers.

"You guess?" I prompt.

"It's just . . . you walked away last time too, and look at where that got you."

"A new boyfriend, and later, fiancé?"

"Wyatt was another terrible rebound, but I'm not here to talk crap about people who can't defend themselves."

I let out a breath and shrug, because I don't want to open that can of worms. When I met Wyatt, this older—much older than me—man, I traded in my friends and family for time with him. I became the girl I said I would never be for a guy, but he wasn't just a guy, he was so much more. He was my mentor, my friend, my lover, and even though he had a controlling aura to him, and I dealt with crazy mood swings at times, he loved me. He was good to me.

"I don't want to talk about Wyatt," I say.

"You never do," Mia counters, raising an eyebrow. I know she's trying to goad me—trying to get me to the place where I lose my cool—because her words resonate something within me that I can't argue with.

"I don't want to fight right now, Meep."

"Because you know you'll lose the battle."

"I can't do this right now," I say finally, taking the glass of Moscato and drinking what's left in one huge gulp before slamming it down with a clink. I take out a bill and toss it on the table.

"You're seriously leaving over this?" she asks, balking at me.

"I have to go get some stuff and get ready to go to Felicia's house for dinner tonight, and I'm not in the mood to argue with you right now."

"How are you going to move on completely if you're still eating dinner with his parents every goddamn week?"

My mouth pops open. I can't believe she's even going there right now, even after knowing how upset this is making me. I try to regain control of the blood simmering inside my body, but the longer I stand there, the more impossible it is.

"Next time I need your advice, I'll ask you. You shouldn't be dishing out so much of it anyway! Your ex-boyfriend left you to marry his ex-girlfriend, and you rebounded with his uncle! How's that for fucked up?" I practically shout.

"I didn't know it was his uncle!" She slams her palms over the table and stands up, so it looks like we're in a boxing ring with the table serving as our referee.

"I . . . I . . ." I put my hands on my head and squeeze the impending headache. "I have to go. I can't . . . I can't right now." As it is, I already regret what I said to her. She didn't deserve that and I know it, but dammit! She knows I hate it when she brings up Wyatt. Even when he was alive, I refused to talk about him with her after a while, because it would always end up turning into a huge argument.

By the time I get to Victor's house, I decide I hate everybody and can only pray nobody else gets in my way, because I feel like I have enough pent-up rage inside me to make a charging bull look tame. The door slams behind me in a thud, and I head for the stairs, ignoring the voices coming from the kitchen.

"Elle?" Vic calls out.

"Yeah. I'm just here for a moment. Picking something up," I shout back, reaching the bedroom door and closing it behind me. I sag against it, feeling like a teenager avoiding her parents, and I focus on collecting my thoughts before the inevitable footsteps come up the stairs. The knock comes shortly after and I sigh, conceding to open it. I regret it immediately when I find Oliver standing on the other side, wearing nothing but a pair of swim trunks and a smile. I refuse to give in to the urge to let my gaze travel the length of his naked torso. My eyes can burn in hell for wanting to do it. My hands can follow them and sit beside Satan himself for wanting to reach out to tame the mussed brown hair falling over his forehead.

"What do you want?" I ask, not even trying to hide my annoyance.

He stops smiling and starts frowning, crossing his arms over his chest. I refuse to look at his defined arms. Absolutely refuse.

"What crawled up your ass?" he asks, and I start closing the door on him, but he stops it with his hand. I exhale.

"I don't have time for this right now, Oliver. If you want to annoy me, come back after nine o'clock," I mutter, looking down at his naked feet. They're probably the least attractive thing on his body, but then, feet usually are.

"Okay," he says, pushing the door wider and letting himself in.

"What are you doing?"

"Annoying you."

"I said after nine. It's six-forty, and I have to go." I grab the bag I have on the floor, filled with pictures of Wyatt.

"Where are you going? Another date?" he asks, as he walks around the room, picking up everything and looking at it—even a pink bra that's draped over my chair. He stays fixated on that.

"I guess you can call it that." I turn to the closet and sift through clothes, looking for something more modest to change into. The black shirt I have on shows off my entire back, and it's not something I would wear to Wyatt's parents' house without him there.

"I like what you're wearing," Oliver says huskily into my ear, making me jump. I turn quickly, both palms up and ready to push him away, but get sidetracked when my nose ends up on his sternum and I can't help but breathe him in. He smells of salty water and a natural scent that's sweet, yet masculine. I only hesitated for half a second, but it's long enough for him to place his hands over mine. He presses them to his warm chest, and my breathing escalates.

"Look at me, Elle," he says, using the deliciously low, demanding voice that made my toes curl and my eyes roll back many moons ago. I have no choice but to tilt my head back and give him my attention. "Forget those lame guys you're dating.

Let me take you out."

My heart, if possible, spikes even further in my chest, overriding all warning of the impending chaos that's sure to come. I try to turn my attention to the poster hanging beside us, but the image of a kissing couple has my eyes darting back to deep green eyes that burn into mine. My stomach does a flip-flop—the way it always does when he looks at me that way. I try to take my hands back, because these feelings are too scary for me to deal with right now, but he holds them tighter, bringing them up to his mouth and kissing the tip of my ring finger. Why did he pick that finger to kiss? I pull harder, and he finally lets my hand drop.

"I can't," I say, my voice raspy.

A myriad of emotions flash in his eyes before they settle on determination, and I'm forced to take a step back—away from his scent, away from his warmth.

"Why not?"

I sigh and finally look away, back down at his naked feet. "I just can't." He knows why not. He shouldn't ask me that question. "What's Vic doing, anyway?"

His body moves into mine so quickly that I don't have time to react, as his large hands clutch my arms and his face drops, bringing his nose to mine. I just stare, wide-eyed, waiting for his lips to close the distance, but they don't. He just looks at me . . . breathes on me . . . lets me breathe on him, and then he groans. And that fucking groan bridges the distance between us and crawls into the core of me, draping over every fiber of my being.

"What do you want, Oliver?" I whisper against his lips. "What do you want from me? You want to kiss me? You want to fuck me? You want to come into my life like the hurricane that you are and tear down everything I've rebuilt before you disappear again?"

His lips brush lightly against mine—just a breath of a touch—yet he's crowding me like he's about to devour me.

He won't though. He never goes in for the kill. He just casts the lure, reels me in and then cuts the line. As expected, his hands drop, and he pulls away from me as quickly as he'd approached. I feel a pang deep inside me that I desperately wish wasn't there.

"I'm sorry," he says quietly, shaking his head in a movement that makes his hair sway back and forth. His eyes are soft on mine now, and I can almost hear his thoughts: *I should never have kissed her. I should never—*

My brows rise in surprise at the apology, though. There are so many things I can say to him, but the sudden, defeated look in his eyes keeps my mouth shut. Finally, I exhale and push off the wall to stand in front of him, keeping enough distance between us to discourage us from reaching toward the other.

"It's okay just . . . don't do it again. The kiss the other day was a mistake . . ." I stop talking and walk past him, putting the bra away and sorting through my underwear drawer, like I'm unearthing hidden treasure or something. This time when I feel him come up behind me, I drop my head and exhale. He really needs to stop sneaking up behind me.

"Oli—" I start, and gasp when I feel his lips on the back of my neck, soft and warm. My heart thunders and I freeze in place, my shaking hands still inside the drawer. I close my eyes and focus on breathing, as he drops another kiss right beside that spot. I never knew the back of my neck was so sensitive. The feeling sends a ripple of sensation down my arms and through my body.

"It wasn't a mistake," he says in a husky whisper that makes my flesh break out in goose bumps. "You've never been a mistake. You want me to tell your brother that I want to date you? Is that what it would take?"

I pull my hands out of the drawer to clutch the edge of the dresser, and a moan escapes my lips.

"That sound," he growls, as he pushes his body against my back. I can feel the hardness of his chest . . . of him . . . against me. "That fucking sound drives me crazy, Elle," he says, sucking the side of my neck. I'm starting to pant, and I don't even care. I don't know what I want anymore. I don't know what I need. I don't know if it matters—if anything matters—when Oliver is making me feel this way. I don't even have time to let guilt sink in, because even that's a foreign feeling right now. A storm of lust rises inside me, and my heart continues to trip over itself as his lips descend on me over and over.

"I can't do this again," I whisper shakily. "I can't . . . oh God, you need to stop." I moan as he drags his hands down my sides, the tips of his fingers grazing my already pert nipples.

He presses against me again, pushing me into the dresser. "Was I a mistake to you?"

"Oliver," I plead in a soft whimper. My eyes roll back as his hands begin a sensual tease—up and down, squeezing and kneading—unhurried . . . as if we have all the time in the world for his seduction. As if we both don't know that as soon as he walks out of this room, whatever we're doing is over . . . like it always is.

"What do you want, Elle? You want me to kiss you? You want me to fuck you? You want to pretend that *I'm* the one who hurricanes through your life?" His voice is guttural as he grinds against my ass. Another moan escapes me.

Suddenly, his words sink in, and my eyes snap open. That's the moment I slip out of his hold and turn to glare at him. His eyes are hooded as he looks back at me, his hair all tousled and sexy. Hell, everything about him is sexy. Oliver Hart is the definition of sexy in my book, but I'm too pissed off to be distracted right now.

"I'm the hurricane?" I say, pointing at myself. "*Me?*" I glance at the clock on the dresser and realize I'm already late, thanks to this . . . whatever we're doing.

"You think you're not?" Oliver counters, now looking at me through narrowed eyes.

"You're delusional." I walk back to the closet and, with my

back to him, I pull the shirt I'm wearing over my head. I hear his sharp intake of breath, and I don't relish it like I normally would. Right now, he's officially back on my shit list.

"No. You are delusional, Estelle," he says, stepping forward so he's behind me again, his voice near my ear. He doesn't touch me this time. "You are so damn crazy, and I want to touch you so bad right now and fuck the insanity out of you."

A shiver runs down my entire body as I pull another shirt over my head. "Not going to happen."

"Not right now, but it is going to happen. Don't go on this date," he says. The soft plea in his voice thaws me a little, and I turn to face him.

"Why? Why shouldn't I go on a date?"

"Because," he breathes, running a hand through his hair. His eyes scan my room quickly, as if he's looking for the answer on my goddamn walls. Just when my anger is bubbling up because this feels like déjà vu all over again, his eyes flash back to mine, and the look in them is so potent that it freezes me. "Because I don't want you to. Because it's my turn. Because I've let you go a million times before, and I don't want to miss this chance with you. Let me take you out. Let me show you how good I can be, and I'm not talking about fucking, I mean me. *One date, Elle.*"

When my heart starts beating again, I let out a rushed breath. "One date."

Oliver smiles. It's the one that makes me swoon—the wide grin that shows off his dimples. "One date."

"Our definitions of dates are wildly different," I say, looking around the room. My eyes glance over everything—anything—so that I don't have to look at Oliver, but then he moves closer, and my eyes snap to his so that he'll stop moving.

"Okay, we'll define it so we're both on the same page."

I let out a small laugh. "Okay, I'll think about it. But if I decide to say yes, I have rules."

He chuckles. "Text me the rules."

"I will."

When I head downstairs, I hear him and Vic in the kitchen and pop my head in to say goodbye. Oliver's eyes take me in slowly, as if I'm the slice of pizza he's about to dig into, and I look away quickly before I get lost in his gaze.

"You're going to Felicia's, right?" Vic asks.

"Yup. I'll be back early. Bye, guys."

"Felicia?" Oliver asks, when I'm already halfway to the door.

"Yeah, Wyatt's mom," Vic responds.

"What?" Oliver asks, bewildered.

I laugh all the way to my car, and when I get there, I see a text message from him.

You played me.

I laugh, but don't respond.

What are the rules?

1- No touching. 2- No kissing . . . If I think of any more, I'll let you know.

Is Friday good for you?

I haven't agreed to this yet.

But you will.

I don't respond. I wonder if he would really ask Vic if he could take me out. For some reason, it makes butterflies ignite deep in my belly. Then I groan, remembering where I'm going and why. Maybe Mia is right. Oliver is the last person I should play this game with. He invented the fucking game. I'm just a newbie hoping for a win.

Chapter 12

Past

Oliver

GROWING UP, THE friend I could relate to most was Jenson—we both came from broken homes. Our families weren't wealthy like Victor's or Junior's, and we had jobs by the time we were fifteen. Even though we had similar backgrounds, Jenson and I still had our differences. He always needed a girlfriend, whereas the last thing I wanted was to be tied down. My parents' divorce probably had a lot to do with it. That, and the fact that when my older sister and I stayed at my dad's house every other weekend, he would openly talk about the issues he had with my mother. His main issue, my sister would say, was that our parents married too young and didn't get to experience life without the other. She was sixteen when she said that to me. I was nine. For some reason, her words stuck with me. Probably because I was always looking for the "real reason" they couldn't work things out.

As much as I loved and respected my father, I always said

I wouldn't end up like him. I wouldn't leave my family just because I had an adventurous itch I needed to scratch. When I was a teenager I had girlfriends, but none of them held my attention long enough to be long term. It wasn't that I wanted to screw around or sleep with someone else. It was as simple as having different interests or the fact that I couldn't stay on the phone long enough to have a conversation without falling asleep. Beyond that, I really liked women. I liked the smell of them . . . the taste of them . . . and I liked trying to figure them out. My sister, Sophie, would hassle me and tell me I was becoming our father—which I didn't appreciate—and then I'd remind her that I wasn't involved with anyone.

"That's the problem, Bean, you're not George Clooney. You can't be a lifelong bachelor."

"Clooney gets some serious ass. I wouldn't mind being him."

"Yeah, but I want my kids to play with your kids at some point," she would remind me.

"Well, I haven't found the right girl yet."

And that was the thing. I hadn't. Not that I was looking, but I'd like to think if I was fucking her, I would know she was the right one for me. It's not like I got women in my bed without having a conversation with them first. All of them made my blood go straight to my cock, but that was about it. The last time I'd been in love was when I was twelve, and according to Sophie, that didn't really count. I just needed to keep having fun while I was in college—everything else would fall into place.

That's exactly where my head was when Vic called to invite me to a party he and his fraternity brothers were throwing. He was attending UCLA, while I was in Cal Tech—which are really close—so we were able to hang out every weekend. I was already planning on going to the party, but when he mentioned Elle was visiting him for the weekend and would be there, I was completely sold. I showered and avoided the calls from Pam, the girl of the moment. I was determined to go to this party and relax with my friends, and taking Pam meant I'd have to babysit, because she was one of those girls who got drunk off of one drink, and then still had ten.

I pulled up to the party and greeted a couple of guys I knew before heading to the back where Vic always hung out playing darts. He came into my line of vision and I had to laugh, because he was guarding the keg like it was a shrine.

"What's up, douchebag?" I said, patting him on the back when I reached him. He backed away and turned to me with a lazy smile on his face that made me chuckle. "Bean! Grab a cup. Actually, grab two. I've been standing in front of this shit for an hour waiting for you to get here."

"You could've told me to bring more beer," I said, laughing, as I reached for a red cup.

"Nah, I got you, I got you." He poured me a beer and finally stepped away from the keg.

"Anyone else coming? Jenson? Junior?"

"Jenson's . . . I don't know what he's doing, but he's back home, and Junior went to visit Rose's family."

I let out a low whistle. "It's getting really serious now."

Vic nodded, his face looking as terrified as I felt at the time about getting serious with somebody.

"Whatever. As long as it's not me, I'm good," Vic said, shrugging.

I chuckled. "You and me both."

"I never thanked you the other day . . . for coming with me," he said, his voice taking a serious note. I clinked my cup to his and shrugged. I'd gone with him to get checked because some girl he'd been fucking called to tell him she had an STD. It wasn't like I went in the room with him or anything, but I could tell he was pretty messed up over the news, so I went for moral support. He didn't want to tell anybody else about it. I'm not sure he would have even told me if he hadn't taken her call while we were out surfing together.

"That's what brothers are for. Have you . . ." gotten the results, was my question, but it seemed too serious to speak aloud at a frat party, and I wasn't sure he was ready to answer.

"Negative," he said, throwing back the rest of his beer. "Everything came back negative."

I let out a long relieved breath. I wasn't sure what I would have felt if he'd had another answer. We weren't kidding when we called each other brothers. I couldn't remember a time when Vic wasn't in my life, which is a big deal nowadays when friends were as fickle as the weather. He was there when my parents divorced, when my dad got sick—and everything in between. His parents took me in for weeks on end in the summer, when my mom was away on work trips and Sophie was off in school. Not that an STD meant death, but it was serious enough to make me realize how lucky we were to have dodged that shit thus far.

"You need to use a condom every-fucking-time, dude," I said in a breath, taking a gulp of my beer.

"I know. I know."

I stood beside him, nodding and facing the yard, which was full of guys in purple shirts and girls drinking and laughing. There was an area to the far left where there was a makeshift dance floor set up with a DJ. Only a couple of people were actually dancing there, and one couple in particular caught my eye. The guy was mainly just standing there, moving in a two-step, while the girl had her hands up, running her fingers through her long, brown hair. She wore a short, tight, black dress that captured every curve on her body, and on her feet, black converse. I was completely mesmerized by her and the way she moved her body. It was like she was doing a striptease without the stripping. Somehow, her dress, as short as it was, covered her nicely shaped ass. I opened my mouth to say something about her to Victor, but then she turned around, smiling, her back facing the guy she was dancing with, and I realized I knew her.

"What the fuck?" I nearly growled.

"What?" Vic said, snapping his eyes to meet mine.

"You let Elle wear that to this party?" I knew I sounded like a jealous boyfriend and I had no right, but here was the girl we were all constantly warned to stay away from and grew up taking care of like she was our own sister, and then . . . whatever . . . and here she was . . . and here was Vic. "What the fuck?" I repeated, glaring at him.

He looked at me like I was crazy and laughed at what was probably a furious look on my face. "She's eighteen. I can't really tell her what to wear, and hello . . . have you ever known her to wear anything more? Besides . . . I've been standing here watching her like a freaking hawk all night just in case that asshole tries anything stupid."

I gathered the hair that had fallen out of the bun I'd put it in and thought about what he said. I hadn't really noticed. We spent that summer together, talking almost every night on her roof and she always looked clothed enough. Well, not really, now that I thought about it. She was always wearing loose shirts and tiny shorts, or pajama pants and tiny shirts. I'd never really seen her at a party, other than her own or Victor's. Those times, she didn't wear make-up or tight ass dresses that would make any breathing male want to bend her over by the bushes and fuck her.

"I haven't really noticed, no," I said, finally.

He laughed. "That's because she's like your sister."

I froze. She was like a sister at one point when we were young, before she grew up. Before that summer happened. I didn't think my heart could take watching another one of those dances, knowing it was her, and that I wasn't that guy.

"Who's the guy?"

"Uh, that's Adam. I think she said his name is Adam."

"She brought him?" Why did that bother me?

"Yeah. Something about Mia not being able to come, and she didn't want to come by herself to hang out with a bunch of horny guys and annoying girls she didn't know."

I laughed. Annoying girls. That sounded like something

she would say, but what did I know? I didn't know this Elle.

"So they're dating?" I pointed at them. They finally pulled apart and walked away from the floor. As they headed in our direction, Elle pulled her hair up into a ponytail and then let it flow through her fingers to drift back down. She was laughing at something Adam said behind her, and I wondered if he was making a joke about her ass, because that's where his eyes were.

"Nah, I don't think so. She's not into the serious relationship thing."

I gaped at Victor, and he gave me a shrug. "You're okay with that?"

He shrugged again, drinking his beer. "What am I supposed to tell her? Go get married, Elle, you need to go get married right now? She's eighteen!"

The thought of Elle getting married right now didn't bode well for me, so I stayed quiet and glanced in her direction again. I could see her eyebrows pull together as she got closer and the smile on her face drop when she saw me. My chest squeezed a little. What had I ever done to her? Shouldn't she be smiling?

"Hey, Bean," she said as she neared me. In that moment, for the first time ever—as I watched her plump lips moving as she spoke—I hated that she used my nickname. The nickname my mother had given me, no less. Bean sprout, she used to call me. It kind of stuck, to the point that all my friends used it when they addressed me. It never bothered me when little girl Elle said it, but grown-up Elle? I wanted her to call me Oliver. I wanted her to *scream* Oliver. And on that note, I cleared my throat.

"Hey, Chicken," I said, my smile growing when she glared as I used her nickname.

Adam chimed in with a laugh. "Chicken?"

Elle groaned. "Long story."

"It's not really that long," Vic said. "She was scared of everything as a kid, hence the name Chicken."

She rolled her eyes and took the cup of beer Vic had just poured for himself, chugging it down quickly. And I stood there, gaping, completely-fucking-entranced by the way she wiped under her mouth using two fingers, and at the wide smile in response to whatever it was Adam was saying. I couldn't concentrate on his words—I could only hear her throaty laugh and see her face . . . her body . . . and I really needed to stop. I knew I needed to stop. Adam said something about the bathroom, Vic pointed, and I seethed as Elle watched him walk away.

"How's the basil?" she asked Vic, who shrugged.

"Your plant, not mine."

"You're kidding me. Victor, how do you expect it to stay alive if you don't care for it?" she asked. "I'm going to go look."

"What basil?" I asked, watching her ass sway as she walked away.

"She planted some basil on the side of my house because her apartment has no proper lighting or something, and she expects me to take care of it. I don't know." He shrugged.

"Huh. I'm going to go see it."

"Good, that way you can keep an eye on her," he said.

I cocked an eyebrow. "What happened to 'she's eighteen'?"

"Well, yeah, she can be eighteen with Adam and shit—not with my fraternity brothers. That's different."

I stared at him, waiting for him to elaborate. He let out an impatient breath and shook his head. "That's sacred. That's like if I make a move on Sophie or something. You just don't do that shit."

I didn't bother to point out to him that Sophie was older than we were, and married, because I understood where he was coming from. She was Elle, the baby sister, and we were Vic's dickhead friends, the ones who liked to sleep around and had STD scares. Not the kind of guys you want around your sisters. It hurt though. The realization of how he felt and how he expected it to be that way, warred with the fact that looking at Elle made me yearn for something I knew I couldn't have.

The loud sounds of the party died down with each step I took toward the side of the house—the direction she'd gone. I stopped when I found her. She was bent over, looking at the plant on the ground, and I took a couple of seconds to admire how good she looked in that position.

"When did you get into gardening?" I asked, walking closer.

Her head snapped up, and she straightened with a shrug and a smile. "It's new. I'm trying to eat healthy. I want to plant my own crops, but it's kind of impossible in my dorm."

I stood beside her and faced the plant. "It looks good."

"Yeah, it smells good, too," she said. I could hear the smile in her voice, and it made me smile.

"So, how has your first semester been?"

"It's been . . . good, actually. Fun."

I turned my body to face her, tucking my thumbs in the front pockets of my jeans. "It sounds like you're having too much fun."

Elle tilted her head to look at me, wearing that tiny frown she got when she was trying to figure something out.

"What makes you say that?"

"I don't know. Adam . . . you dancing . . . Vic saying you're not into relationships . . ." I shrugged.

She laughed, her eyes lit in amusement. "That's something, coming from you."

"What's that supposed to mean?"

"You've never been into relationships. You have all the fun in the world."

"That's different."

"Different how? Is it because I'm a girl?" she asked, crossing her arms over her chest.

"No," I said quickly. "It's not that." It wasn't. The women I fucked were all single and not into relationships—it was what we had most in common. But this was Elle. This was . . . *Elle.*

"So what is it?" she challenged.

I groaned, running my hand over my hair and leaving it there. "I don't know. I . . . don't know. You're right. You should do whatever you want."

"Your hair's gotten longer," she said, her eyes trailing from mine, to my bicep, and then my head. I smiled.

"You can braid it better now."

She smiled. "Turn around."

I did. My shoulders stiffened when I felt her hands on them. "I can't reach. You're going to have to kneel down," she whispered against my neck. My eyes fell closed as I tried to contain the fire beginning to blaze through me. I turned and walked to a bench at the side of the house. It was gross, and Vic had been trying to get rid of it for years, but right now, I was glad it was there.

Elle sat beside me, and I turned my back so she could let my hair down. I cringed when she pulled on the rubber band.

"I told you to stop using these," she said, sighing heavily as she ran her fingers through my hair. She massaged my scalp as if she was washing it. I resisted the urge to moan at how good it felt. Women loved to pull on my hair, and I never complained about that, but there was something about the way Elle touched it that made a tingling sensation run through me. When she was finished combing it through, she dropped her hands. The pause was long enough for me to turn my body and face her.

"You're not going to braid it?" I asked, frowning as I took in the faraway expression on her face.

She shook her head, her eyes dropping to my chest. I moved closer, until our faces were inches apart, but she still didn't look at me.

"Elle?" I asked, my voice a whisper.

Her eyes snapped to mine and for a beat, I got lost in the way the different colors in them swirled. They always reminded me of a marble. My favorite marble—blue, green, and brown. The way she looked at me made my heart pound. It was like a world of wonder lived in those eyes. I wished I could see myself the way she saw me. Maybe I would be a different person if I could. Maybe I would be a one-woman man—a man who wanted to go visit her parents for the weekend and get serious right now. Looking at Elle—right there at that moment—made me want to be that guy.

"I was, but it brings back memories," she whispered. "Braiding your hair, I mean."

I nodded and swallowed, pushing my hands down over my thighs so I wouldn't touch her.

"Do you remember when I asked you if you would kiss me when I was eighteen?" she asked in a whisper. She reached out and tapped the tips of her fingers over my knuckles as if they were piano keys. It made my heart beat faster.

"Yeah," I matched her whisper, but mine sounded hoarse.

"Would you?" Her eyes bounced to each of mine, her hands stilling over mine. "Would you kiss me, Oliver?"

My heart was beating so fast, I couldn't think. My lips parted slightly, and I nodded. I was always the chaser—the one sweet-talking girls—but this girl always seemed to have me at a loss for words. She threw me off balance. We moved toward one another until the tips of our noses touched. We held each other's gaze and, a millisecond apart, we closed our eyes. Our mouths touched . . . my lips slid between hers . . . her tongue slipped into my mouth . . . and as soon as it touched mine, I felt the fire ignited earlier, roll through me at full blaze.

Kissing Estelle felt like what I could only imagine kissing a cloud was like—light and sweet, and all consuming. Our mouths moved together in sync, as if we'd been kissing since we were born. Our hands framed each other's faces, like we were scared to pull away because the moment would be over. I'd never wanted to melt and disappear into a girl's mouth as much as I wanted to right then. When I finally broke the kiss—because my hands were developing a mind of their own and I didn't want to do something I would regret tomorrow—her eyes popped open. She looked at me like she was just seeing me for the first time—or maybe that's just how I felt because I wanted her to look at me like that. I kissed her again, this time more urgently, and groaned into her mouth when her hands pulled my hair. We pulled apart one last time, our chests heaving, when we heard someone calling out her name.

"That's Adam. He probably wants to leave," she said, panting.

"Are you going to go have fun with him?" I asked, dipping my head and taking her bottom lip between my teeth. She moaned and pulled on my hair, readjusting so she could straddle my hips. My hands moved to her thighs of their own accord. Everything in me wanted her so bad—all of her. And for so much more than just a make-out session.

"I'm having fun with you," she said against my lips, grinding down on me.

"Fuck, yes," I said in a moan, when she did it again.

Our tongues met and, as Estelle moved, I guided her hips to meet my thrusts. It was crazy. We were crazy. Anybody from the party could turn the corner and find us there, dry humping on that dirty bench, but we didn't care. We weren't *really* having sex, anyway, even though I wanted to. I wanted to pull my dick out of my pants and slip inside her more than anything, but this was Estelle, she didn't deserve a quick fuck at a frat party. Her name got louder, and we tore away from each other quickly. She sat back beside me as we caught our breaths, and finally a figure appeared in the corner.

"Elle, I've been looking everywhere. You're still looking at that damn plant?" Vic said, walking over to us.

"Yeah, well, we were talking," she said, standing up and straightening her dress.

"Adam is throwing up everywhere. You might want to take him home," he said.

She sighed heavily. "Are you serious? I don't bring a girl with me because I don't want to babysit, and then the guy I bring acts like a drunk sorority girl?"

I chuckled. "You want help?"

She shrugged. "I guess. If you don't mind."

I stood and followed to where the guy was. We waited for him to finish puking and I helped him get to the car—a shiny black BMW, which apparently he owned. It happened to be parked beside my beat-up Maxima and, for some reason, this drunk little shit having this car and trying to make a move on Elle bothered me. She'd never been a materialistic girl. I knew she didn't need much, but it made me feel a little inadequate and reminded me why I was waiting to settle down. I wanted to be at a secure place in my life when I settled down. I wanted the car, the house—and anything else my mind could conjure up as a necessity—out of the way before that happened, and I knew it wouldn't happen any time soon.

When she got into the driver's seat and started the car, I walked to her window. We looked at each other for a long moment, and then she smiled shyly.

"I always wondered what it would feel like to kiss you," she whispered. I grinned and looked around the driveway. Everybody was inside the party, so I dipped my head into the window and kissed her again, not caring that Adam was sitting there. He was passed out anyway.

"And?" I asked when I backed away.

"It was . . . everything." Her face lit up when she said it. "But don't worry; I know it was a one-time thing."

My smile vanished. I wanted to tell her it could be more. We went to nearby schools. It could be more. Then I remembered who she was and that her brother would never approve of me dating his sister. With my track record, I wouldn't approve of me either. And she was only eighteen. It was her first semester of college, and I was about to graduate and go to medical school.

"You're the one who wants to have fun now that you're a college girl," I said jokingly, kind of hoping she'd say otherwise. Instead, she smiled brighter.

"That, I do. See you next time, Bean."

Adam groaned beside her, and we both froze and glanced his way. He stayed put.

"Yeah, next time," I said, as she drove away. I sighed. My heart felt heavy as the taillights disappeared around the bend. I wondered if it would ever again stagger and skyrocket the way it just had.

Chapter 13

Estelle

Present

I HATE FIGHTING.

I hate being wrong, but I hate fighting more than I hate being wrong. I'm just not good at the grudge-holding thing. I get mad, scream about it and let go. Mia, on the other hand, gets mad, screams about it, and clings on to her anger like a leech. Needless to say, we haven't spoken in a couple of days. I'd managed to avoid Oliver the past few days at the hospital, while I painted vinyl records and surfboards with the kids. I saw him a couple of times by the nurses' station, though, and once leaving Jen's office. I caught glimpses of what his life must be like—the flirting, the multitude of sexual partners, the late night rendezvous he probably has in the hospital during the night shift. They aren't things I necessarily want to imagine, but that's just where my mind automatically goes when it comes to Oliver.

Two of my friends, Micah and Dallas, are standing in the

middle of the hallway of the pediatrics floor, both with the same disgusted looks on their faces that I had when I saw the walls. I could tell from the way Micah keeps running his hands through his long blonde hair that he's nervous about taking this project on. Dallas is just full-on gaping, as if the walls are taunting him. Micah turns first and shoots me a *what the fuck did you get us into* look that I have to laugh at.

"But for real," he says when I reach them. My arms swing around his middle, and I squeeze.

"Thank you, thank you, thank you," I say against his back and then do the same to Dallas.

"Honey, this thank you better come with a blow job," Dallas says as I pull away, laughing loudly until I hear a throat clearing behind me. I turn to find Oliver standing there with a strange look on his face. That makes me laugh harder, because clearly, he'd heard Dallas.

"Hey," I say. "This is Micah and Dallas. Guys, this is Oliver, my brother's friend—the one who got me into this whole thing."

As they nod at each other, Dallas, who's just slightly taller than me, gives Oliver a quick onceover, and Micah throws out a "hey man" that makes him sound like a stoner straight out of Woodstock. Oliver returns their greetings politely before his eyes return to mine.

"May I speak to you for a moment?" he asks, the intensity in his eyes making my stomach twist.

"Sure. Guys, the paint is in there. I think we should start with the room on the far left first. I'll be right back," I say, pointing to the room before turning to follow Oliver with a frown. "Where are we going?"

He opens a door and signals for me to go inside, but I stand rooted in place. This side of the hospital is vacant because of the paint project, but I don't want somebody to see us and get the wrong idea.

"Come in."

"We can talk here."

Oliver closes his eyes and takes a deep breath as if he's trying to calm himself down. When he opens them, they look more tired than before, if possible. "Please, Elle. Just humor me."

I shake my head, but do as he says, because I don't want to leave the guys alone for too long. He's invited me into some sort of storage room, with a bunch of filing cabinets lined up along the walls.

"So?" I ask, turning to face him. He's leaning against the door with his hands in the pockets of his white coat, just staring at me. "What?"

"I haven't heard from you. I haven't seen you, and then when I finally do, some guy is talking about you giving him a blow job?" He doesn't sound upset, just confused and maybe a little hurt, I think, which is ridiculous and impossible—because this is Oliver we're talking about.

"And?"

"And I miss you."

My heart trips a little at his admission and the way he says it, all smooth and low. Then I remember Wyatt and his "I miss you's," which weren't said often, only when he was away on one of his many trips, and only after it'd been a couple of days since we'd spoken. I never questioned him or what he was doing. I never wondered if he'd been with another woman, and even the times Mia planted that seed in my head, nothing grew from it, because for some reason, I didn't care. I always wondered if there was something wrong with me for not caring.

"You don't miss me, Oliver. Besides, aren't you dating someone?" I remind him with a glare.

He rolls his eyes. "It's just a thing, I wouldn't call it dating."

"Just fucking," I say, sounding more bitter than I intended. "Not that I care," I add quickly. Oliver smirks, and I feel my face growing hot. "I have shit to do," I say, finally coming to my senses and stepping forward, but he doesn't move away from the door.

"Are you having fun with him?" he asks, nodding his head toward the outside. Having fun with him. It's funny how I can straight-out ask him if he's fucking somebody, but when he asks me, he uses the term *having fun*. It reminds me of when we were teenagers, and Mia's mom would call her boyfriends her *little friends*. "Or is it the guy with the long hair that you like? I know you have a thing for that."

I take a step back. I do have a thing for guys with long hair, probably because of him. I should hate guys with long hair because of him. I should, but of course, I don't. Oliver's hair isn't long anymore, but it's still long enough to run your hands through and tug on if his head is between your legs. He has a sandy brown scruff going on over his jaw that isn't just a five o'clock shadow anymore. It would probably feel delicious against the inside of my thighs.

"Why are you looking at me like that?" he asks, the huskiness in his voice snapping me out of my fantasy.

"Huh?"

He takes a step forward so he's right in front of me, my eyes at the level of the Dr. Hart ID on the pocket of his left pec.

"Elle. Look at me," he says. A slow, curling desire winds its way around my belly. I have two options: push past him and leave, or look into his eyes and acknowledge the desire that heats the air between us like a blowtorch. I choose the latter because I'm a moron, and because clearly, I like to have my heart shredded repeatedly. "You want me. After all this time, you still want me."

"I don't have time for this right now. They're waiting for me," I whisper, trying to pull away from the electrical current that is his gaze.

"One date, Elle. One date. I'm keeping my word and not touching you, I promise."

"You're already fucking someone. Do you really need another?"

His eyes narrow slightly. "For your information, I'm not. Do you really think this is about fucking you?"

I don't know, I want to say. History tends to repeat itself, but I hold my tongue on that part.

"I don't know what it's about," I respond, dragging my eyes away. I feel like I'm suffocating in this tiny space with him. I try to brush past, but he grabs my arm.

"One date."

I close my eyes and shake my head, regretting it when I feel tears start to prick them. "I'm not ready."

He drops his hand, looking pained. He'll live; he always finds things to fill his time with. As I open the door, I look at him over my shoulder.

"By the way, Dallas, the blow job guy, is gay. Micah, the guy with the hair, was one of Wyatt's best friends, and he is *so* not my type."

"He's cute," Dallas says later, while we're priming the walls, and I know he's talking about Oliver, so I make a grunting, annoyed sound that makes him laugh. My eyes sweep over to Micah, who doesn't comment.

"I'm just saying, I would totally do him," Dallas adds.

"He would probably do you too if he swung your way. You're older, kind of good looking with your nerdy boy glasses and your bow tie . . . yeah, I think he would." My words make him smile and roll his eyes.

"What did he want to talk about?" Micah asks, and my heart starts thumping in my ears. His tone is always nonchalant, so I can't read him properly, and that kills me.

"Just stuff."

"You dating him?" he asks. I suck in a breath. In a sense, I feel like Micah is the string telephone between Wyatt and me, and as soon as I feel like I'm cutting the string, he tightens the knot so I can't.

"No, I'm not dating him! I'm not dating anybody."

Micah sighs heavily and puts the roller down before turning to face me. "He's not coming back, you know? He's not on one of his trips around the world where he'll be back next week. You have every right to move on."

"I'm not ready," I say, my voice cracking as I pick up a roller back and continue painting. I hear the metal roller handle he's holding clatter to the floor, followed by approaching footsteps. I know he's behind me, but I refuse to turn around. I know if I do, I'll cry. I know if he keeps talking, I'll cry. I don't want to cry in here. I want this project to be about hope and life, not pain and loss.

"That wall," Micah says, standing beside me as he points at the wall. "That wall is your life, Elle. The blue isn't ugly, and it's not sad, but we're painting over it because its time is over. The nurses who walk in here won't forget how it looked. The kids who stare at these walls all day won't forget, and maybe they'll miss it sometimes, but we have to give them something that makes them happy to look at. Life is short, and brutal, and painful, and it takes loved ones away from us as quickly as it brings them into our lives, but it's also beautiful. Wyatt would want you to move on and be happy. Date, get married, have kids, travel . . . do whatever makes you feel alive. The longer you mourn, the less you live, and you know how short our time here can be."

Imaginary fingers curl around my throat and squeeze so tightly that I can't even respond. I don't even realize I'm crying until Micah pulls me into his chest, and a loud, wet sob escapes me. I hear something drop on the other side of the room and feel Dallas' arms wrap around us so that we're standing there, all three of us crying for the missing pair of arms that would've covered us all. I call it a night shortly after that, because I can't look at the wall without crying. As I head out, I see Oliver leaning his elbows on the counter with his face buried in his hands. I wonder if he's tired or if one of his patients isn't doing well.

I keep thinking about the damn blue wall, and even though I have reasons not to, I want to comfort him. Sorting through the negative memories in the past, I focus on the good ones and cling to those. Without further hesitation, I walk up behind him and wrap my arms around his middle, laying my cheek over his back. His body stiffens.

"We go out as friends. No date," I say against him, and feel him let out a long breath. I drop my hands when he straightens and turns to face me, his eyebrows furrowing as he scans my face. "Okay?" I ask in a whisper. He doesn't respond. Instead, he brings one of his hands up to cup my cheek. I shiver, as he runs the pad of his thumb over it slowly.

"Okay. A friends date," he responds. He holds my gaze as dips his head. I start to lose composure. Oliver knows my date rules include no kissing, and we're not even on a date, friends or otherwise. But, when his breath falls over my lips, my eyes flutter closed. He doesn't kiss me though. His lips land on the very corner of my mouth, like they did so many years ago on the roof of my parents' house. You would think with the one-man band going on inside my chest, that he'd done something more risqué. My eyes open slowly as he backs away from me, his eyes examining me as if I'm some sort of ancient artifact.

"It's still a yes, right? I didn't break any rules."

I nod slowly, enthralled by him, despite inner thoughts screaming *NO.* If that was his friendly kiss, I don't think I would survive a real one from him, even now that I know better.

"You'll send me the rest of the rules? Even if we are just going out as friends?" he asks, with a sparkle in his eyes that makes me nervous.

I nod again.

"At a loss for words?"

"You caught me off guard," I whisper.

He tries to hide a smile, but I see the dimples deepen in his cheeks, so I know it's there.

"You just made a really bad day a whole lot better for me," he replies, cupping my face and running his thumb over my bottom lip.

"You want to talk about it?" I ask, leaning into his touch.

He shakes his head and smiles sadly. "This is enough."

I can't help it; I smile back. We stand like that for a moment, staring into each other's eyes, his finger on my mouth and my heart in his hands, until the hospital speaker calls out his name.

"I should go. You have work and, unlike some people, I need sleep."

Oliver nods, drops his hand from my face, and steps toward the patient rooms.

"Good night, beautiful Elle."

"Good night, handsome Oliver," I say with a smile.

He grins as I turn to walk away.

"Text me when you get home," he calls out. I leave the hospital feeling much lighter than I did when I walked in. When I get to my car and press a hand to the spot his lips touched, I swear I can feel it tingling. I close my eyes and try to remember if Wyatt ever made me feel that way. I loved him—I really did—but every time I'm around Oliver, it's something I question. It makes me feel terrible for even comparing the two. Maybe I just loved them differently. Maybe Oliver has been more of a familiar, teenage-hormones kind of love and Wyatt was more of an adult, predictably stable kind of love. I can't decide which is best, or if either of them are, really. Not that I have to. Wyatt is gone, and there's nothing I can do about that. So why does going on a just friends date with Oliver make me feel like I'm making the ultimate betrayal to his memory?

Chapter 14

I'M PACING THE gallery when a woman opens the door and makes me stop in my tracks. She smiles as she lifts her sunglasses into her hair. She's older—probably the same age as my mom—and carries herself with the grace of a prima ballerina.

"Are you the owner?" she asks, looking around once before settling on me again.

"Yes," I respond, and walk to her. "Estelle Reuben. Have you been here before?" I ask. She looks familiar, but I can't place her. In the past, Wyatt and I hosted painting reveals in our gallery, so I figure maybe she came to one of those.

"Actually, I haven't. I think we may have met once in New York," she says, tilting her face to examine mine. "You're Wyatt's . . ."

"Fiancé." I fill in the blank. Fiancé, ex-fiancé, fiancé before death, I never really know what to say to a stranger who knew of me.

"I'm sorry for your loss," she says, smiling sadly. Her face muscles don't move much when she smiles, and it makes her look a little more grim than it does compassionate, but I return it nonetheless.

"Thank you. Do you collect?" I ask, figuring she must, if we met in New York.

"Yes. I've had my eyes on that one for a very long time." She lifts a delicate hand and points at my main attraction, the eye that watches over the gallery.

"Oh," I say in a whisper.

"How much for it?" she asks. "I've tried to buy it in the past to no avail."

My eyes widen as realization washes through me. "Priscilla?" I say, turning to face her. Priscilla Woods has been calling—and has had her husband's assistant call—for almost a year now. I keep turning down their offers, although they're big sums, because she wants my two favorite paintings, and I haven't been ready to give them up.

"You remember," she says smiling. "I'm in town for a couple of days, so I figured I would stop by to see if you're ready to sell these pieces to me."

"That one isn't for sale," I say, clearing my throat to make sure I'm heard.

"And the other? The shattered hearts with wings?"

I look away from her, toward where the painting hangs on the opposite wall. "It's called Winged Kaleidoscopes," I reply, suddenly feeling a lump settle in my throat. Wyatt painted it shortly after we got engaged. He painted three, sold two, and kept one for the gallery. I was never sure if he would sell it, even though the meaning behind it always made me tear up and smile. Ultimately, it was his painting to do with what he pleased.

"It's beautiful," she says, and she walks to stand before it. "It reminds me of a rebirth of some sort."

I nod and swallow, hoping to stay put together enough to get through a conversation. "It's very much a rebirth." It's a rebirth of my heart, of my hopes of love, of my love life, and the birth of our relationship.

"It doesn't have a price tag," she says.

"Some things don't have a price."

She turns to me and tilts her head. "Nothing tangible is priceless."

"Maybe not, but the memories behind them are."

My response makes her nod in understanding. Her eyes dart away from mine and look back to the painting. "So you're not willing to let go of the memories it holds?"

I stare at the painting in silence. I know that no price will ever be enough to cover those memories, but they'll forever be embedded in my brain, so maybe I should stop thinking about his paintings in terms of that. In the past couple of weeks, I've managed to turn over a new leaf. I feel like I'm headed in the right direction, yet when I'm faced with something like this—the reality of letting go, *really letting go,* of the past three years of my life—I stall like a car switching gears. I take a long breath, inhaling the ever-present smell of wood and paint, and when I let it out, I have my mind made up.

"I'm ready to let go of it," I say, my voice steady and determined.

Priscilla turns around and claps her hands in front of her with a happy squeal—the exact opposite of everything she looks like—with her fine pearls and perfect bob. It makes me smile a little, and I feel less sad about selling the painting.

"I can deliver it to your house," I say, knowing it's sold, because when somebody with money sets their eyes on something, they don't walk out without it.

"I live in New York," she responds. "I wouldn't expect you to fly all the way over there to deliver something."

"We do it all the time. I wouldn't feel right shipping it to you. Not this one."

She offers me a small smile. "I'll be taking it myself. We own a jet, so it wouldn't even fly in a closet. It will be well taken care of."

The way she speaks about it—as if it was a child—makes me feel slightly better about the sale.

"I'll draw up the paperwork for you."

"Do I have time to run across the street? I'm supposed to meet my girlfriend for lunch," she says, looking at her watch.

"Of course. I just need some information from you. I'll have it ready and packed up by the time you finish."

"Perfect. I can't wait to hang this on top of my fireplace and show off my new painting," she says.

Her painting. I try not to let the words puncture me, but they do anyway. When she leaves and I finish the paperwork, I take down the painting, gripping the edges of the canvas as I set it down on the floor. I fold my legs beneath me and let my fingertips graze each shattered heart, colorful and beautiful, and the wings that lift them up. Tears slide down my face as I touch each one and say my goodbyes. I begin to cover it, one layer, two layers, three . . . stopping to wipe my face with each wraparound I make. I think about the serious look on Wyatt's face as he'd mixed the watercolors . . . the look of elation as he'd gotten to the ivory wings when his vision came together on the canvas.

"Do you like it?" he'd asked. His face had beamed when it became clear that I loved it.

"I never want to sell it," I said, as he laughed and wrapped his arms around me, squeezing me into him.

"One day we will. When we get sick of looking at it."

I hope he doesn't think I got tired of looking at it, because I'm not. I don't think I will ever tire of staring at his paintings, but this isn't about that. This is my goodbye, I say to myself as I stand up and, with a heavy heart, hand a piece of my past over to somebody else. She will never know the history behind it, but she will appreciate it nonetheless.

Chapter 15

ON DAY FOUR of Mia-hiatus, I call her, and after we've had a long conversation about things, I drive over to her studio. I push the door open when I get there and take a moment to admire the photographs she has hanging on the wall. She's changed them all since my last visit. To the right, there's a black and white photo of a woman lying in bed. She's facing away from the camera, and the white bed sheets are bunched up at her bottom, so all you see is the curve of her naked back and lush black hair covering half of her shoulder. The lighting and the pose create a photo that is absolutely stunning. The wall facing the door features a family: The dad is wearing brown corduroy pants, a navy blue, button-down shirt, and, on his head, a Chewbacca mask that covers his face. The small boy beside him is dressed similarly and wears a storm trooper mask. Mom stands on the other side of their son and wears tight brown pants, a white shirt, and has styled her brown hair like Princess Leia. As I laugh at how adorable it is, I startle when Mia rounds the corner to greet me.

I glance down and notice she's wearing a red wrap dress and no shoes, which is funny because I'm wearing the same dress in black. We give each other a quick onceover and laugh.

"Hi," I say sheepishly.

"I'm sorry I'm such an asshole, and I'm sorry I wasn't there when you sold that painting," she replies, repeating what she said in our phone call.

"It's okay. I was fine. I'm sorry I said what I said—it wasn't my place."

We both let out a breath and walk forward with our arms held out, wrapping the other in a tight hug.

"You're such a bitch sometimes," she says against my neck.

"It's why we're friends." We pull away from each other, and I look back at the wall in front of us. "I really love this picture."

Mia smiles. "Isn't it awesome? It's their Halloween card this year."

"That one is stunning," I say, nodding at the one of the woman's back.

"Yeah, boudoir shoot for her soon-to-be husband. Lovely girl." She turns her blue eyes to me. "When are you going to let me shoot one of those for you? You'd be perfect."

I make a noise. "I would suck at that. I don't know how to look sexy on purpose."

Mia laughs. "That's what makes sexy, sexy! If you try too hard, you end up looking like an idiot. I'll help you though—you know I know how to work my magic."

"Yeah, clearly," I say, waving around her studio.

"Hey, do you want to be in a shoot for me this weekend?"

"A shoot? I came to take you out to lunch and grovel for forgiveness, not schedule a sexy shoot!"

"I know, but I have this model I'm shooting, and the girl just canceled on us because she's too sick to do it, and to top it off, this is a major shoot for a local magazine, and I'm supposed to have these pictures to them by next week. This is huge, Elle. This could be my moment."

"Shit," I say, letting out a slow breath.

"Yeah, shit. Every model I've worked with has given me a 'maybe,' and I can't deal with maybe right now."

She looks like she's about to cry, and I hate to see her this stressed over a job.

"Okay. I'll do it," I say. I mean, I've done this for her before. How bad can it be?

"Ah! Thank you!" she says, giving a little jump and hugging me again.

"Is this . . . okay, remember that time you made me take pictures with a guy on the beach? Is this like that?" That wasn't so bad until Wyatt showed up. We'd been frolicking in the water and doing our best not to look at the camera and pretend we had chemistry—which is hard to do with a guy you don't know, no matter how cute he is.

By the time we got comfortable with each other—comfortable enough to go in for the make-believe "we're about to kiss" shot—Wyatt showed up. He made me so nervous, I couldn't get back to feeling natural with the guy. Needless to say, that was strike one for him in Mia's book. It was terrible.

Mia's laugh snaps me back from my thoughts. "No, this will be indoors and much more intimate, so it's a good thing you haven't found a boyfriend yet."

"Yeah, thank God for that," I say halfheartedly, before I let her get back to work and head to my own studio. I make a mental note to grab a sandwich along the way.

Later, as I'm setting up for the kids to arrive, I get a text message from Oliver that makes me frown.

Rule #1- no short dresses.

I stare at it for a long moment, look down at myself, then outside to see if he's stalking me.

Are you stalking me?

??

Are you watching me from somewhere

right now?

The phone starts to vibrate with his name on the screen.

"Does that mean you're wearing a short dress right now?" he asks in a whisper.

"Yes, and from the sound of your voice, I'm guessing you're in the hospital."

"How short?" he asks, ignoring my statement.

"Friends, Oliver," I remind him.

"Just tell me how short it is, for the love of God. I need a visual."

"Just above my knees."

"What color?"

"Black."

I hear a door open and close before his breath is back on my ear. I shiver as if he's standing behind me.

"Is it tight?"

I laugh. "Are you going to try to have phone sex with me at three o'clock in the afternoon? From work?"

He exhales. "I sent you a text message to tell you not to wear a short dress to our friend date, and you're telling me you're wearing one right now, in plain sight, for everyone to see."

"And? You act like I'm wearing lingerie."

"No, but every male in Santa Barbara is going to be looking at those legs of yours and wishing they were wrapped around their waist, and seeing the tops of your tits and wishing they could pull the dress down to get a better look . . ."

"Oliver!" I interrupt, completely flustered. I'm starting to get hot flashes and breathe heavily, and he's not even there to do any of those things to me. "Friends!" I shout. "Friends! I'm not going out with you if you keep saying these things to me."

He doesn't speak for so long that I actually look at my screen to make sure he's still there.

"What does me saying these things do to you, Estelle?" he asks, his voice grating over me, making me shiver involuntarily.

"Nothing," I whisper.

"Nothing?" I close my eyes at the challenge in his voice, knowing I should have just ignored the question altogether. "It doesn't make you wish we were alone somewhere?"

"Why would I wish that?" I ask, hoping my voice sounds steadier than it feels.

"Because if we were, I'd slip my hand under your dress . . ." he pauses and drops his voice even lower. "Into your panties."

"Who says I'm wearing any?" I ask in a breath.

"Are you not wearing panties, naughty Elle?" The smile in his voice makes a blush creep over my face.

"Maybe."

"If I slip my hand under your dress and find that you're not, I wouldn't be able to resist. I'd have to pull the dress over your head and find out if you're completely naked beneath it."

"And what if I am?" I ask quietly. *Why am I playing this game? Why, why, why am I entertaining this? Why am I enjoying it?*

"You'd be in a lot of trouble," he says with a rough growl that makes my heart skip.

"Oh yeah? What kind of trouble?" I tease.

"First I'd want to taste you," he starts.

"No kissing on friend dates," I taunt with a smile.

"I wouldn't be kissing your mouth," he says in a voice that makes my heart lurch, before he continues, "I'd take my time, kissing my way down your body until I reach your ankles, and then I'd move back up slowly, my tongue tracing the inside of your thighs . . . tasting every inch of you . . ." His words are a purr, and I'm panting at the vivid picture he's painting for me as if I can feel his hot tongue on my sensitive skin. "I'll savor you until you beg for my lips and mouth to fuck that—"

"Oliver!" I snap, a moan escaping my lips. I totally asked for that—I know I did—but hearing the actual words from him make me feel too hot, too bothered, too . . . much. I take a breath and manage to squeak out, "Don't you have lives to save?"

"I'm on break," he responds nonchalantly, as if he hadn't just said all those things to me. "I do eat lunch, you know."

"You're phone-sexing on your lunch break?" My eyes pop open and blink rapidly to adjust to the light in my studio.

He chuckles. "I'm skilled like that."

"Okay . . . I'm going to let you go now so you can finish enjoying your lunch break."

"You don't have to. I have a raging hard-on right now, and I have to hide in this dark closet until I figure out what to do about it before I can go about my day."

I sigh, sagging down to the seat behind me. Images of him flirting with all the nurses flash through my mind before I can stop them. "I'm sure there are many willing nurses . . . and hospital execs willing to help you out with that."

Silence again, followed by a harsh exhale. "I wish you wouldn't think so poorly of me."

"I wish you wouldn't have put those thoughts there to begin with, but that's life, Bean."

"I hate it when you call me Bean," he whispers, his voice suddenly morphing into something deeper, something sadder.

"Why?" I whisper back, even though I'm completely alone.

"I have my reasons," he says, before clearing his throat. "Anyway, the problem is gone, so no need to call for backup. Not that I would have."

"Okay, well . . . have a good day," I say, not knowing what else to say.

"You too."

I put the phone down, and as I'm about to pick up a piece of broken glass to start on my sculpture, it vibrates again.

Next rule: no "Bean" on our friend date.

Okay.

No Chicken, either. Only Estelle and Oliver.

Winged creatures flutter inside me.

E & O

Thank u. It's been a rough week. I needed that smile today.

When he says things like this, he makes me want to cry. I know his job is hard, and the fact that he wants to continue with pediatrics once he finishes his residency is something I can't fathom. Seeing him looking so defeated the other day was so unlike him. And now this message? It breaks my heart.

::curtsies:: I'll be here all day.

In your dress?

LOL. In my dress!

Neither of us responds after that and, as I continue to make my usual shattered, kaleidoscope heart, I smile. He's the reason I started making these in the first place, even though Wyatt was the one who taught me how to perfect them so that the heart wouldn't fall apart. I can't help but wonder if that was a sign somehow, but I don't let that idea hang around for too long. There's no point in believing in destiny if you're too stubborn to give in to it.

Chapter 16

MY FRIEND DATE with Oliver ends up falling on a Saturday. We've only seen each other in passing since our last text message-slash-phone conversation, and I've mainly been focusing on painting the rooms with Micah and Dallas.

Oliver gave me three rules for our date: no short dresses, wear comfortable shoes, and no lipstick. I had to outright laugh at the last rule, and of course, I didn't abide by it. I dressed in jeans, low black boots, and a frilly, white tank top with a dark green jacket over it in case it gets cold later. I left my hair down and straightened it, and put on my make-up—dark red lipstick included. As I looked in the mirror, I smiled at my reflection. Before I met Wyatt, I never wore lipstick. He was the one who suggested it, along with more grown-up clothing. I liked the change. He was older than me and more knowledgeable. He'd lived a fuller life, so any time he made a suggestion, I took it to heart.

Before Wyatt, I dressed however I wanted—short dresses, tight skirts, big heels, you name it. He slowly got me away from those things and into more, what he would call "adult clothes." Mia thought I was an idiot. She said that, because we were only twenty-one, we could (and should) show off our assets.

"Especially you, with your dancer's body," she'd say.

I still wore Chucks and Doc Martens, and I got my nose pierced once. I just no longer walked around showing off too much leg or too much cleavage, and there was nothing wrong with that. I'm thankful for Wyatt and everything he gave me, but I decided I wouldn't change who I was for anybody again—especially a man.

I stomp down the stairs and grab a water bottle, drinking it as I flitter around looking for a snack.

"You look nice," Vic says as he opens the fridge.

I turn around and smile. "Thanks."

"Going on a date this early?"

I look at the time, it's ten, and Oliver should be here any minute now. And suddenly I start getting nervous. The whole reality of it slowly begins to sink in—Oliver will be picking me up for a friend date at my brother's house—his best friend's house. Clearly, we hadn't thought this through as much as we should have. I'm twenty-five. I'm not a child anymore, but to Victor, this is the ultimate no-no. I know because I've heard it time and time again. I know it because as much as he loves Oliver, and even goes as far as introducing him as his brother whenever they're together, he wouldn't like the idea of him dating me.

"Not really a date," I say. "I'm going out with Bean for a little while."

Victor frowns as he searches my face but nods slowly. "You guys seem to be bonding over the hospital thing?" He poses it as a question. A very curious question. Too curious coming from my attorney brother. I give him a tight smile and nod in response. The doorbell rings before he gets a chance to say anything else, and I practically sprint toward it.

"See you later," I call out over my shoulder as I grab my purse and open the door. I step outside without even looking up at Oliver, who's standing so close, the smell of his cologne hits me like a wall. I need to lock the door before I acknowledge him though. We need to get far away from here before Victor comes out and says something that would make us forget about this friend thing, forever.

"In a rush?" Oliver says with a chuckle as I sort through the million keys on my ring. My eyes snap to his dark jeans and trail up slowly to his narrow waist and to the burgundy polo clinging to his lean body. I glance at his face, flitting across the scruff that sort of hides his dimples, and the way his long hair brushes his high cheekbones. Those amazing green eyes are lit up in amusement. Fuck. He looks too good for a friend date. His eyes stay glued to my lips when I part them to respond, and he opens his mouth to say something at the same time, but before either of us can speak, the door opens and Victor peeks out.

"Huh. I thought you were kidding," he says, looking at Oliver.

"About?" I ask.

"What's up, man?" Oliver says at the same time, bumping his fist with Vic's.

"She said she was going out with you, but she was acting like she was hiding something from me, so I assumed she was lying."

My heart threatens to jump out of my chest, so I look away, focusing on the mountains in the distance.

"I'm not a child, Victor," I snap, as Oliver makes his own response.

"Why would she be hiding something?" Oliver says, his voice full of confusion. "Are you hiding something from us, Elle?"

My head jerks up to glare at him. "Are we going somewhere, or are you guys going to start grilling me? This is beyond ridiculous." I turn my glare to Vic, who laughs, shakes his head, and steps back inside the house.

"Have fun with Miss Grouchy Pants," he shoots over his shoulder.

I flash him my middle finger, which makes him laugh harder, and I stomp down the steps and head to Oliver's black Cadillac. I pull on the handle when I hear his footsteps approach, but the door remains locked. He stops beside me, and I see the keys in his hand, a thumb hovering over the unlock button.

"I'm not really into starting dates—friend or otherwise—on a bad foot," he says, beckoning me to look at his handsome, serious face.

"I'm not really into starting friend dates by getting grilled by both my brother and the dater."

His lips twitch. "The dater?"

"You know what I mean," I mutter.

Oliver smiles, a full-on devastating event. "I don't. I'd rather you clarify, so I don't get any funny ideas."

"Oliver."

"Estelle."

"You know the rules—no kissing, no touching, no funny business."

"And you know mine. No short dresses, no lipstick . . . yet here you are wearing red lipstick. *Red.* Total date color, by the way."

I bite the inside of my cheek to keep from laughing, but fail. "Red is a date color?"

"On those lips it is."

He holds my eyes for a moment—a really electrifying moment, where a current zips along my pulse—before he unlocks the car and reaches to open my door. I slip inside and wait for him to go around.

"Nice car," I say when he gets in and revs it up.

"Thanks. It was a med school graduation present from my dad."

I nod. "How is he?"

I only met his dad once, in passing, but have heard enough about him to know he's still feeling the effects of the strokes he'd had.

"He's . . . fine. Remarried. He seems happy, and his wife is nice, too. She stays on top of his health, so that's good."

"How are your mom and Sophie?"

He flashes me a quick smile before turning his attention to the road ahead. "They're doing really well. Sophie's pregnant again, and Sander is getting bigger by the minute. Mom's good too, she's so over the moon with them, that she cut back on work and stays home to help Soph."

"Wow. I'm impressed. I guess people do change."

"You'd be surprised at how much," he says in a low voice that resonates deliciously through me.

"So," I say, slapping my hands over my thighs. "Where are we going?"

"First, breakfast. Then a vineyard."

I turn my face to look at him. "You're trying to get me drunk on a friend date?"

I can tell he's trying really hard not to smile, or laugh. "You wore red lipstick on this friend date."

I laugh, sigh, and groan all in a matter of three seconds. "You're impossible."

"You make me this way."

"Let's talk about something else," I say, looking out the window. "Does this car have Bluetooth?"

Oliver chuckles. "Yes, Princess Estelle, is it up to par with your inspection?"

I stop moving my hand over the dash and set it back on my lap, feeling a blush creep into my face.

"I liked your old car better," I say.

Oliver's eyebrows hike up and he turns to gape at me. "You like my beat-up Maxima better than this?"

I shrug. "It was more cozy. This reminds me of the Batmobile, and there's nothing wrong with the Batmobile, but I like cozy."

He shakes his head and mutters something under his breath, but starts to look for my phone to hook up to Bluetooth. He already knows it's because I want to play my own music—I don't even have to explain. I used to bring my own CD whenever I was in the car with him. Oliver listens to two things: heavy rock and rap, and while I'm okay with both, I prefer the classics. The Steve Miller Band hasn't even gotten to the hook before they're interrupted by a call from Mia.

Oliver looks at me with a question in his eyes.

"If you don't mind," I say. He presses the button, and before I say hello, Mia's frantic voice comes through.

"What underwear are you wearing?" she asks.

My face goes hot for the second time this morning. From the corner of my eye, I see Oliver bite down on his lip.

"What?" I ask. "Mia, you're on speaker phone!"

"I don't care. This is an emergency. Do you not hear the shrill tone in my voice? What are you wearing under your clothes?"

My eyes snap to the side of Oliver's face, then out the front window, and finally, I pull my shirt slightly and look down, because I completely forgot what underwear I have on.

"Can you disconnect the phone?" I say to Oliver, who shakes his head in refusal. "Please. This is like . . . monumentally embarrassing."

"Just answer," he whispers.

"Who's that?" Mia asks.

"Oliver. We're in his car, and you're on the fucking Bluetooth."

She laughs. "Oh my God! I am so sorry, Bean!"

"What?" I shout. "He's not the one being harassed!"

"Oh, but now he is. So tell me—underwear?"

"White lace bra and matching boy shorts," I say, almost through my teeth, not missing the way Oliver's eyes snap to me with an approving look. I want to slap him for it, but I know nothing good would come of that, so I just cross my arms over my chest like a petulant child.

"Well, you know that favor you owe me," she begins. "The

male model can only come at noon. Will you be available at that time?"

I look back at Oliver, who shakes his head. "Can we do it later? Like at. . . . six?" I say, asking him more than her.

"Elle! This is huge. I'll have to make more calls, and nobody can do quick shoots because they're all in LA for some sort of fashion thing!"

I huff out a breath and close my eyes, leaning on the headrest. "Let me call you back."

"Please let me know within the hour. Please."

"I will."

Oliver disconnects the call as we park in front of a little shack by the water.

"What was that about?" he asks, turning the car off and turning to face me.

"She has this photo shoot that has gone wrong in every way imaginable, and she asked me to do it for her, but apparently can't find a guy to shoot with me on such short notice."

"Do you want to do it? I mean, we can eat and go there instead . . ."

I sigh, looking out the window. "I know this isn't what you had planned for our friend date."

"But you want to be there for your friend. I get it, Elle. We can go over there after."

I turn back to him with a smile. "Thank you."

He shrugs like it's no big deal. "Are you hungry?"

"Starving."

We head inside and sit down in the balcony, where we're steps away from the water. There is a group of surfers out there tending their boards, while others are in the water waiting for better waves.

"This okay?" Oliver asks, nodding to the surfers.

I smile. "It's perfect."

"Okay. I wasn't sure." Realization dawns on me when his eyes move back toward the beach full of surfers.

"We can talk about it, you know? I'm really okay."

He smiles softly. "I don't want to make you uncomfortable."

"I'm fine."

He nods. "Have you gone back after it happened?"

"To the beach?" I ask, frowning. "Of course. I was there recently . . . a couple of days after the anniversary."

Surprise flashes in his green eyes. "I wanted to reach out to you after it happened. I'm sorry I didn't. I kept tabs through Vic, but I should have been there. Every time I thought about showing up at the gallery or seeking you out, I . . ." He sighs and turns his face away, his gaze back on the water. "I kind of panicked."

When the waitress comes, and we order our drinks and some food, I know I can just drop what he said. It's an out for both of us to go back to treading on more comfortable ground, but his words keep playing in my head.

"Panicked why?" I ask quietly, breaking a piece of bread and lathering it with strawberry jam, as he does. I feel his eyes on me and I look up to see him shrug.

"Because of the last time I saw you."

"At my parents' house," I say, nodding in understanding.

When the waiter comes back with our drinks, we drop the subject, because that one is too much for a friends-only date.

"So, Doctor Hart, how are you doing in your residency so far? Do you get quizzed? How does that work?" I ask, smiling. Oliver chuckles, as his eyes light up and those dimples flash in amusement.

"I'm proud to say all of my quizzes are behind me, but they do stay on my ass enough to know if I mess up . . . which I don't," he adds with a wink.

I grin. "Of course you don't, Mr. Perfect."

"*Doctor* Perfect," he corrects, raising an eyebrow. We share a laugh over that, but it dies down quickly when his gaze turns serious again. "Can I ask you something?"

"Of course," I respond, just as the waiter sets down our food. He ordered egg whites and bacon scramble, and I'm having Eggs Benedict over avocado. We push our plates toward the middle of the table so we can share, like we used to. Everything feels so . . . natural.

I smile, watching as he takes a bite of the avocado and eggs. He groans, making a face of pure bliss, and then smiles and cuts a piece to feed me. I place my hands on the edge of the table and lean into the fork, my eyes on his as I do. As soon as the explosion of flavors hits my tongue, I match his moan and close my eyes.

"That is so good," I say once I finish chewing. I smile when I notice Oliver's eyes are still on my mouth. "You had a question for me," I prompt. He swallows and nods.

"Was he really controlling over you?" he asks. I guess my face shows how taken aback by his question I am, because he adds a quick "If you don't mind me asking" to his statement.

"I wouldn't say he was controlling . . . not in a bad way, anyway . . . I'm sure Vic has painted a terrible picture of our relationship for you—this guy goes out of town constantly and leaves her alone without calling her for days and days and then comes back and tells her she can't dress the way she normally dresses and has to give up dance classes," I say, mimicking my brother's angry voice. "But he didn't make me do any of those things. I did those things because I wanted to."

Oliver's face twists into something I've never seen before. It's like grief or something, I don't know—but the sight of it makes my heart drop to my stomach.

After a moment, I whisper, "What are you thinking?"

He looks away from me, into the ocean, and when his green eyes find mine again, that look hasn't gone away. "I'm thinking . . ." He stops himself, as if he's having this tug of war in his mind over whether or not to tell me. I nod, encouraging him. "I'm thinking that I don't think I could go days and days without hearing your voice."

His answer is so not what I expected. The way it makes me feel, is so not what I was expecting. And the fact that I like both things makes me feel conflicted.

"What are you thinking?" he asks after a moment.

"That this is nothing like the last date I went on."

Oliver chuckles. "With that Derek guy?"

"Why must you have such a good memory?" I ask, smiling and shaking my head.

"Did you ever go out with him again?"

"Nope. Definitely not my type."

"What is your type?" he asks, his eyes dropping to my lips, which I lick because they're suddenly dry.

"I don't really have one. I just know he's not it," I say, shrugging.

"I think you do have one."

"Really?" I say. "Enlighten me, oh, wise one. What is my type?"

Oliver smiles, that lazy smile, and leans back in his seat, pushing his cup of water away slightly. "You like guys with long hair."

"You're only saying that because Wyatt had long hair," I say. He gives me a pointed look. "And you had long hair."

"Have," he corrects.

"It used to be longer."

"You want me to grow it back?"

I shrug, ignoring the butterflies circulating inside my stomach. "Doesn't matter to me. What does Jen like?"

Oliver smiles wider, scratching the scruff on his chin. "I never really thought to ask for her opinion."

The fact that he's not denying that there was something going on with her makes me want to chuck my silverware at him. His deep chuckle snaps me out of my murderous thoughts.

"What?" I ask, sounding snappier than I intend.

"You're so cute when you're jealous."

My mouth pops open. "I am not jealous. I don't get jealous—ever. I couldn't care less what you do in your free time."

He keeps smiling at me, both eyebrows raised now. I close my eyes when I feel my face heat, because I can't stand to look at the laughter in his eyes.

"Elle," he says. I jolt and open my eyes when I feel his large hands covering mine on the table. "I already told you I'm not sleeping with anybody. Now tell me—what do you like?"

"It doesn't matter what I like. Ask one of the nurses," I throw out and regret it immediately, because I realize that I do sound jealous.

Oliver laughs again. "Their opinions don't matter either."

"Yet mine does." I raise an eyebrow.

"Yours does," he responds, his smoldering look beginning to affect me in a way I can't handle well.

"What else is my type?" I ask, taking my hands from under his and putting them on my lap.

"You like older men."

"Again, you're just saying that because Wyatt was older."

"Too much older," he counters.

"No such thing."

His jaw tightens and he throws a curve ball my way. "Do you know how shocked I was when I found out you were engaged to him?"

My stomach flips. I know the answer to this. I could never forget it, but I somehow manage to shake my head slowly, suddenly wishing the wind would take me far away from here before I get lost in the look he's giving me. "How shocked?"

"Very."

"Why?"

Oliver closes his eyes and breathes out harshly. Just as he opens them again, the waitress comes back with the bill. He pays, and we thank her as we leave out the side door, closest to the beach.

"I always thought you were mine," he says. His words are so quiet they almost get lost in the gust of wind that attacks our faces, but I hear them as if he was screaming them to me. What do I say to that? How in the world could I possibly respond after all this time?

I'm thankful when Mia's phone call interrupts us. I close my eyes. "I forgot to call her back," I say, to him . . . to the beach . . . to no one in particular, before I answer.

"Elle, twelve is all I got. Nobody else can come at that time."

I look up at Oliver, who's staring down at me, and mute the phone. "Are you sure you're okay with me cutting this short? Do you want to go with me?"

"And watch you pose with another guy?" he says with a smile and a shrug. "Fuck it. Why not?"

I beam at him and un-mute the call. "I'll be there at twelve, but Oliver is coming with."

Mia laughs loudly. "This should be fun."

Chapter 17

F UN IS WAKING up on Christmas morning, or taking a ride in a brand new car, or having drinks with friends . . . or even that first cup of coffee in the morning that gives you the sometimes-false feeling that maybe the day will be awesome. Fun is a lot of things. Taking off your clothes and knowing that you agreed for an ex-fling, or whatever he was, to watch you in your underwear in bed with another man, also in his underwear? That is the polar opposite of fun.

"Elle, you can come out now!" Mia says, pounding on the door for the second time. I open it a little, just enough for me to poke my head out and take in the room. The bed is covered in fluffy white sheets, the window behind it is open to let in the natural light, and in the middle of it all, Oliver is talking to the half-naked model guy. He keeps nodding his head at whatever the model guy is saying.

"Is the guy gay?" I ask Mia in a low whisper.

"Marlon?" she asks with a laugh. "Most definitely not, according to the females he's worked with before."

My eyes widen. I'm already picturing his unwanted boner poking me in the ass. "What does that mean?"

"Relax. He's a total professional. I mean, he's fucked some

of them, after the fact. Not on my bed . . . on theirs."

"Oh." I pull my robe shut and follow her out to the room. Both Marlon and Oliver turn their heads to look at me. Oliver is serious, while Marlon flashes me a huge, model face Colgate smile as he walks over to me.

"I'm Marlon," he says, extending his hand out to me.

"Estelle," I respond, shaking it.

"I know you don't usually do this, but relax, I'll take care of you," he says, pulling me toward the bed. I flash a look at Oliver, who raises his eyebrows and shakes his head at the whole thing.

"How long is this going to take?" I ask Mia.

"About an hour, so get comfortable, Bean."

"I'm not sure comfort is a possibility right now."

Mia looks over at him with a smirk. "Would you be more comfortable if you took over for Marlon?"

As Oliver seems to consider it, Mia tells me to take my robe off, so I do. It slides off and pools at my naked feet. Marlon is already sitting in the middle of the bed adjusting his boxers.

"Can I?" Oliver says suddenly. I look over my shoulder, wide-eyed.

"Are you serious?" Mia asks, gaping at him.

"If Elle is okay with it. I'm not here to dictate your shoot."

Mia doesn't think twice before ordering him around. "Take off your shirt. I need to make sure you're still in good shape before I kick Marlon out."

I'm about to put in my two cents, when Oliver pulls his polo over his head and my words, along with my sight, get lost somewhere between his sternum and the dips of his narrow waist.

"Yeah, still hot," Mia says. "Marlon, off the bed. You're not needed."

"What?" he says in disbelief. "What do you mean I'm not needed?"

"Sorry. You and Elle have zero chemistry, and I need major

chemistry on this shoot."

"We only just met," he argues, as he gets out of bed.

"And I already know the chemistry isn't there," Mia says. "I'll call you next week when Miranda is back and schedule something then."

"Okay," he says with a shrug. "Have fun," he says to me.

When he leaves to get dressed, Mia turns to me and says, "Just to be clear, I wouldn't kick him out of bed under normal circumstances, if you know what I mean."

I laugh. "Neither would I."

Oliver clears his throat behind me, and I look at him with a smile and a shrug.

"All right, Ollie boy, strip and get on the bed. Elle, make yourself comfortable on it. You want music? I'll play music anyway, so just nod."

"You're such a pain." I laugh, as she taps her iPod and *Just Breathe* by Pearl Jam stars playing. I stop laughing and glare at her. "This is the kind of music you're going to play?"

She shrugs. "My shoot, my rules."

Oliver walks over to me on the bed, wearing a pair of black boxer briefs and nothing else. It takes every ounce of everything inside me not to devour his body with my eyes. He's not even really muscular like Marlon, but he's perfect, in that lean, California surfer–dude-and-former-baseball-pitcher kind of way. He gets on the bed and practically crawls to me like a fucking lion, and I'm starting to feel like a cat in heat, so I look away.

"You okay?" he asks, low enough for only me to hear.

I nod, still not looking at him.

"You don't feel like I completely took over the shoot, right? Or like I'm being controlling or anything, right?" he asks.

I meet his gaze with a frown, and realize I don't feel that way at all, despite the fact that he sort of did and he is sort of being a little controlling . . . sort of . . . right? I mean, he's a goddamn doctor, not a model. This isn't even his world!

"I'm not mad or anything, if that's what you're asking."

"That's not what I'm asking."

He settles himself so that his legs are around my body, not touching me, but just . . . around, and my legs are together and bent. I bring them closer to me and place my chin on my knees.

"You're different people, you know," I whisper.

A smile tugs on his lips. "So you agree that it was a good call for me to let the model with a thing for fucking the women he shoots with leave?"

"I didn't say that," I respond, hiding my smile behind my leg.

"But you agree. I know you," he says, running his hand up my leg ever so softly until he reaches the hand I have resting on my knee. He holds on to the tip of my ring finger, and I'm reminded of the last time he touched it.

"You have an obsession with my ring finger. Have you noticed?"

He drops my hand suddenly. "Do I?"

I nod, not breaking eye contact. "You always touch it."

He doesn't say anything, but something in his eyes makes my insides stir and his words from earlier—the ones he doesn't think I heard—come back to whisper at me.

I always thought you were mine.

I wish I had the balls to ask him about that, but I don't, and Mia's clicking camera interrupts us anyway.

"Okay, here's the deal, I'm going to sort of guide you through this, but I want this to be as natural as possible. We'll do a couple where you guys are looking at each other first, and then we'll see where it goes."

"I'm kind of worried about your 'we'll see where it goes,'" I mutter under my breath, earning a laugh from Oliver.

"All right, darlings, let all that pent-up sexual tension come out and play," she says, stepping away.

Oliver and I stare at each other, wide-eyed, wondering what we've gotten ourselves into. Or at least I thought we were both wondering that, until his shock dissolves and his face darkens, and I'm left with a thrashing sense of holy shit as Mia walks away to open the blinds. Suddenly it hits me that I'm in my underwear with Oliver—who is also in his underwear—and we're surrounded by needy music. I gulp in a deep breath.

"You okay?" he asks, his voice too low, too husky, as his fingers run over my calves.

I shiver, close my eyes, and nod.

The bed shifts, and I feel him move closer. When I open my eyes again, his nose is almost touching mine.

"Perfect!" Mia says. "Hold that pose!"

The look in his eyes holds me there. I can't really think of even blinking anyway.

"Elle, do you mind taking off your bra?" Mia asks, lost behind the lens, and Oliver inhales sharply, his eyes widening at the request. "You're not showing your boobs in the pictures, I promise."

"Ummm . . . okay." I have zero qualms about nudity, though I have to admit that this entire thing is making me nervous as hell.

"You need help taking it off?" Oliver asks.

"No."

"Actually, that would make for good pictures," Mia chimes in, and I turn to glare at her. She shrugs. "What? Bean, you've seen your fair share of tits before, right? You don't mind?"

"This is definitely the most awkward form of punishment I have ever received. I think I'll take the spanking next time," I say to Mia, making her smile and Oliver laugh.

I drop my head as he wraps his arms around me and finds the clasp of my bra.

"You need to look at him," Mia says. I take a breath, and with what I find in his gaze, it takes everything in my willpower not to look away or close my eyes again.

His fingers unclasp my bra, and as soon as it loosens, he brings his hands up to my shoulders and ever so slowly, drags the straps down my arms, never breaking eye contact with me.

My stomach flips, my heart is in my throat, and I feel like I may or may not vomit because of the amount of nerves circulating inside of me right now. I just pray really hard the last one does not happen.

"Okay?" he whispers, his breath on my mouth.

"Perfect," I whisper back.

Our noses touch.

"Elle, put your right hand over your boobs like you're shielding them. Bean, keep looking at her like that and fix her hair on the side facing me," Mia says.

I bring my arm over myself as one of Oliver's fingers thread into my hair and the other cups the side of my face. I'm completely lost in his eyes. I'm mesmerized by the way he's handling me, looking at me. I can't seem to do anything else but breathe and stare back.

"You are so beautiful," he says. His guttural voice mixed with the lust in his eyes make my stomach dip and my lips part. Oliver takes it as his cue to inch his face closer and brush his mouth against mine.

"Perfect," Mia says, reminding me that we have an audience. "Shit. I'll be right back. I need my back-up battery, and I left it in the fucking car."

I pull back, not taking my eyes from his, and drop my hand from my chest. I can tell he's having a really hard time not looking down. I smile at him, wondering how long it'll take for his eyes to drop, but they don't. He continues to look into my eyes, search my face, touch my hair, my cheeks . . . He scoots forward and pulls my legs apart so that they're overlapping his in a scissor on either side, and our naked chests are almost touching.

"How much longer do you think we'll have to do this?" I whisper, my eyes flickering between his mouth and his eyes.

"I don't know. I'm kind of hoping it takes all day."

"It definitely makes for an interesting friend date," I say with a smile.

He flashes his charming half-smile. "You still think this is a friend date?"

The door opens and shuts, and we turn our heads at Mia's return. She stops dead in her tracks when she sees us. "Holy shit. That pose! If I can get a couple of shots with that pose, I think we're done!"

Oliver and I face each other again as she sets up the camera.

"Why'd you do it anyway? Take over Marlon's spot. I mean, other than the overprotective, big brother thing."

He gives me a confused look, which almost looks comical with the way his mouth drops. "You think this is a big brother thing?"

I shrug. "You tell me."

"Elle, I'm sitting in a bed practically naked with you, doing everything in my power to keep myself from getting hard because we have an audience, and as you can see, nothing is working." I look down, of course, and gape at the large condition inside his boxers. "Yeah. So obviously, I don't see you as a little sister. I can't believe you would even . . ." He trails off with a huff.

"Okay. Look at each other again," Mia says. "Same pose and hold it."

His hand goes back to my hair, mine goes back over my boobs, and we look into each other's eyes again.

"I want to kiss you so bad right now," he whispers against my lips.

"Don't," I say in a breath. "That's a rule."

"I don't like rules."

"Oliver, please don't."

"I love it when you call me Oliver," he says, his bottom lip settling between both of mine. He doesn't move though, just stakes out there until I have to close my mouth over his lips. Then he groans and moves his mouth against mine, and before I know what's happening, I'm on my back, and he's on top of me deepening the kiss that wasn't supposed to happen. But when his tongue touches mine, and his fingers thread into my hair, I can't help but reciprocate, and we end up in a tangled mess of sheets and tongues and rough hands down my sides, and mine down his toned back. It isn't until we hear a loud cough that we snap and tear away from each other.

"Well . . . that was . . ." Mia says, fanning her face with her hand. "I can honestly say that I've seen a lot of shit happen in shoots, and that was by far the hottest. Okay, lovelies, we're all done here. Go get dressed. Elle, we need to talk."

Oliver pushes himself off me and brings me up with him. We're both still catching our breaths from the kiss, but now that the lights are on again and the moment is broken, I feel the weight of what just went down, and I can't bring myself to look at him. Instead, I look around, trying to locate my robe, which I wrap around myself as I stand up. Heading to the bathroom, I refuse to turn and look at him. This is what we do, anyway. We have our moments and then nothing. And this wasn't even supposed to be a moment, so I have nobody to blame but myself for the way my heart feels like it's going to break at any moment.

In the bathroom, I look in the mirror and bring my hand to my lips. Why does he make me feel this way every time? I close my eyes, think of Wyatt and his lips . . . his touch . . . and I feel guilty for having this moment with a man he would never approve of. Not that Wyatt knew Oliver, but he knew of him. He got an earful from me about Oliver when we first met, and after that, he just never liked him. He was furious when he found out I extended an invitation to the grand opening of the gallery to him, because he said Oliver didn't deserve to breathe the same air as me. He said that I was too good for somebody like him. At the time, I believed it. I believed it because when we want to believe something, that's what we do. Wyatt loved me despite my brokenness. I loved him because of his. But now I'm back at square one, and I can't figure out if there's anything really left of me to love.

Chapter 18

I WALK OUT of the bathroom and find Mia and Oliver engrossed in a quiet conversation. From the look on her face, I know she's telling him to stay away from me, as if I'm some damsel in distress who can't fend for herself. When they hear me approach, they stop talking and turn their attention back to the camera in her hand.

"The pictures look incredible," she gushes, turning it so I can see the little screen.

"Wow. I can't even believe it's us. We look so . . ." My eyes snap up to Oliver, who's staring at me with a look I want to get lost in forever. I look away quickly, back down at the rest of the pictures.

"Won't this be bad for you?" I ask, looking at him again. "I mean, for work. For your residency or future work."

He shrugs and looks at the pictures. "I want copies."

"For what?" I ask a little too defensively.

"Your faces aren't going to show all that much," Mia says, interrupting us. "Trust me, when I'm done editing these, you're both going to want to frame them."

"What magazine did you say this was for?" I ask.

"V!"

"Holy shit," I breathe, looking at Oliver, who looks impressed.

"I know. I'm so excited!"

"Yeah. Exciting. I feel like I might throw up," I say quietly.

"Why? They're beautiful pictures."

"Yeah, but I'm posing half naked with Victor's best friend!"

"And?" she says.

I look at her like she's crazy and turn my attention to Oliver, who's looking the other way now. Of course, he hadn't thought of that.

"When does this come out?" I ask.

"In . . . a month? Right before Thanksgiving."

I nod. I guess if I tell my parents and Victor about this before they have a chance to see it, it won't be so bad. Victor will definitely need time to process it.

"Okay. What else do you need?"

Mia looks at Oliver. "I need to talk to Elle. I can take her home if you want."

He looks at me, scratching the back of his neck. I shrug, he shrugs back and then says, "Sure," before giving us each a kiss on the cheek and leaving.

That's when I start to feel murderous. How can he just leave?

"Can you believe this shit?" I say after he's out of earshot. "We just did all of that." I signal to the bed. "And he still leaves in the middle of what was supposed to be our date, right after my brother and these pictures being viewed by the public is brought up. I don't even know why I bother."

Mia rolls her eyes. "You know exactly why you bother. He's like your drug. No matter how far you go or what crazy measures you take to stay away from him, you always end up back where you started."

"Not this time," I say with finality. "Nothing has really happened this time."

Mia laughs. "Elle, what I just saw, I mean, what I just captured, says otherwise," she says waving her camera around. "You can't make this shit up."

"It doesn't matter."

"You said you needed to move on."

"Yeah, but not with him. You said so yourself, it's a bad idea."

"Maybe I was wrong. Maybe it's not a bad idea."

"Oh, really?" I roll my eyes. "You got all that from a few pictures?"

"No. I got all that from talking to him. I think he's grown up."

I wave frantically in the direction of the door. "He just left! Again!"

Mia shrugs. "Yeah, because I asked him to. Do you feel guilty for entertaining the idea of hooking up with someone?"

"I don't think so. I think it's just him I'm afraid of."

Mia leans forward and gives me a hug. "Love is supposed to be scary."

"Love is supposed to be comfortable," I reply.

"Do you really believe that?"

"Wyatt was comfortable."

"Wyatt didn't make you go on tantrums and break your brand new Isaac Mizrahi Target plates because he didn't call, or go into seclusion for weeks on end when you heard he was going to be living four hours away."

I drop my arms and stare at her, feeling like she just said the most significant thing in the world.

"Do you think it's possible to have different kinds of love?"

"You mean like head over heels in love and then just in love?" she asks.

I shrug, following her out the door. "Yeah, like soul mate love as opposed to just regular love."

"Soul mate love?" she asks, laughing. "As far as I'm concerned, the only soul mate I have is you. And maybe Robert, since he's my twin, and you know how we twins are."

"I don't think . . . I mean, I don't want to think that I didn't love Wyatt with everything I had. That makes me feel so bad, you know? He died so young, and to think I wasn't the love of his life makes me sad."

"Oh, honey," Mia says, pulling me to her as we walk side-by-side to her car. "You loved him so much, though. You gave up so much for him, Elle. Dance, your friends, time you used to spend with your family . . ."

"Yeah, but he gave me a lot too. The studio . . . he taught me how to hone my craft . . . and he left me his house."

"I'm not saying he wasn't a good guy for you, but was he your forever guy? You know I can't agree to that."

We drive in silence, only singing along to her Taylor Swift CD when a song we both like comes on. When we get to my brother's house, I'm a little sad that Oliver's car isn't there. He really ran off. Again. Unbelievable.

It isn't until after I shower and climb in bed, that I decide that I can't leave it alone. Not this time. I send him a text message and look at my phone until he responds.

I can't believe you left.

Mia said you needed to talk. I would have stayed if you wanted me to.

I wanted you to.

Why?

I stare at the phone as if it's going to explain why men are so stupid, and when it doesn't, I decide that I can't give him an answer either. I toss it on the nightstand and pull the covers over my head. The sun is just going down, so it's still early, but I feel drained. I sleep until something wakes me . . . a whisper on my face . . . the caress of a hand on my head. My eyes pop open, and I push myself to sit quickly.

"It's just me."

I gasp and look at Oliver beside me.

"What are you doing here?" I whisper, looking from him to my slightly open door. "Where's Vic?"

He shrugs a shoulder and puts a finger over my lips to silence me. "He passed out already. Can I stay?"

I frown. "What's wrong with your bed?"

"You're not in it."

I push aside the way my heart is thundering inside me. "I've never even seen your bed."

"Would you like to?" he asks, dropping his voice.

"Stop looking at me like that."

"Like what, lovely Elle?" he asks, trying to smother a smile.

"Like you want to swallow me whole."

"Has it ever occurred to you, that maybe I do?" He moves closer, and I hold my breath. "But no funny business tonight. I promise. Scout's honor."

"You were never a Boy Scout."

He grins. "Okay, but I promise I won't try anything. I just want to be with you tonight."

"The last time you said that—"

"I was an idiot."

I close my eyes. "What about my brother?"

"What about him?"

"What if he comes up here and catches you?"

Oliver's hand grabs my waist, and he pulls me to him so that we're nose to nose. "What would you want me to do if he does?"

"I don't know," I whisper, my breath catching at the dark look in his eyes.

"Do you want me to tell him that you're all I think about?" he asks, matching my whisper.

I shake my head, and our noses kiss. I'm not ready for Victor to know about whatever this is yet.

"Tell me why you wanted me to stay."

"Because we weren't done with our friend date."

Oliver chuckles. "That friend date had me going home and taking the longest shower of my life."

"I took one too," I say in a whisper, my cheeks burning as I look at him through my lashes. His face turns completely serious, and he groans.

"God, Elle, why'd you have to say that to me?"

I laugh. "Say what? That I touched myself thinking about you?"

His eyes hood a little. "If you want me to keep my word, you need to stop talking about that."

"Okay." I grin and turn around so that my back is on his chest. He snuggles me close, creating a nook for my body. "Tell me a story," I say, yawning.

"About what?" he murmurs, dropping a kiss on my head.

"Anything. Like the ones you used to tell me when we were young."

"Okay." He pauses and holds me tighter. "Once upon a time, there was this little girl named Cassia. She used to walk around talking to herself."

I nudge him. "To the plants, not herself."

He laughs. "Oh, that's right. She used to talk to the plants. One day this little boy named Jeter asked her—"

"Jeter?" I ask, looking at him over my shoulder. "Like the baseball player?"

Oliver laughs and shakes his head, snuggling into me. "I forgot how many interruptions these stories lead to," he says against my neck.

"Well, you're always talking about how weird I am, but listen to your stories."

His sigh sends a shiver down my body. "Okay, let's move on to joke time then."

I groan. "I hate your jokes."

"You're not supposed to tell me that!" he scoffs as his hands trail down my body. "What are you wearing anyway?"

My eyes snap open, and I'm glad we're cloaked in darkness. "It's one of Wyatt's shirts," I whisper.

Oliver's hands stop moving over my stomach. "Did you keep a lot of his things?"

I turn around in his arms and prop my elbow up on the pillow. He does the same. "Only his shirts. I gave his parents back his pictures and a couple of other things I didn't want. But I can't seem to get rid of the shirts."

"Is it because you miss him?" he asks.

"Is it bad that I was wondering the same thing the other day? That all these questions are suddenly popping up in my head?"

Oliver brushes my face with the back of his hand. "Like what?"

"You really want to know?"

"Of course. I want to know everything you want to tell me."

I stay silent a moment longer, and once again wonder why he really took Marlon's spot in the photo shoot. Maybe he was just protecting me from a creeper, and it wasn't really his way of marking his territory. This is Oliver, after all. He doesn't really mark territory; he just goes over it on a bulldozer and leaves before he can even notice the damage.

"Okay. Well, when he first died, I felt like I couldn't breathe—especially at night when I was alone—but as time went on, it got better . . ."

"And now?"

"And now sometimes I don't miss him at all," I whisper. I feel ungrateful . . . un-loyal. Like it's a disgrace for thinking it, let alone voicing it aloud, especially to Oliver. I turn back around and settle into Oliver's warmth again.

"It's okay for you to find happiness after him. You know that, right?" he says, his voice on my neck again.

I swallow. "I guess so. Sometimes I feel guilty about it though. We lived together. We were engaged. It was a big commitment."

Oliver stays quiet for a long time before speaking up. "For a long time, I couldn't imagine myself ever getting married. It's no secret that I've always had an aversion to commitment," he says quietly. "Unless you count school and work—those things I can commit to—but women . . . growing up, I never found one I wanted to commit to." He whispers the last part, and my heart lodges in my throat before he continues. "Except this one girl. She always looked at me like I was somebody, even though I wasn't. And of course, my luck would have it that the one person I feel like I can actually commit to is the one person I can't have. I tried so hard to stay away from her." He drops a kiss on my shoulder. "I kept reminding myself what would happen if my best friend were to find out about my feelings. I kept them to myself for so long, even after the girl asked me to kiss her. And after I asked the girl to let me kiss her. And after she let me touch her in the bathroom of a party. And after she touched me in a stranger's bedroom."

"Why didn't you ever tell her how you felt?" I whisper. He tucks his face into my neck, and I close my eyes when I feel his breath on me.

"Because I was an idiot."

"Hey, Oliver?"

"Yeah?"

"Do you think I can sleep with your shirt tonight?" I whisper.

If possible, he squeezes me tighter and buries his head further into me. I'm about to take the words back and say I was just kidding or something, when he pulls his arms away and sits up. I follow his movement and watch through the darkness as he pulls his shirt over his head. I do the same, slowly pulling mine over my head and tossing it to the furthest corner of the room, by the closet.

"Hey, Oliver," I whisper again.

"Yes, Elle?" he whispers back. I can make out the way his chest rises and falls, but not much else, so I inch closer.

"I want you to touch me." I screw my eyes shut. Not because I'm shy by any means, but because I haven't had this in so long. So, so long. And I'm scared at what his reaction will be. Worse, I'm scared of what mine will be if he gives in.

He throws his head back and exhales. Just when I think he's going to tell me he can't, or that my brother will wake up at any moment, or that he needs to go, his hands reach out and graze my arms.

"Only if you want to," I add when his hands stop moving.

His deep chuckle vibrates the bed. "Only if I want to," he repeats, leaning closer, his hands splaying over my ribcage on either side. "God, Estelle, you don't know how bad I want to."

Pushing my body forward, I brace myself on his shoulders. His thumbs brush just under my breasts, so I lean in a little more, hoping he gets the hint. His laugh lets me know he totally gets the hint and is purposely ignoring it.

"Bean, please," I whisper-pant as my hands grip him tighter.

"Bean isn't in right now," he whispers, dipping his head and plucking tender kisses from my neck to my clavicle, over my shoulder and back in.

"Oliver, please," I say, throwing my head back when his lips reach the hollow of my throat.

"Tell me what you want, baby. Tell me where you want me to touch you," he murmurs against me in a voice that sets me on fire.

"Everywhere. Just . . . anywhere."

His hands finally move up so that his thumbs brush over my nipples slowly, causing a shiver of pleasure to rock through me.

"More," I say, pulling him down on the bed so I can straddle his legs. I rock against him as I bring my lips to his. He groans against my mouth, plunging his tongue into it and exploring like a starved man looking for his next meal. The pressure on his hands doesn't increase though. He just continues to softly explore my body as if I'm made of glass. His fingers feather up and down my sides, over my breasts, along my neck, down my stomach, and stop right above the elastic of my panties.

"Please keep going," I say in a voice that's not mine. My legs are quivering, and he hasn't even really touched me where I need him to. Oliver moves his head back and pulls my face into the moonlight coming through the window. He searches my face, and I nod frantically as he smiles.

"If I do this, are we still on a friends date?" he asks. The fact that he can make jokes when I feel like I'm falling apart is a little infuriating, so instead of answering, I grab his hands and push them down so that he gets the hint. Oliver shakes his head. "Is this still a friends date?"

"I don't know," I whisper, rather loudly, my impatience beginning to get the best of me. "I don't care. Just touch me!"

He grins and moves a hand into my panties, his moan matching mine when he finds how wet I am already. "You're hazardous to my health. You know that?"

"It's a good thing you're a doctor then," I whimper when he plunges his finger inside me. He does a little hook with it that makes my eyes roll back.

"You like that?" he asks against my neck. He increases his tempo when I nod against him.

My hands move from his shoulders down his chest and into his boxers. Before he has a chance to say anything, I close my hand over his length and squeeze.

"Jesus fucking Christ, Estelle," he groans, shifting his weight to give me better access.

"You're so hard," I whisper, leaning forward to kiss him again.

"You're so wet," he says against my lips.

"You're so big," I say. I had forgotten how he looked, how he felt. He chuckles breathlessly, as I continue to move my hand to match the rhythm he's making with his.

"You're so tight," he groans, his thumb circling over my

clit as he moves his other fingers inside me.

"I'm going to . . . I'm going to . . ." I pant just before my vision becomes bright lights. I keep moving my hand over him until he's grunting, and I feel hot liquid over my hand.

We sit there for a moment, wordlessly, only the sounds of our heavy breaths audible in the room. Finally, he drops a kiss on my forehead and gets up to go clean himself. I don't know if he expects me to follow, but as I look at his broad shoulders walking out of the room, I can't help but wonder if that was a mistake. He brings back a wet towel and wipes my hands thoroughly, and when he comes back again, he takes the place he had before.

Neither of us says a word as we settle down again, his arms around me as I lay in the little cocoon that might as well have been carved out and made for my body to fit in.

"I like you in my arms," he says, finally, his breath against my ear.

My eyes close. "I do too." Too much. Way too much.

"We broke a lot of your rules today."

"We did. Too many of them," I say, smiling into the darkness.

"When do we go on our next friends date?"

"You're sleeping in my bed tonight," I remind him.

"You wore red lipstick."

I laugh. "You and the stupid lipstick."

"I'm just saying—a woman only wears that color on dates when she wants to get laid."

I shake my head, laughing, and he laughs along, holding me tighter. We're quiet for a while, and I think maybe he's fallen asleep. I feel myself relax, and sleep begins to drag me under again. When I wake up the next day, to the sun blasting in my face, I realize I'm alone in bed. A sense of sadness threatens to wash over me, but I push it aside. This was my own doing. I asked for it. I pushed him for it. Those thoughts don't alleviate the pain I feel though. I close my eyes again and exhale. When

I open them back up, I spot Wyatt's discarded shirt, thrown in a corner like some washed up memory, and suddenly I get even sadder. He may not have been the perfect man, and we may have had a lot of differences, but Wyatt never made me feel like I wasn't special to him. He never walked out after sex without giving me a kiss or telling me how lovely I was. He would have never, ever just left me alone in bed without acknowledging that we shared something special.

Tears brim in my eyes as I stagger to the closet and pick up the shirt. I hug it to me, asking it for forgiveness, because that was a total dick move on my part. Then I start crying because I'm talking to a shirt while wearing another man's shirt. A man I let touch me, a man that once again left me without a good-bye. The door opens suddenly, and I look up just in time to see Oliver walk in. The smile on his face instantly drops when he takes me in—the crying face . . . me clutching my dead fiancé's shirt for dear life . . .

"I thought you left," I say in a hoarse whisper.

He doesn't move, doesn't speak . . . just stares for a moment longer. Finally, he walks over to me and wraps his arms around my head, pulling me into his hard chest.

"I wasn't going to leave without saying goodbye," he says against my hair. I think of all the times he did . . . all the times *we* did . . . and wonder if this time it'll be different. "I had a great night."

"I did too," I whisper against him.

He drops a kiss on my head. "I don't want to mess this up, Elle. So I'm going to give you some space, okay? Not because I don't want you . . . not because I don't think last night was incredible . . . but because I don't want to push you." He tilts my face to look at him, and my heart lodges in my throat as I wait for those green eyes to spear through me. "I want this to happen."

"Okay" is all I get to whisper before he drops his hand and walks out the door. I'm not sure what to do with any of that. I don't know what "that" is. All I know is that I'm scared to want him as much as I do. I'm terrified that I'll get burned again.

A couple of days later, I wake up and throw on the navy scrubs Nurse Gemma gave me on a day that painting got extra messy. When I show up at the hospital, I see her at the nurses' station, and she laughs.

"You here to offer back up?" she asks.

"Not unless you want the malpractice lawsuits to start pouring in."

"Never give Estelle anything with a needle. Noted."

I laugh, shaking my head. "I'll be quick today. I just want to make sure it looks perfect."

"Last day," she says, smiling. "I won't lie; I'm going to miss having that Micah guy around."

"Well, there's always the maternity wing."

"Nooooo! Don't send him over there! I have to stake my claim over him first!"

After talking a little longer, I finally make it to the room we've been working on, and pull the blinds open to check on the progress of the drying paint. I smile at the beauty of what we created and select a small brush to touch up the clouds that are missing some color.

"I heard you were in here," Oliver says behind me, almost making me paint outside of the lines.

"Never sneak up on a person holding a paint brush."

He chuckles. "Sorry. You want help?"

I stop moving the brush and shoot him a frown over my shoulder, which makes him shrug.

"I can fill in."

"Grab a brush. The clouds need another coat."

He does as I ask and stands beside me. I look over at the

cloud he's painting and move on to the next one, which is a couple of steps further away.

"You look great in scrubs, by the way."

I try not to smile and fail. "Thanks."

"You would make a good nurse," he adds.

I stop painting and turn to him with a raised eyebrow. "But not a good doctor?"

"Entertaining that question would mean that I'm saying doctors are more important than nurses, and they're not. If anything it's the other way around . . . either way, I'm not going there. I will say, though, that you would be good at any profession where you deal with people."

"I'll keep that in mind if this painting thing doesn't work out," I say with a smile.

"Meaning never?" he responds with a chuckle as he moves to the next cloud, on the opposite side of the room. "What do you think you would be if art didn't exist?"

"Dead."

Oliver lowers his paintbrush and looks at me. "Don't ever say that."

Somehow, with one look, he makes me feel the intensity in his words.

"Okay, fine, probably a teacher or a school counselor."

He nods and goes back to painting. "For the record, I think what you do for a living is perfect. This whole project is really incredible."

"Just doing what I can." I shrug.

"Why are you doing it?" he asks, walking toward me. "I know how much you love working with kids, so I knew coming here and painting with them would be something you would like . . . but this? This is a lot, Elle."

I turn away from his gaze—back to the cloud in front of me—and look at the wall as I answer. "It sucks to be having a bad day and have to get up in the morning and go about your business because it's expected. Imagine having an illness and having no choice but to come here and be stuck looking at the same four ugly walls, every single day. It makes all of my bad days seem so stupid when I hear these kids talk about what they're dealing with, and they don't even complain about any of it," I say, letting out a breath as I drop my hand and turn to face him. My heart skips a beat at what I find in his eyes. I walk to him and brush my fingers under his left eye. "You look so tired."

"This is what twenty hours straight looks like, but it's like you said, they don't complain, and that gives me no reason to complain either," he says.

I drop my hand and rock back in my heels, still looking at him. "You're a good man, Oliver Hart."

His lips curve into a smile, and I watch his hand come up. I brace myself for his touch, but he drops his hand before it reaches my face. "You're a great woman, Estelle Reuben."

"Art is pretty selfish. I create things for myself and hope others like it, but it's not like I'm thinking about the greater good when I make anything. What you do, on the other hand, is completely selfless."

His green eyes twinkle. "That's where you're wrong. This job may seem selfless, but helping those kids makes me feel like I'm leaving my footprint. When I help them leave in a healthier state than when they got here, that's . . ." He sighs, looking away for a moment. When his eyes meet mine again, he looks completely happy. "It's everything. It makes me feel like I matter."

"You do matter," I say with a smile.

"So do you. You think art is selfish, but I think it's pretty giving. I can't do this." He waves his hands around the room. "I spend sleepless nights and endless days in here making sure these kids are getting better, but aside from the days that I announce that they can go home, I won't put a smile on their face like this will."

His words make my heart soar. I turn back to the wall and

finish the cloud I'm working on before walking back to the supplies and dropping my brush there. Oliver has a way of making even the smallest things you do, seem like they're making a worldly difference. It's part of his charm, I guess.

We say goodbye, teetering on unchartered territory. I've never gotten one hundred percent of Oliver. As far as I know, only his job gets that. In the past, we've been friends . . . and then more than friends . . . but this feels like something else. I'm scared to let go and get more than what I bargained for. I'm also scared that I won't.

Chapter 19

Past

Oliver

I COULDN'T REMEMBER the last time I'd cried, if ever, but when I went to visit my dad in the hospital and saw the way half of his body was slouched, that's exactly what I felt like doing. He may not have been an ideal father to us, but he was always larger than life. Between seeing him all crumpled up, trying to ace all of my finals, and my job as an undergrad student helper—which consisted of everything from tutoring to helping them pick their classes—I was stressed.

This particular morning, I'd settled myself into a corner table in the coffee shop by my mom's house, and was working on a Quantum Physics paper and trying to keep my mind off my dad's condition, when Estelle sat down in front of me. I looked up in time to see her cross her legs and smile at me as she closed her mouth over the straw of the cup she'd been holding.

"What are you doing in this neck of the woods?" she asked.

I let out a deep breath and put my pen down. I hadn't seen

her in a couple of weeks. The last time we'd hung out was in a crowded Chili's. I'd gone with Victor and took a girl with me because I had no idea Estelle would be there. She hadn't acted like she cared. She'd been talking to Mia and Jenson most of the time, but it had felt awkward to me, having her there after we'd kissed so many times . . . after I wanted more all of those times . . . and there I was with someone else. I felt relieved seeing her now, and having her talk to me as if everything was totally okay, which was something I'd feared wouldn't happen after that night.

"You cut your hair," I said after a beat.

"Only the front, and I'm already regretting that decision." She brushed the long bangs out of her face.

"It looks good on you."

"Are you meeting someone here?" she asked, looking around. She looked hesitant suddenly. I smiled, wondering if she meant the girl from Chili's.

"Would it bother you if I was?"

Her eyes widened before her face settled into a small, thoughtful frown. "Not really."

"Are you meeting someone here?" I asked, hoping she wasn't. Why? I didn't know. She was free to date whomever she wanted, but that didn't mean I wanted to witness any of it. Her mouth turned up slowly as if she could read my thoughts. I was starting to think she could.

"Nope. I just left a terrible date."

"Why was it terrible?" I asked, leaning in a little closer, both of my elbows on the table, as hers were.

"He talked about himself the entire time. Total jock move. All the girls want him, all the guys want to be him," she said, mimicking a guy's voice as she rolled her eyes. I laughed.

"That sounds pretty terrible. Why would you even give a jock the time of day?" I asked, raising an eyebrow.

"I can think of one jock I like . . . but he's sooo nerdy," she said, her eyes dancing in so much amusement that I had to chuckle.

"Tell me more about this nerdy jock."

"Well," she started, dropping her gaze. She started using the condensation from her iced coffee to draw circles on the table as she spoke. "He's really good looking, if you like tanned surfer dudes with long hair . . . and ridiculous dimples . . ." She looked up at me and smiled shyly in a way that made my heart stop. "He's a really good guy, but rumor has it he's not much into relationships."

"It doesn't sound like he's good for you. You can't base a relationship on hard abs and dimples."

She grinned. "I didn't say anything about hard abs."

I shrugged. "I put two and two together. What else do you like about this nerdy jock?"

"I like how smart he is. I like the way he makes me feel when he talks to me . . . when he looks at me . . ." A blush spread over her cheeks. "When he kisses me."

I tried to ignore the hammering in my chest. "You think pretty highly of a guy who's not into relationships . . ."

"We all have our downfalls, and that just happens to be his," she said, shrugging as she looked away.

"What if he was into relationships?" I don't even know why I asked. It didn't matter. Not only was I not into relationships, I was totally against them.

Her gaze cut to mine again. "I have it on good authority that he's not."

I nodded sharply and exhaled, looking away.

"Did I upset you?" she asked, her words bringing my eyes back to hers.

"No. Why?"

"You look . . . I don't know . . . you're acting weird."

"I'm . . ." I ran my hands over my face. I wasn't planning on telling her or anybody about this, but the way she looked at me with those beautiful, nurturing eyes made me want to lay it all out there for her. "My dad's in the hospital."

She gasped and reached for my hands. I let her take them. Hers were small and cold, but her touch warmed through me. "Again? Is he going to be okay?"

I let out a short laugh. "He had another stroke. He should be fine if he takes care of himself this time. He's so stubborn though. He won't quit smoking. He won't diet or exercise. It makes me crazy." Estelle squeezed my hands and gave me a small smile.

"He's going to be fine. I have faith that he'll change."

Her words made me smile. She'd only met him once. She had no idea what he was like.

"Do you think people can change?"

Her eyes flickered between mine. She moved forward until half of her torso was over the table, closer to me. I wanted to take my hands out of hers and pull her face to mine. I wanted to kiss her and get lost in the feel of it, the way I always did. Her face stopped centimeters from mine.

"I know they can. They just have to want to," she whispered in a breath against me.

"You have a lot of faith in people."

She backed away, leaning back into her seat. She smiled, wide and confident, as she picked up her cup and put her lips around the straw again. "I sure do."

You make me want to change, I didn't say. *You make me believe that I can.*

The next day, at the same time, we ran into each other there again, and the following day one more time. We sat down, talked, made each other laugh, and went our separate ways after. She made me smile on days that laughter seemed impossible. She made me see hope in things I didn't know existed. That was when she truly became my Estelle. She just didn't know it. Hell, neither did I.

Chapter 20

Present

Estelle

A WEEK LATER, my painting team is done with the rooms and the hallway. We've turned an ocean into a field filled with flowers and kids playing. Everyone has been working around the clock to make sure we meet the deadline, so needless to say, when we're finally done, we all cheer loudly about it. We walk out of there, with our arms linked to one another's, fighting the urge to close our eyes in exhaustion.

"I am so ready for sleep," Micah says, leaning his head on mine.

"Me too," I say with a yawn.

I nearly trip over my own feet when we round the corner, and I see Oliver talking to a nurse I haven't seen before. He's standing against the wall, and she's leaning into him like he's her next meal. I catch his eye and he straightens a bit, but I look away and lean into Micah, walking out of the hospital before he can approach me—not that I expect him to. It kills me to admit to myself that I feel anything when I see something like that happen. It kills me, because I'm really not the kind of girl who gets jealous over anything, yet when it comes to Oliver, I feel possessive.

I go home and sleep like the dead. I don't hear my phone calls or text messages or shouts from my brother downstairs telling me I need to eat. I don't even care about any of it, until I realize I have a missed call from my realtor, and I call her back frantically, hoping for good news.

"Hello?"

"I don't want you to get your hopes up, but we have a possible buyer."

"Oh, thank God! Finally!"

She goes on to tell me how much they offered and lets me know she'll get back to me as soon as she needs me again. I stretch and go downstairs, half expecting not to see my brother there, but unfortunately come face to face with not only him, but his friend Bobby from work, as well. And I look like shit.

"Hey, Elle, good to see you again," Bobby says, smiling as his eyes run up and down my body.

"Hey. Sorry you had to see me in this condition, but I've been sleeping for like . . ."

"Eighteen hours," Vic interrupts.

"No shit."

"Yes, shit."

"Wow. I guess I was really tired."

"Yeah, I guess. Bean called asking for you."

I frown and pop my head out of the fridge. "And?"

"And I thought that was odd," Vic says with a shrug. "You've been hanging out a lot, right?"

"Not really." I go back into the fridge, looking for nothing in particular.

"He says he tried calling you and couldn't get through."

"I'll call him back later. I think he's working tonight anyway."

"Yeah, isn't tonight Grace's night?" Bobby asks with a laugh over a mouthful of muffin.

Vic doesn't respond, just looks at me for a reaction I don't give him. Inside I'm screaming "Who the fuck is Grace?" but I can't let that show. If anything, this cements the reason my brother shouldn't know anything about Oliver and me. It just bugs me that they seem to know his every move. It makes me realize that I don't.

"Mom called too."

"Okay, Vic. What are you, the freaking operator? I'll call everybody back when I feel like it." I turn around and head back up to my room.

"Damn. Maybe she needs more sleep."

Vic scoffs. "She was born bitchy."

143

Chapter 21

WHEN ALL ELSE fails, run home to your mother. At least those were my thoughts when I woke up this morning. I didn't consider that, once I pulled into her driveway, I would be accosted by her and asked a gazillion questions I didn't want to deal with. *Have you been eating well? How has it been staying with your brother? Is he eating well? How did it go with Derek? I'm setting you up on another date, you'll like this guy, I promise. How's the studio? I heard you did a great job with the hospital.* And lastly . . . *Come in, let me feed you!*

Which of course, I did. I sat in the dining table overlooking the mountains and the ocean behind them. Vic and I were water babies, but my parents preferred the Santa Barbara Mountain View. They owned a house in Malibu that we used to drive to on weekends. Sometimes we were with them, but mostly we were with friends.

"Vic says you've been hanging out with Oliver a lot," my mom comments, using her nonchalant voice, as if curiosity isn't coloring the undertones of her voice.

I groan. "Vic is so annoying. We see each other a lot in the hospital. We hung out once outside of work. Big deal!" Her laugh makes my eyes snap to her. "What?"

She shrugs. "Your brother didn't think anything of it until I mentioned it was odd that you were hanging out. You used to hate him, didn't you?"

"No I didn't." I frown. Where the hell would she get that idea?

"I thought you did. You were always talking about what a player he was."

"Because he was," I say, giving her a "no shit" look.

"And now?"

I stare at her for a while, my hands playing with the napkin on the table. People say I'm a carbon copy of her, and that if they cloned me I wouldn't have looked more like her than I do. The thought makes me smile, because my mother is really a beautiful person, inside and out. Even with her demanding career as a professor, she's always managed to put her family first. Like today, when she saw my car pulling into the driveway, she immediately called out sick. I'm used to telling her everything, but for some reason, I can't talk to her about Oliver. I just can't. He's like a third child of this house. It's not like Wyatt, where I could come and complain about him or say beautiful things about him, and it wouldn't matter either way because he was an outsider to everybody. Oliver practically lived here growing up. And even though absolutely nothing is going on, as usual, I would hate to paint him in a bad light.

"I don't know, Mom," I say, finally. "I honestly don't know. I'm sure Vic can tell you better than I can."

"But you see him at work."

"Yeah, and?"

"Does he have a girlfriend? Or girlfriends?" she asks, rolling her hazel eyes.

I shrug. "You know him. He flirts with anything that walks, so I guess."

"Do you think he sleeps with all of them?"

My eyes widen. "Okay, this is getting awkward, and again,

I don't know."

"Sometimes guys like him get a bad rap, don't you think? I mean, he's always been such a good boy."

I make a noncommittal wave of my hands. "I don't care. Why are we talking about this?"

Then she smiles, really wide, and I sink back in my seat. I'm half expecting her to tell me she's setting me up with him on a date.

"Because, this guy, Zach, sort of has that reputation with the ladies, but I hear he's not a player at all," she starts.

"Mom."

"And he is so cute, Estelle!"

"Mom."

"He owns a gallery in Malibu."

"Zach Edwin?" I practically shout.

My mom smiles, nodding and raising her eyebrows as if she just tasted all the cookies in the jar and didn't get caught.

"How the hell do you know him?" I ask a little too enthusiastically for my own good.

"Well, it's a funny story, Bettina and I were doing some shopping a couple of weeks ago and happened to step in his shop. He has gorgeous things in there, by the way, but the piece that caught our eye was a heart—one of your hearts. We stepped in, pretending we didn't know anything about anything, and asked him how much the heart was." She pauses for dramatic effect. "Four thousand dollars."

My mouth drops.

"He says he sold the last one for three thousand, and this is the only one he has left, but the person he bought them from didn't leave a card so he can't get in touch with who made it. Elle, are you all right?"

I shake my head, my mouth still hanging open.

My mom laughs and taps my hand with hers. "Can you believe that? I'm assuming he bought them from Wyatt."

I swallow, recollecting myself. "Yeah, Wyatt mentioned

selling him a few pieces years back but . . . wow . . . four thousand dollars?"

"So you haven't gotten a cut from that?" my mom asks, frowning.

"It wasn't on consignment. He sold it to get rid of them, because I had made too many for a show we were attending, and Wyatt thought selling to Zach would be good for me later on. Obviously I never followed up, and Wyatt probably forgot his cards, as usual, but oh my God."

"I know!" my mom squeals.

"Okay, so how did the date thing come about?"

"Oh. Well, I told him my daughter was the one who made it, and he was very impressed."

"Uh-huh?"

"And then I got on my phone and showed him the website to your studio. He saw your photo, and I just saw his eyes light up."

"Oh my God, Mom," I say, burying my face in my hands.

"So I told him the short version about Wyatt and that you're dating now. I asked him if he would be interested, and he jumped on the chance."

"Oh my God, Mom!" I say again, still talking into my hands.

"Have you seen him, Elle?" she asks. I peer at her through my fingers and nod. "He's good looking!"

"He's freaking hot, but I can't go out with him! This isn't the fifteen hundreds. You can't just go around trying to court me to people!"

"Why the hell not?" she says, frowning. "Haven't you seen those shows on television where people are actually paying to be set up with others? Millionaire Matchmaker or something?"

I stare blankly. "No, I haven't had the pleasure of watching that. Just . . . I don't know, I mean, I would love to sell him some of my work, but I can't date him!"

"Is it because he's a player?"

"What? No!"

Zach does have that whole player reputation, with good reason. He doesn't usually date people in the industry, but the one girl he dated, he married, cheated on, and divorced within a year. After that, he'd been known to sleep with models, actresses, and whoever else walked into his shop on two slender legs and a short skirt.

"Are you sure?"

"I'm positive! I'm not looking for anything serious, so why would I care about his reputation?"

"I don't think his reputation is who he is. I'm telling you, he's a charmer, but I don't think he sleeps around as much as we're led to believe."

"Are we done? I'd really like to eat my pancakes in peace now," I mumble.

"Of course, dear. More coffee?"

"Sure. Where's Dad?"

"He left at sun up. Long day today. Three celebrity clients."

"Fun."

"Yeah, I'm sure we'll hear all about it when he gets back. Are you staying here tonight?"

I sigh and pour syrup on my pancakes. "Yeah, I think I will."

"You're sure you don't want to meet Zach? He lives a couple of blocks away."

My gaze cuts to hers. "You're kidding."

"What if he just comes over for dinner? That way it won't be a date, but a way for you to talk about your art."

"Since when are you interested in art? You hated when Wyatt used to come over and talk about art."

She gasps, placing a hand over her heart. "I never hated when he came over! I just didn't like how he spoke to you sometimes."

"Really? How's that?" I say, stabbing a piece of pancake. I don't mean for her to answer, but she does anyway.

"Like you were a child."

My chewing slows. I was a child. He was eleven years older than I was and had the experience of an eighty-year-old.

"He didn't speak to me like I was a child," I say.

"You were his muse . . . his light, I guess. I see that now, but at the time, it was unnerving, the way he wanted you stuck to his side every time your father's friends were around. As if he thought they would take you away from him. You never got that vibe?"

I shoot her a look. "Of course I did. Men are like that."

She tilts her head, seemingly weighing out my words. "I suppose they are. Anyhow, he obviously loved you in his own way and helped you a lot. But, just think, Zach Edwin!"

The rest of the day is spent shopping with my mom and Bettina (Mia's mom), talking about Zach and how he's coming over for dinner. Mia called threatening to kill me if I don't call her as soon as he leaves. At one point, between trying on shoes at Neiman Marcus and having drinks at Chili's, my brother gets wind of the whole thing and calls me to tell me he'll kill me if I hook up with Zach because he heard he hooks up with everybody, including a client's ex-wife. I turn off my phone after that. I have enough chatter to listen to from Bettina and my mom as they go on and on talking about all the guys Mia and I could have married by now. I don't know if they forget that I was engaged, or they just choose to ignore it because I wasn't engaged to somebody of their liking.

At night, I wear one of the dresses I bought earlier, a short—but not too short—flowery dress that hugs my torso but opens up and flows past my waist. My mom insists I wear a pair of red heels with it because it'll make my legs look miraculous (her words). When the door swings open at seven o'clock, I practically jump on my father before he has a chance to put his briefcase down. He laughs, his big Santa Claus-like laugh comes straight from his core, and he hugs me tightly.

"Someone missed me," he says, smiling when he lets me

go. His once sandy brown hair is now covered in salt, and the lines of his face are marked with every time he's laughed—and there have been a lot of those. His brown eyes shine when he looks at me, and it makes me feel like a kid again.

"You're the only other normal person in this house," I whisper-shout dramatically as he continues to chuckle and shake his head.

"Nobody told you to stay alone with you mother," he whispers back conspiratorially.

"And Bettina!"

His eyes widen. "Oh Jesus, you need a drink."

"Or twenty."

He laughs again, putting his hand over my shoulder.

"Thomas! You're home!" my mom says, smiling widely as she saunters over to us, wearing a knee-length black dress.

"Are you trying to give a man a heart attack, Hannah? What are you wearing?" he asks, dropping his arm from my shoulder and reaching for my mom.

Watching them is like watching Gone with the Wind. You know, that last part, where Rhett Butler holds Scarlett O'Hara's face in his hands? That sums up my parents. Every. Single. Day.

"Oh, stop it, Tom, you know Elle hates public displays of affection," my mom coos as she throws her arms around his neck.

I laugh, shaking my head. "I do not, but I'll be outside if you need me."

"Why do you insist on setting her up on these stupid dates?" I hear my dad whisper to her as I walk away.

"Because, she needs to move on!"

"She'll move on when she's ready, honey. Your meddling isn't helping. And now I have Victor calling to say he's coming over to intervene," he says. I freeze with my hand over the doorknob. I have a moment of clarity, where I think maybe I'll call it a night and go home, but then remember where home is right now and decide to walk outside and sit in my parents' yard.

Growing up, I had two types of friends: the ones who had overbearing parents and the ones who had parents who didn't care what their kids were doing. I always wanted to have the second type of parents. Mine weren't strict, unless I got bad grades, and they only meddled when . . . well, they always meddled. When Wyatt died, I was grateful for that because I would have probably gone weeks without eating had it not been for them practically spoon-feeding me. Needless to say, I'm not surprised Vic decided to follow me home after he learned about the Zach thing, especially after he made the comment about his client. This is more than his normal big brother overprotection; it's about work.

My dad joins me outside after he's showered and hands me a glass of white wine.

"Figured you'd need it," he says, toasting me with his own.

"Thanks," I respond, taking a sip and leaning back into the cushions of the seat.

"I heard you did a great job at the hospital."

I glance at him and smile. "I think we did."

"I'm proud of you, Elle. I know I always said art was a waste of time and you should have stuck with something else, but then you go and do things like this, and I can't help but to be proud of you."

"Thank you," I say, leaning over and giving him a kiss on the cheek.

"Your mom isn't going to give up until you find a new boyfriend, you know? I think you should just pretend you're in love so she can let this go already."

"Mom isn't going to stop until I have kids."

"I thought you didn't want kids," he says, taking a sip of wine. He doesn't look at me when he says it. His eyes are far off into the distance. He doesn't see the crumbled look on my face. Wyatt didn't want kids. I turn my body away and mimic his pose, staring at the mountains—at the spot where I know the ocean is, but it's too dark to see right now.

"I haven't decided yet," I say finally.

"Sometimes we give up a lot of ourselves for the people we love," my dad says. "It's hard knowing when to stop doing that, because you feel like if you love someone, you should be okay giving things up for them." I nod and sip on my wine. "When I married Erika," he says, recalling his deceased wife—the woman he lost years before he met my mother. "I gave up everything I loved. I gave up school and got a job because I felt I needed to provide for her. That's what men do, you know, we provide for our woman—for our family. Then I lost her to a drunk driver and thought—what is my life now? I have nothing. And the thing is, I didn't feel that way because I lost her, I felt that way because of the things I'd given up for her."

I gulp a big sip of wine, knowing exactly how he feels. "And with Mom? And us?"

"Well, by the time I met your mother, I was back on track. She was younger, so I waited for her to graduate, I didn't want her making the same mistake I made with Erika. I never wanted to be the reason she looked back on her life and regretted the things she didn't do."

"Do you think all men are like that? Waiting for the right time to do things?" I ask, thinking of Oliver.

"No, not all of them. I think your brother does. I think he's waiting for his career to blossom before he settles down with somebody, and if he had met someone already, I would tell him he's an idiot for doing that at his age, but he hasn't met anybody that makes him reconsider, so I guess he's on the right track."

"Yeah, I guess."

"My point is, Elle, you probably gave up more than you think when you were with Wyatt, and that's not a bad thing. It's the way of life. I just don't want you to jump into a new relationship with that mentality. No matter how good looking your mom says the guy is." He flashes a smile that I return.

"Well, we both know Mom's taste is often a little screwed

up," I say, making him laugh.

"Ain't that the truth."

Chapter 22

Past

Oliver

I'VE ALWAYS CONSIDERED myself lucky to have Victor for a friend. He's been selfless, ruthless, and above all, loyal. When I didn't have any place to go after I graduated and my lease was up, Vic didn't hesitate for a moment.

"You're living with me," he'd said.

"Okay, let me know how much I owe you. I only need a place to stay for a couple of weeks," I'd said, and he'd looked at me like I was crazy.

"You're my brother. You don't owe me shit!"

And that was how I ended up sleeping in the small cottage beside the house he'd been renting for the summer. Summer break—*the last hurrah,* he was calling it. The last hurrah before I left for medical school, and he settled down in law school at UCLA. Life was good during those weeks—wake up, catch some waves, eat something, drink, party, and hook up with the girls that hung around. We were treating grad school like some men would treat their last weekend as bachelors, which was funny because we'd been self-proclaimed lifers. "Who needs one woman when we can have ten?" those were Vic's words, followed by Jenson's, "Bros before hoes." Junior was the only one who couldn't participate in our crazy summer, since he'd been tied down to the same girl since the first semester of school. As much as we made fun of him, I think we were all slightly jealous that he'd found a girl he actually wanted to be with every day.

I dressed that night, much like I did every other night, but I was exhausted from being in the sun all day, and I needed to get up early the next morning to start hauling my stuff upstate. One drink . . . maybe two . . . then sleep, I promised myself as I walked over to the main house, where the party had already started.

One drink, maybe two, then sleep, I repeated, the mantra becoming like second lyrics to the song bumping off the speakers. One drink, maybe two, I was about to tell myself again when I spotted Estelle walking into the house. I felt a slow smile creep up on my face as I watched her finger comb her hair, wild from the wind outside. Her lips were pressed into a sexy pout as her eyes wandered over the room. She shrugged off the jacket she was wearing, which revealed a low cut black shirt that pressed her tits up, and a short sequined skirt that showed off every curve of her legs.

I guess she felt me staring, because her eyes caught mine a beat later, and she smiled that wide smile of hers. It told me she was up to no good tonight and that she wondered if I was fair game. One drink, maybe two, then sleep, I said to myself again, this time kicking the frontal lobe of my brain, in the hopes I'd knock some sense into myself before I reached her. My treacherous feet walked toward her, as they always did, and she stood there waiting for me, as she usually did.

"I haven't seen you in a while," I said, my eyes taking in those marbled orbs of hers, as she slowly looked me over from head to toe. "What's the verdict?" I asked when her eyes finally stopped at mine. She blushed slightly and looked away, laughing.

"You look good," she said, turning her gaze to mine again.

"You look great," I said, and she smiled. "How have you been?"

It had been maybe two months since we'd last seen each other. Two months since our tongues did the song and dance they usually did whenever we were at one of these parties . . . or at the movies . . . or anywhere that afforded our sneaking around. We'd never gone too far, usually kissing and touching over clothes before we were interrupted by one thing or another. Our hiatus wasn't a coincidence. I'd been going to Cal parties instead of Vic's because the guilt of everything I felt whenever Estelle was around was starting to weigh down on me. Like the time I saw her at the mall a couple of months ago and cornered her in a long hallway that led to the bathroom. I only wanted to talk to her about stopping this madness between us, but then she pulled my face to hers and kissed me so deeply, I forgot my fucking name right then. She was dangerous for me. What I felt when I was around her wasn't right. I had my life planned out, and the things she made me want didn't fit into them. Not yet.

"I've been pretty good," she said. We started walking to the kitchen and grabbed red cups with beer when we reached the table. "How about you? I heard you're leaving for Berkeley soon. I knew you would get in."

I smiled. The last time I saw her, I was still waiting for my application. "It almost seems surreal."

She tilted her head and looked at me for a long moment before her lips turned into a small, warm smile. "I'm proud of you, Oliver."

My heart thumped a little at that. I smiled and drank some beer.

"You still all about having fun?" I asked. I didn't necessarily want to hear about her love life, but I wanted to know everything she was up to. Everything I'd missed.

Elle laughed as we reached a bench outside and sat down. "I guess you can say that."

"Still haven't met *the one?*" I asked, hoping my voice sounded light—unlike everything I felt squeezing inside me.

"Maybe I have, maybe I haven't. How would I know if he's the one?" she said with a smirk and a shrug.

I looked away, out into the distance where I knew the beach was just steps away. "I'd like to think we know when we meet that special person."

"Have you met her? The one?" she asked.

I swallowed, closed my eyes, drank more beer, and let out a breath.

"I decided a long time ago to avoid meeting her until the time was right," I said in a low voice, as if I was confessing a crime to a priest.

Estelle scooted closer to me, until our arms were touching, then she rested her head on my shoulder. "Is there ever a right time?"

"I don't know," I whispered, turning my face to smell her hair.

"I met a guy," she said suddenly, quietly, and my heart dropped.

"Yeah?" I said, drinking the rest of my beer.

"He's . . . different. He's nice. Older."

"How much older?"

She lifted her head to look at me, and the movement had us sitting nose to nose. A jolt ran through me, and I inched closer. Because I'm a bastard. Because I'm selfish. Because I wanted those lips to be mine, and those eyes to be mine, and that voice to only be heard by me—even if it was only for one night.

"Older than me," she whispered, her nose brushing against mine. "Older than you." I reared back, taking a quick moment to glance around, as adrenaline at the possibility of getting caught coursed through me. I berated myself for a moment—a quick, fleeting moment—that got lost as soon as I looked back into her eyes.

"Do you like older guys?" I whispered, my lips feathering over hers.

Her eyes flashed. "I like some."

"Yeah?" I asked, plucking at her bottom lip with my teeth.

"Yeah," she said breathily.

"Do you think he's the one?" I asked in a whisper, planting a kiss on the edge of her lips.

"No," she said, repeating my movement and dropping a kiss on the edge of mine.

"Have you ever been in love, Estelle?" I asked quietly, backing away slightly to search her wide eyes.

"Have you?" she whispered, staring at me, waiting.

"I . . ." I didn't know what to say, and before I could say anything at all, boisterous voices came from behind us, and we inched away quickly. We turned to see some guys cheering on another as he chugged his beer. The crowd cheered and hollered, but died down quickly, and we looked at each other again.

"I really want you to kiss me," she said, bringing her eyes to mine.

If possible, my heart spiked harder against my chest. I dipped my head until we were nose to nose. "I really want to kiss you again."

"I want you to do more than kiss me this time."

I held my breath. "Estelle . . ."

"Please."

I closed my eyes at her plea. I took that moment to tune out the loud party and focus on why this couldn't happen. *Victor is your best friend, and you promised you'd take care of her, not hurt her. He will kill you. He's your brother. How would you feel if he did this to Sophie?*

But then I felt Estelle get even closer to me. I felt her soft breath over my ear, and as her hand reached down between us and settled right over my dick, I couldn't breathe, let alone think.

"I want you, Oliver," she whispered. My eyes popped open in a flash and when I looked at her, I knew I couldn't deny her even if I wanted to. Even if I should.

She stood, grabbing my hand and started to walk toward the cottage. I looked over my shoulder to make sure nobody saw us. My eyes scanned the party and looked for Vic specifically, but I never found him. Then I felt like an asshole for doing that. I was about to disappear into a room with his little sister, and I was making sure he didn't see us. I was supposed to protect her from the big bad wolf, yet here I was, feeling like a wolf myself. But I couldn't help it. I didn't see red lights when it came to Elle, I only saw green and go, and felt things that made me want to be a better man for her, even though I knew I couldn't.

The door opened and closed behind us. As soon as we faced the other, she jumped on me, wrapping her legs around my waist and throwing her arms around my neck as she smashed her lips to mine. I held her, grabbing her ass as I plunged my tongue inside her mouth. I couldn't help but moan when she bit it lightly, sucking it in and out of her mouth. I set her on her feet only to let her take my shirt off. Her eyes blazed as she looked at me, from my face down to my torso. Her small fingers touched every line I had, leaving a trail of fire behind every spot she touched.

"You're ticklish," she said, looking up at me in wonder.

I wasn't, not really, but when she touched me like that, my muscles contracted, so I shrugged and let her think I was. I didn't want to rush her, so I let her undress me completely. I let her take the lead and decide what came next.

"You're beautiful," she breathed, as I stood naked in front of her. Her hand reached out and grasped my cock, and it jumped. I groaned, biting my lip and throwing my head back, asking all the gods to please give me enough control not to come in her hands as she stroked me. Finally, my control broke, and I stepped forward, reaching for the hem of her shirt. I waited, watching as she nodded for me to take it off. I did, then stayed fixated on her bare chest. I'd pictured what she looked like a million times, and none of those did the reality justice. She was just . . . perfect. I unzipped her skirt and let it pool at her feet around the strappy heels she wore. Then I dipped my head and kissed her—a slow, leisurely kiss that deepened as my hands trailed down her body. My lips left hers and made their way down to her neck, her collarbone, the valley between her breasts . . . then I pulled each nipple into my mouth. She grabbed onto my hair with a deep moan of encouragement, so I continued plucking kisses down her body, and over her panties, which I pulled down with my teeth. I pushed them down her calves and then her feet, where I unstrapped each shoe and helped her step out.

I was still on my knees, making my way back up when a surge of desire hit me like a ten-foot wave. I stopped and looked into her eyes when I reached the inside of her thighs to push them apart. She watched me in rapt attention, as if I was some sort of beautiful puzzle she had to figure out.

"Bed?" I asked as my hands stroked her thighs softly. She nodded, lips parted, those multi-colored eyes glazed over. I stood and carried her to the bed like a bride. Neither of us spoke as I moved down her body again, my mouth kissing her, teasing her, communicating how much I wanted her. Her body thrashed against the bed . . . against my wet lips . . . and she pulled my hair as she said my name over, and over. *Oliver, oh, Oliver.* I'd never heard such a beautiful melody.

My fingers replaced my mouth as I moved back to her breasts, tweaking her nipples, and squeezing them lightly.

"So good," she whimpered in a pant, and I smiled. I wanted to make her feel good. I positioned myself between her legs and paused. I never paused. I always looked for a condom, put it on and continued. I never paused and wondered if I could possibly get away with no condom. I never paused and wished that there would be no barrier between us. But this was Elle. *My Elle.*

Her hands moved down my chest and to my cock, where she squeezed again. "I'm on the pill," she said quietly.

"Do you do this often? No condom?" I asked, matching her tone. My heart was tripping over itself in anticipation. Why had I asked that question? Did it matter? Since when did I care what my lovers did with other partners?

She shook her head. "Never."

I let out a sigh of relief. Never. I felt high. I could give her something she'd never had. I wasn't the one who took her virginity. I wasn't the one who'd had the pleasure of her first kiss—but this, I could give her. I bent lower and teased her folds with my cock.

"Please, Oliver," she said, doing a shimmy below me. "Please."

I dipped my head and kissed her again, letting her taste herself on my lips, moaning when she pulled my hair to bring me closer. "We'll go slow," I whispered against her.

"No. I don't want slow," she said, her eyes wide. She moved her hips up. I grinned.

"I want slow," I said, pushing myself inside her with one deep thrust. Her body bowed off the bed with a yelp. I pulled back, and she sighed, I pushed back in, she yelped again. "You still want it fast?" I asked, groaning when she clenched around me.

"I still want fast," she panted, meeting my thrusts. I pulled out completely, then pushed back in slowly, and smiled when she growled at me. My thrusts were long and hard. I relished the way she felt around me. I tried to absorb her heat, her wetness—everything I could—so I took my time. I took my time until she trailed her hand down her flat stomach to the spot where our bodies were joined and began to rub, and then I lost it. I lifted her leg and started to move—really move. She screamed my name, I groaned out hers. She clawed at me, and it made me move faster. Then she started whimpering *Oliver,*

Oliver, I can't, I can't, as her head swayed side to side and her eyes rolled back. I pulled out of her, and she gasped, and looked like she was going to kill me, so I scooted back and sat down, picking her up and positioning her over my hips. We never lost eye contact, and when she took me in and started to move, I was a goner.

The way her eyes searched mine said, *do you feel this? Can you feel it too? Am I making this up?* The words were never verbalized. They were spoken with our tongues against the other's. *Are you still searching? Do you still believe someone else is better for you?* My hands framed her face as hers did mine, and we held each other there as she reached the brink of her orgasm. I fell right behind her. It was slow at first, then all consuming and powerful. We looked at each other as we caught our breaths, still searching . . . questioning . . . wondering things we didn't dare ask.

Chapter 23

Present

Estelle

"IS THAT A new dress?" Vic asks as I take a seat across from him at the table.

"I got it with Mom yesterday. Mom and Bettina."

Vic groans. "God, what a pair. And they managed to pick up a douche for you to date while you were shopping."

I laugh, because he's not completely wrong. Zach coming over last night solidified my belief that the dating pool available right now is less than spectacular. He's good looking, charming, and talks about himself ninety-percent of the time. He used the other ten percent to tell me how much he could profit from my kaleidoscope hearts. By the time Victor got there, I was ready to go to sleep, but I stuck around because he was so flustered. On his way to our parents' house, he'd gotten a flat tire and had Oliver pick him up because he'd already been riding on his spare. That led to a confused Oliver standing in the dining room, looking between Zach and me with a weird look on his face. I wasn't sure if he was jealous or if he was just put off by how much Zach talked. At any rate, he excused himself pretty early, and as soon as he left, I went upstairs.

"All he did was talk about himself," I say, shaking my head.

"Like a true artist," Victor says, and grins when I slap his shoulder. "You have great luck with dates, huh?"

"You dated him longer than I did. I went to sleep," I say, raising an eyebrow.

"Whatever. You're not dating him. He's a womanizer and a cheat, and I'm pretty sure he's involved in some weird shit."

"You say that about everybody. 'I'm pretty sure he's involved in some weird shit,'" I mimic, rolling my eyes.

He shrugs. "I'm usually right."

"You're worse than Dad. You're never going to approve of anybody I date."

"That's not true," he says, his brows furrowing. He looks up at the sound of the door closing behind me, and before I turn around, his eyes lock with mine. "As long as he's a good guy, not a player, and isn't involved in weird shit, I approve."

"Approve of what?" asks Oliver, whose voice makes me shiver. I stand up and head to the kitchen, glancing back and greeting him with a smile.

"Vic is telling me who I can and can't date. Don't worry, so far, you are not on the list of contenders."

Vic spurts out a laugh and mumbles something about, "That'll be the day." While Oliver just stares at me like he can't believe I just said that, it takes everything in me not to flash him my middle finger. Instead, I turn my attention back to the pantry and sort through the cereal. I don't know what I'm so mad about, but it seems like every time my heart involves itself in Oliver, everything inside me goes haywire. My already loose screws rattle. My already questionable judgment vanishes. And lastly, the possessive chip I never knew I had, surfaces. The only thing I remember is Bobby mentioning "Grace night," and that's enough to make me want to throw something at the man who's not even mine.

"Mom only has healthy grain cereals in here," I call out. "What the hell!" I say when the pantry slams shut in front of me, and I find Oliver glaring at me. I frown. "What?"

"Who's on the list?" he asks, and it takes me a couple of seconds to realize what list he's referring to. I laugh.

"What does it matter?"

"It matters," he presses.

I raise an eyebrow. "How was 'Grace night?'"

Oliver's eyes widen in shock. "What?"

I open the pantry again, effectively making him move out of my way.

"There is no Grace night," he whispers loudly. I feel his eyes burning the side of my face as he glares at me over the pantry door. "There is only Mae night, Danny night, Patrick night, Justin night . . . do you want me to continue? Because I spend most of my nights doing rounds in a hospital, unless I get really lucky, and then it's Estelle night." His words make my heart quicken, but I refuse to look at him. "Now tell me, who's on the list of contenders?"

"You really want to know?" I ask in a quiet voice, closing the pantry.

He crosses his arms over his chest. He's not wearing his scrubs today, but instead, a navy t-shirt that hugs his frame, and jeans that cling to his hips as if they were tailored. His hair is wet and brushed back, and his stubble looks cleaned up. He looks like a goddamn model, and I hate it. Stupid boy. Stupid cute boy.

"I'm asking."

"Go ask my brother," I say, nodding in that direction.

"I'm asking you."

I cross my arms over my chest and stand in front of him. "And I'm telling you to go ask him, because I don't know who is on the approved list. Is there a reason for you shutting the pantry in my face, or are you just here to annoy, Bean?"

He opens his mouth and closes it, then opens it again. "I want your list. I don't care about Victor's list. I know I'll never make it on his. I want your approved list."

I can't come up with a comeback for that, so I'm glad when my dad walks in clearing his throat, and I have to drag my eyes away from the intensity in Oliver's. Dad's brown eyes bounce between us, and his brows raise in question.

"Interrupting something?"

"No," Oliver and I say at the same time.

"I heard this is your last week at the hospital," my dad says, using his enthusiastic voice, as he rounds the corner and opens his arms to hug Oliver. "Congratulations, my boy. I knew you had it in you, despite those late nights out."

I groan and fake gag. Can the people in this house not stop talking about this guy's past? Jesus.

"Thank you," Oliver says, laughing. "Now it's time for the real world."

"Do you know where you'll be working?" my dad asks as he opens the fridge. Oliver turns his body to face me as he answers.

"I've gotten some calls, but I'm holding off for the right one," he says. I scoff like a bratty schoolgirl and turn around.

"Dad, what's up with the Lucky Charms?"

"Your mom won't buy them anymore."

"What? Why?" I ask, opening the freezer. "You guys have nothing to eat!"

My mom's laugh rings throughout the house. "We have nothing you like to eat, but we have plenty to eat. Sit down, I'll make you some eggs."

"I hate eggs," I mutter under my breath. As I stand with my back against the counter, Oliver's fingers brush mine, and I feel a jolt that makes my eyes snap to his.

"You like eggs," he says.

I shake my head. "I really don't."

"With goat cheese?" he asks, his fingers now intertwining

with mine.

"I like them a little bit if they have goat cheese," I whisper, trying to untangle my hand from his, but he makes it an impossible feat. "What are you doing?"

"I want to be on that list," he says quietly so only I can hear, but my eyes automatically pop around the room, making sure nobody is paying attention.

"Then get on it."

"Your list or his?" he asks, throwing a nod in the general direction of where Victor is.

"Whichever one matters most to you."

I reach up to push his hair out of his face, threading my fingers through it so that it stays back. His eyes close at the movement, and my heart spikes at the intimacy of it all. My dad clears his throat again, and I push away from Oliver, giving us enough distance to look like nothing is going on. Because nothing is going on. *At all.*

"Do you want coffee, Oliver?" my dad asks.

"Yes, please."

As I walk past, Dad twists his lips into a smile. "Your brother would kill him. You know that, right?"

I grab on to the edge of the counter. "He has no reason to."

He laughs. "You sure about that?"

And with that, I scurry over to the table and sit in front of my brother, as usual. Oliver sits beside me, as usual, and my mom and dad sit in their seats as she places the food in the middle of the table—scrambled eggs, sunny side up eggs, poached eggs, toast, jelly, and butter. I go for the toast. Oliver takes it upon himself to serve me some scrambled eggs, because they have goat cheese and bacon. I thank him and eat with one hand while I fidget with the napkin on my lap with the other. My dad is looking at us like we're about to announce my pregnancy, and the entire breakfast feels awkward.

"I like that dress on you," Oliver whispers, and my face flames.

"Oliver, Tom says you'll be finished with your residency soon. Will you stick to pediatrics?" my mom asks.

"Definitely. I love working with kids, so I'm trying to find a small practice to join."

"You must see so much in the hospital though," my mom says sadly.

"It's not easy," Oliver says, his hand reaching for mine under the table. "It really makes you realize what you have and how lucky we are to be healthy."

"I bet. I'm sure it sheds a different light on your life," my dad comments.

"It does," Oliver responds, squeezing my hand. I feel like he's squeezing my heart. "It's made me see a lot of things clearly."

"I think this year has opened our eyes to a lot of things," my mom starts, until Victor interrupts.

"Did I miss the memo about this being a Thanksgiving breakfast?"

I bite my lip, trying not to laugh, and glance up at Oliver, who's apparently doing the same. Our hands squeeze tighter together.

"It doesn't have to be Thanksgiving for you to be grateful," my mom says.

"Vic is just upset because that girl he's been seeing hasn't come around in a couple of days," I say, sticking my tongue out at him when he makes a face.

"Whatever. At least my mom doesn't have to play matchmaker for me."

"She doesn't have to for me either!" I say, shooting a glare at my mom.

"Prove it," Vic says. "Prove it. Go out tonight and get yourself a date the old fashioned way."

I laugh. "By go out, I'm assuming you mean to a club, and that is the last place I want to get a date. Besides, since when do you want me to date?"

"Since you started pointing out my dating life when you have none."

I roll my eyes. "I'm happily single, thank you very much."

"I'm just saying—I have no issues finding women who want to date me."

"I have no issues finding guys who want to date me either."

He raises an eyebrow, but makes no further comment.

"I'm serious, Victor."

He raises his hands up. "I'm dropping it, Elle. Are we still going out to celebrate me closing this case?"

"I guess we are, right?" I say with a shrug.

"Maybe you'll find a date there."

"You are so infuriating."

"You never know. Maybe you'll find love in a hopeless place," he says and laughs.

"Mom, you're not going to say anything to your idiot son?"

"Estelle!"

"Estelle, what? He's being a moron!"

"I think your brother just wants you to move on with your life," my dad chimes in. "He just has a weird way of showing his feelings. Besides, who's to say she isn't moving on with someone right under our noses?"

Victor scoffs. "One, we would have noticed. Two, we don't know anybody she would date."

"This is not happening," I say, muffled into my hands, while Oliver laughs beside me.

Victor calls Jenson, who seems to be in town every weekend, to join us. His invitees end up being: Mia, Jenson, Victor, Oliver, Bobby and me. Oh, and whoever Oliver and Jenson decide to bring along, because God knows they don't travel without a date unless they're going to find one there.

"Why the hell would he want to go to a club?" Mia asks, as we sort through her closet.

"Because obviously Victor has no life outside of his workplace, which, may I remind you, consists of divorcees trying to screw each other over."

"Ugh. Why is Jenson even here again? It's getting annoying. I like it better when he stays on the east coast," she says, and suddenly stops looking through clothes, to sit on her bed. I face her and take in the sad look that invades her face any time Jenson is mentioned.

"You don't have to go," I say. "Just sit this one out."

Mia brings her gaze to me. "Are you sure you'll be okay?"

"I'll be fine. I'll have three body guards, and I can't blame you for not wanting to see Jenson."

She sighs. "I'm just not ready."

I take a seat beside her and hold her hands in mine. "I know." I don't mention how Jenson seems upset every time Mia's name is brought up, because there's no point. "I hate that he makes you so sad."

Mia smiles. "Me too, but that's life."

The conversation shifts to my outfit and hair as I start getting ready, and for a while, we both let go of the ghosts of our pasts.

Chapter 24

WHEN I GET to the club, I'm escorted to the VIP area, where Victor, Bobby, Jenson and Oliver are talking to some women at the table beside them. I watch for a couple of beats, but the loud house music and dim lights make it impossible for me to understand what they're saying. The fact that none of them feel my eyes on them enough to look up is telling though—they're all completely lost in conversation. Oliver throws his head back in laughter, and I swear I can feel it rumble from his chest to mine. Or maybe it's the speaker I'm leaning against. Either way, it's enough for me to finally shuffle my feet in the opposite direction and head to the bar. I'll go back over there after I've supplied my body with the liquid courage it needs to sit next to them . . . next to *him.*

As soon as my ass touches the stool, I ask for a drink and start looking around, watching the bodies move and the women strut across the dance floor in search of their next victim. Two drinks later, I get up and walk back to the VIP area, giving a wave to the girl who walked me in before. She smiles and escorts me back to where Vic is, and I stand directly in front of them so they'll hear me over the music.

"Hey."

Victor looks away from the woman practically sitting on his lap, but then, it seems like all of the women are sitting on the men's laps right now. I try to avoid getting in a twist by not letting my eyes drift to Oliver.

"Finally! You made it," my brother says, looking genuinely happy as he stands to pull me into a hug. "This is my sister Estelle. She can vouch for us and tell you that we're all single."

I must be making a face, because the one clinging on to him laughs loudly. "Hi, Estelle. I'm Marie." Then all four women introduce themselves to me.

"So they are single," a brunette says. She looks a little drunk, with her way too-wide smile and her grubby hands on Oliver's lap. Still, I smile, though it feels tight on my face.

"Sure. Some come with more baggage than others do. Take your pick." I shoot Jenson a pointed look, and he shakes his head at me in disbelief. I guess it was a bitchy thing to say. I groan. "I'm just kidding. I'll see you guys later." I give them a small wave and one last smile before heading to the same bar I was at earlier. I feel somebody take a seat beside me, but don't acknowledge him. I keep sipping on my drink and tapping the counter with my fingernails as I debate whether I should stay a little longer, or leave and call Mia so we can go somewhere.

"What's a beautiful woman like you doing here alone?" he asks, and my eyes practically jump out of their sockets, because he has the sexiest British accent I've ever heard. Not that I've heard many, movies aside. I pivot in the seat and find a good looking, older man. He looks like a businessman, which has more to do with the suit he's wearing than anything else.

"Not alone. I just needed a little space from the people I'm supposed to be here with."

His lips twitch. "That bad?"

My eyes trail over his features, and notice thin lips, dark eyes, short, light curls on his head, and the lack of hair on his face. I wonder if it feels as smooth as it looks. His smile broadens, as mine does.

"I'm here with my brother and his friends. Celebrating some big work thing. It's pretty bad."

"In that case, would you like another?" he asks, looking at my now almost-empty glass of vodka tonic.

"Sure," I say, smiling. "Are you here alone?"

"With a couple of blokes from work." He points over to a table close to where Vic and the guys are sitting.

"You're sitting in VIP and came all the way out here to refill your drink?"

He leans forward so that his mouth is beside my face. "I saw you and thought I should come introduce myself before someone else got a chance to."

I smile and focus my attention on the drink the bartender places in front of me.

"Miles," he says, offering his hand.

"Estelle."

"Beautiful name. What do you do for fun, Estelle? Other than avoid boring celebrations with your brother."

My eyes find his, and I flash him a smile. "I dance."

He raises an eyebrow. "Show me."

I stand, gulping down the drink in a less-than-ladylike manner, and grab his hand, pulling him to the dance floor with me. I glance over my shoulder to where the guys are, and see they're still talking, save for Victor, who's now dancing with one of the girls. The only one who takes notice of me is Oliver, and the look he's giving me is enough to set my insides on fire. Miles grabs my hips, and we begin to sway to the music. Finally, I close my eyes and ignore Oliver's gaze, along with everything else. I let the music travel through me, and I let my body take over to the point of forgetting where I am and who I'm with.

"You're really good at this," Miles says into my ear. "What else are you good at?"

I can't keep the smile off my face, but I keep dancing and ignore his question. We stay on the dance floor and, as the songs get more provocative, so do my moves and Miles' hands on my body. Where they were once on my waist, they've gravitated down to my ass. I turn around in his hold and pull his hands higher so they're at my waist, and as I do, I spot a tall figure walking toward us. Normally it wouldn't be weird, since we're in the middle of a crowded club, but I'd know that strut anywhere. My heart picks up a little as my gaze finds Oliver's. I look past him and notice Vic and Bobby are both wrapped up in the ladies beside them. If they notice Oliver is gone, they don't show it. He doesn't stop until he reaches me.

"I need to speak to you," he says, leaning his face between my dance partner and me.

"We're dancing," Miles says, frowning, but he stops moving so the three of us are standing.

"And now you're not," Oliver says in a voice that makes the hairs on the back of my neck stand up.

Miles takes it as a challenge and cocks his eyebrow at me, saying *can you believe this guy?* And honestly, no, I cannot believe this guy.

"Oliver, what do you want?" I ask. He doesn't even look at me. He continues to glare at Miles.

"I'd like to leave my days of fighting back in middle school, so if you could just do me a favor and take your hands off of her ass and step away, we'll be okay," Oliver says.

Anger simmers in the pit of my stomach as I watch the exchange. The only thing I can think about is "Grace's night." The words repeat themselves inside my head. "Grace's night" followed by Bobby's amused chuckle, and suddenly I'm livid, just like that.

I take a step back and shoot him a murderous glare. "What is your problem?"

"I take it you know each other," Miles says, shaking his head. He looks at me one last time. "When you're finished playing whatever game it is he wants you to play, you're welcome to join us at our table." Then he turns around and disappears into the crowd, leaving me gaping at the empty spot where he was standing.

"Elle," Oliver says, but I put my hand up to stop him and turn around, walking to the back of the club.

The line for the women's bathroom is insane, as usual, so I look both ways and figure out my next plan. When I see a figure coming up behind me, I bolt to the nearest exit, shivering at the wall of cold air that hits me.

"Estelle!" he shouts as the door closes behind him, the noise of the club fading along with it.

"What do you want?" I say. What could he possibly want? I'm holding my arms together as the residual alcohol travels through my system, warming me against the outside air. Suddenly I am so upset with everything—with everyone. This was supposed to be a night out. Maybe even a night where I could show Vic that I can get a guy by myself, without Mom's help, without school, without art, just me. And it's stupid. It's stupid because I'm at a dance club trying to prove things I didn't realize I needed to. What was I going to do, anyway? Have a one night stand with some random guy? Find a real chance of starting over at a place where conversation is completely optional, and dry sex is the norm? A laugh escapes my lips at my stupid, idiotic thoughts. And another one follows when I remember who's behind me—the only guy I want, but shouldn't. The one I don't *want* to want. The one I'm *terrified* to want.

When Oliver doesn't respond, I turn around and face him. He has his eyes closed as he runs a hand through his hair, brushing it back as if he's doing outtakes for a Pantene commercial. He looks exhausted, like a man who had an eighty-hour workweek and still managed to come out tonight to help his best friend celebrate a win. But when he opens his eyes and looks at me, it's as if he gets a second wind.

"I know I'm fucked up, Elle. Or at least I have been in the past," he says with a short laugh. He strides over and I stay still. I don't want to interrupt anything he's going to tell me in that voice, while he's looking at me with those eyes. "You have no reason to open yourself up to me. I know I can't have you, Elle. I know I shouldn't have you. The job offers I'm getting are in San Fran, which means I'll probably leave soon . . . again. Your brother would never approve of this . . . of us . . . of me being with you," he says, sighing. He runs his hands through his hair again as he stands in front of me. He's so close that the only thing between us is my crossed arms. He drops his forehead to the top of my head and lets out a long breath that fans over my face. "So why do I want you so bad?"

"How many times are we going to go through this?" I whisper. *How many times am I going to let you break my heart?*

"Just give me one date," he says just as low, moving his face so that our noses brush.

"Just one date, and then what? You leave the next day?" I say, stepping away.

"Give me time to figure that part out," he says, his eyes pleading with mine. I shake my head.

"I can't."

"Why not?"

"Because last time we did this, you left me!" I say a little louder than I intend. He flinches. "We had that night, and you freaking left me! I woke up the next day and you were gone. All of your shit was gone! You didn't even leave a note, just a 'Bean left to Berkeley today, he says he'll catch you next time' from Victor who thought we hadn't even seen each other at the party. Do you know how bad that hurt?"

He looks away. "I thought we established that I'm fucked up."

"Yeah, well, stop fucking us all up along with you!"

His eyes flash to mine. "You got engaged a year later!"

"Oh, was I supposed to wait for you? Did I miss the memo where you told me you would come back, and we could actually have a chance at something? I'm so sorry, King Oliver. I must have missed that one, along with the apology for leaving me and then making me miserable at my own—"

His lips smash into mine before I can finish the sentence, and I back him into the wall behind him. He moans when I press my body flush against his and dip my tongue into his mouth. My head clouds with his scent, his taste, and the hint of iron in our mouths that our nipping teeth have made. We kiss like we're hungry . . . starving . . . for each other. Through the haze inside my head, I hear our names being called out, but I don't process it until I hear the voice getting louder, closer, and our phones start to vibrate (his in his pocket, mine in the wristlet I have on).

"Elle?"

"Bean?"

Jenson's voice cuts through us, and Oliver gasps against my mouth and pulls away, or pushes me away. It feels about the same. The vibrating of our phones grows frantic. I look down, taking it out, and see Vic's name on the screen. My eyes flicker to Oliver, who says Jenson is calling him. We nod at each other and answer our phones at the same time.

"Yeah, she's with me. We're outside," Oliver says into his phone.

"I'm outside," I say to Vic.

"Oh. Is Jenson there with you? He went out for a smoke."

"No. I haven't seen him."

"Are you coming back with us? I didn't get to hang out with you inside."

"You were a little occupied inside," I say and open my mouth to agree, when he cuts me off.

"Okay, well we'll see each other at home. Tell Bean the girls we were talking to are coming over," Victor says, and my stomach turns.

"Sure. I'll tell him," I say, looking at Oliver, who's watching me intently.

As soon as I hang up and put my phone back in my purse, Oliver reaches for me, but I put my hands up to stop him.

"Don't bother. Victor says you have company tonight. He wants you to know the girls are coming over," I say, sauntering out of the alley and to the front of club. I catch Jenson standing, gaping at us with his mouth hanging open and everything. I don't even care that he saw us right now. Tomorrow I'm sure I'll give it more thought, but right now, I feel like I need to get out of here.

"I'm taking a cab," I say as I reach him and open the door to the first one I see. I glance over my shoulder and catch the torn look on Oliver's face before I slide into the car and close the door—then I head to the only place I've been able to call home for the past two years. Thankfully, I still have a key.

Chapter 25

Past

Oliver

THE DOWNFALL OF ambition is sometimes letting life pass you by and only realizing it did so after the fact. Like the seasons, people change—their lives change—and suddenly you're stuck between fall and winter, not knowing whether you should step forward or back. I didn't go home on my breaks during my first two years of school, because my mom and Sophie came to see me at Berkeley. Then the guys came up for Spring Break one year, and the next we went to Vegas. Being back home felt weird at first, as if everything stayed the same except for me. That's what I thought until I met up with a stressed-out Victor at Starbucks one morning.

"If you don't stop bouncing your leg, I'm going to stab it," I said, looking up from the textbook I had in my hand.

We were supposed to be studying—him for the LSAT, me preparing for a Genetics final.

"I'm just . . . sorry. I'm just dealing with a lot of shit right now."

I put the book down and leaned back in my seat. "Talk."

He closed his eyes and breathed out through his nose, long and heavy. I didn't know what to expect him to say. Maybe he'd failed a class. Maybe he'd gotten a girl pregnant. Maybe he got himself a hamster. With Vic, there was no telling.

"She's engaged," he said finally.

"Okay?" I drew out slowly, waiting for him to elaborate.

"Estelle," he said, his brows bunching up. "She got engaged."

A couple of things happened at once: my mouth dropped, the air left my body, and the barista dropped the coffee she was making, causing a stir in the coffee house.

"She's what?" I said.

He nodded, raising his eyebrows like we were on the same wavelength. Little did he know, while his wavelength was down where the familiar territory lay, mine was leaping into the mountains where warning bells rang. I felt like huge claws were squeezing around my neck. Estelle was engaged. My Estelle.

"To who? I didn't even know she had a serious boyfriend," I said, trying to keep my voice even, trying not to get upset, because then my ears would get red and he'd know something was up. Where the fuck have I been? Where the fuck has . . . why hasn't anybody told me anything?

"She's been dating that painter, Wyatt, on and off for a while now."

"Yeah, more off than on though, right?" Was I crazy? I'd heard it wasn't serious. Or maybe I just assumed that.

Vic shrugged. "Well, it's fucking serious now. They're moving in together, engaged . . . it's just . . . she's my little sister, you know? One thing is for Junior to go and get engaged, but when Elle does it, it's like . . . I don't know. I feel like I'm going through a midlife crisis."

I couldn't even laugh or joke about what he'd said. I was

too hung up on *Estelle is engaged.* Estelle is moving in with somebody—somebody that's not me. Somebody that obviously has his head on his shoulders and was smart enough to not let somebody that perfect pass through his life without locking her down.

"Aren't they always breaking up?" I said again.

"I guess he wants to make it so they don't," he said, biting on the tip of the pencil in his hand. "He's such a pompous dick, too. He thinks he's better than everybody."

"Really? And Estelle is moving in with him?" I looked down at the discolored wood between us on the table.

"She says she loves him."

My chest squeezed, but I nodded and made a sound to show I was listening.

"She says she's happy with him and that he's taught her so much. I think she's just comfortable with him. I mean, he's older, he has all this success, and they're opening that gallery together."

"They're opening a gallery together?" I asked. This couldn't be going any worse.

"Dude. I haven't shown you the pictures?" Vic asked, taking out his phone and scrolling through photos. The one he landed on happened to be the picture they used to announce their engagement. Estelle had her hand over the guy's chest, and they were both smiling widely for the camera. He had long blonde hair, like mine . . . a beard, like mine . . . and a girl that should have been mine. Estelle had her dark hair down in loose curls that winded down the front of her thin frame. Her hazel eyes were as wide and smiling as her beautiful mouth. I looked at the rock on her finger and quickly looked away. It felt like a boulder on my collarbone. I couldn't breathe. I put the phone down and looked the other way.

"So I guess she's happy," I commented, picking my book back up. I could feel Vic staring at me from across the table. I half expected him to call me out on why I was acting weird. I prepared myself a little speech where I would tell him that I was in love with his sister and that I knew he didn't approve, but I didn't care. I said I would do it. Call me out, I begged, but he didn't. He sighed and leaned back in his seat.

"I feel like an old man. My sister getting married—"

"Engaged," I corrected. "A lot of people get engaged and don't get married."

Was I a dick for wanting that? Was I terrible for hoping the engagement would fall through? Why did it bother me so much anyway? I hadn't been there. I left. I left. I had nobody to blame but myself.

"You wanna come to the engagement party tonight?"

He might as well have asked me if I wanted to wear a pink leotard to a football game.

"What? You might as well keep me company," he said, laughing at the look on my face.

Because I needed to see her despite the circumstances, I agreed. Of course, I agreed. I would go and ask her not to marry that stupid painter. Or maybe I just needed to see her to make sure that she was truly happy. To make sure that the spark between us no longer existed. Maybe whatever we had in the past was gone now that she had something real. Maybe I waited too long. Of course, I waited too long. Every second it took to get ready to go to Vic's house became the countdown to doom. I changed my clothes five times. *Five.* I felt like Sophie. On that note, I called my sister. I'd never told her about Elle because I knew she wouldn't approve, but I needed to tell somebody, anybody. I needed to lay it out there for the universe to hear me, and maybe telling Sophie would make it real. Maybe telling her would stop the engagement . . . stop the wedding—I don't know.

"If you're not calling to tell me you're coming over to feed Sander, your voice is not welcome right now," she said, sounding completely wiped out.

"Soph, I fucked up."

She stayed quiet for a long moment. "Did you . . . okay, I can't think of how you would fuck up, so enlighten me, oh perfect one, what did you do?"

"You remember Estelle, right?"

"Uh-huh."

"Well, we kind of hooked up in the past. A few times . . . more than a few times," I admitted quietly.

"Ohmygod don't tell me you got her pregnant."

"No! God. No," I said, my voice slightly defeated. Would that be the worst news ever? For me to have gotten her pregnant? Normally I would have said yes, but today, I wasn't so sure.

"Okay, so? Victor caught you and gave you a black eye?" she guessed again.

"No!" I said, groaning. "She's engaged!"

More silence. The only tell I had that she was still on the line was Sander's cooing.

"And you're upset about it because you can't hook up anymore?" she asked.

"I'm upset about it because I think I'm in love with her," I said, my voice quiet. I hadn't even admitted that to myself. "I mean, I don't know for sure, but I think," I added.

Sophie laughed. "Well, this is . . ." she sighed. "This is something . . ."

"Sophie!"

"Bean, you call me in the middle of feeding to tell me that you're possibly—but don't know for sure—in love with the little sister of your best friend from third grade and that she's engaged to be married to somebody else. I mean . . . I have no words. When did this start? When did you figure this out?"

"It started years ago, but it's never been anything real, you know?"

"Only real enough for you to freak out when you hear she's engaged?"

My eyes screwed shut.

"How can you not be sure you're in love with her? Do you guys keep in touch?"

"No. No. We haven't spoken since . . . in a while. Since I came home last time . . . and even then, it was quick hi and bye—awkward because I was leaving a restaurant with a date, and she was getting there to meet hers."

"And now?"

"And now . . . she's engaged to some prick."

Sophie laughed again. "And you're Prince Charming."

"I don't know what to do. I'm going to her engagement party, and I don't know what to do."

"You're going to her engagement party?" she said. "Are you crazy? What do you think she'll say?"

"I don't know. I'm hoping she'll take her ring off and throw it in the guy's face."

"Ollie . . ."

I groaned. My sister only called me that when she was about to cajole me and say something I didn't want to hear.

"Maybe you should let her go. Maybe she wasn't the one."

"She was! She is!" I said, pacing my room.

"If you feel that way, why didn't you try anything sooner?" she asked with a sigh.

"Do you remember what it was like when Dad left?"

"Dad didn't leave. They got a divorce. There's a difference."

"Whatever. Do you remember when that happened? What he would say? How he felt like he was unaccomplished and couldn't provide Mom with anything?"

"Oh my God. You actually listened to the crock of shit Dad fed us when he was probably drunk?"

"Of course I did! I was a kid! He was my dad! And all my friends were so . . . I don't know. I just had this vision of what I wanted to be when I grew up. I wanted to be successful so that my wife didn't have to work unless she wanted to."

"So you planned out this entire 1950's reality for you and

your future wife without taking into account that life actually moves on with or without you?" she said after a long pause.

I let out a harsh breath. "Fuck. Fuck. Fuck. Fuck." I spewed, kicking the wall beside my closet.

"Well, that's my cue," she said when Sander started crying. "Good luck tonight. And Bean?"

"Yeah?"

"Sometimes we let the first ones get away, but it teaches us to cherish the second ones that much more."

I mumbled a yeah, thanks, and promised her I'd visit tomorrow. I couldn't deal with the idea of letting Elle get away. Was it so bad that I wanted to keep her? I finally stuck with what I was already wearing and left my house. Instead of taking my car, I walked to Vic's. I needed to think about what I was going to do once I got there. Thinking didn't help. If anything, the rustling wind in my ear confused my thoughts that much more. When I finally got there, I didn't know what to do. Normally I went in through the back door, but today I wasn't here as Victor's friend, I was here as Estelle's . . . something . . . so I used the front.

Thomas, Victor's dad, wore a shocked expression on his face when he opened the door for me.

"I don't think you've ever used this door," he said with a frown.

"I figured I should, since it's been a while."

"You're still our boy, no matter how old you get or how many lives you save, Doctor." He laughed the same laugh Victor had, with his shoulders quaking and his perfect, straight teeth shining.

"So, big day," I said.

"Big day . . ." he agreed, looking around. There were only a handful of people there, but I figured this was only the beginning. "Vic is in the game room with Mia's brother, and Estelle is in the kitchen. Her fiancé is . . . around."

I had no intention of meeting him, but as soon as the words

left his mouth, the fiancé from the photo appeared in front of us. I sized him up quickly. He was definitely older than me, skinnier than me, a bit shorter than me, but he had a smile that demanded attention. I knew that smile, because I saw it on my own face when I looked in the mirror. So evidently, Elle had a type. If he hadn't given her the ring on her finger, I would have smiled, too.

"Wyatt! This right here is Oliver, one of Victor's oldest friends," Thomas said, swiveling around and signaling at me.

Wyatt looked at me with the most serious brown eyes. At first, he frowned, then, as if something dawned on him, he smiled. "Of course. Oliver! I've heard a lot about you. Good to finally put a face to the name," he said, offering me his hand, which I took and squeezed a little tighter than I normally would have.

"Interesting. I just heard about you today, and I guess on that note, I must say you're a lucky bastard," I replied, earning a raised eyebrow from him. I should have probably toned down the mirth in my voice, especially being that Elle's dad was standing right there, but the filter over my mouth was non-existent.

"You know what they say about the early bird," he said, and with a wink, walked away. I wanted to clobber him.

"What does she see in that guy?" I muttered under my breath, low enough that I thought Thomas couldn't hear me, but his healthy chuckle rang out. He clapped a hand on my back and walked me toward the game room.

For what seemed like an eternity, I watched Robert and Victor play some stupid video game where they shot up everything that walked by. Such pointless garbage.

"I'm going to grab a beer. Want something?" I said, getting up.

"You sure you don't want to play?" Vic asked, even though he knew I would only play Madden. When I didn't respond, he shouted for me to bring him a beer.

I walked to the kitchen and greeted the people I knew. Mia, who was having an argument on the phone, managed to roll her eyes and signal at me in a way I understood was code for *can you believe this shit?* I saw her mom and Elle's, hugged them quickly, and talked to them about Berkeley. I spotted Wyatt through the window. He was outside on his cell phone, smoking a cigarette. I paused. Elle was marrying a smoker?

Every hint I caught from this life of hers seemed the opposite of what I would have guessed it would be. I pictured her painting, making her beautiful sculptures, eating those granola things she liked to eat, and drinking lattes. I didn't picture her with . . . this guy. Maybe there was nothing wrong with him. Maybe I was just looking for an excuse to hate him, but I didn't like the way he'd greeted me as if he knew me. Like he'd heard every stupid mistake I'd made when it came to Elle, and he'd righted all my wrongs.

When I rounded the corner to the kitchen, I finally saw her and paused at the doorway. She was definitely one of those women who got better with time—like a good scotch. She was wearing an ivory dress that reached her knees, and it hugged her body like a glove. Her shoes were gold with spikes on the heel. Her hair was down her back in natural waves, but the front was cut shorter, and every time she bent over, she had to blow it out of her eyes. I waited for her to stand upright before I barged in, because when it came to us, that's what we did. We didn't knock, and we didn't ask for permission. We just invaded.

"Hey," I said to her back. She gasped and stiffened, taking a moment before turning around to look at me.

For what seemed like an eternity, she just stared at me, eyes wide, clearly questioning what the hell I was doing there.

"Hi," she said finally, her voice a croak before she cleared it.

"I heard you're . . ." I couldn't even say the words. My eyes fell on her finger. The ring was glaring at me. Yelling.

"Yeah," she said.

Our eyes met again. I didn't know what to say. I couldn't congratulate her on something I wasn't happy about.

"Are you happy?" I asked, inching closer to her. She took a step back, hitting the counter behind her with a gasp.

"Don't," she said, putting her hands up defensively. "I . . . yes. I am."

"So he's the one?" I asked, my voice steady, my heart coiling, my eyes begging.

She tore her gaze away from mine. "He makes me happy, if that's what you're getting at."

I moved closer. "Is that what it takes to be the one?"

Her eyes flashed back to mine, and I swear, in that moment, I lost whatever doubt I had left. Right there, in those eyes, in the turbulent sea she created with just one look.

"What it takes is showing up. What it takes is not walking away every time something possibly meaningful happens. What it takes is . . . Jesus, Oliver, I don't even know what you want me to tell you!" she whisper-shouted at me.

"Tell me he's the one. Tell me he makes you feel the way you feel when you're with me," I urged, getting closer to her face.

She let out a short laugh. "I haven't seen you in what? Over a year? And you come in here looking at me like that and talking about how I feel when I'm with you. What am I supposed to do with that, Oliver?"

I grabbed her elbows and held her there so that we were breathing on each other's faces. The smell of cookie dough and wine infiltrated my nose, and I could only close my eyes and picture what it would taste like on my tongue.

"Let go of me," she said, in a low voice. "You are not going to kiss me. You do not get to kiss me. Not today."

"This may be the last chance I get to kiss you," I said softly, my lips falling over her cheek. "This may be the last time I get to hold you."

"Oliver, please," she said between a whisper and a plea.

"Does he make your heart race like I do?" I whispered beside the corner of her mouth. "Does he make you feel like you can't breathe sometimes?"

"I like breathing, thank you very much," she whispered, but sagged against my touch.

"How often do you think about me, Elle?"

"I'm not answering that," she said, closing her eyes as my lips brushed against hers.

"You're not stopping me from kissing you," I said, in warning.

"I should. If he comes in here, he's going to be upset."

"He shouldn't have left your side to begin with."

She pressed against me, pushing me back slightly. The sound of heels clinking against the floor startled me, and I dropped my hands from her elbows, taking a step back.

"Are the cookies ready, honey? I have nothing else to give people," her mom said, appearing beside us.

"Yeah, here. I'm making one more batch of pigs in a blanket and then I'll be done," she responded.

Hannah stopped beside me with the tray in one hand and held my chin. "Doesn't he get more handsome every time he comes home?" she said, pinching my cheek as she walked away.

Estelle glared at her mother's back as I smiled slightly.

"He seems to know a lot about me," I said when we were alone again.

Her face clouded. "He knows enough."

"Enough to know he should worry about me and you being alone together?"

"Enough to know you're trouble. Deadly. Hazardous to my health."

I sighed, running a hand through my hair. This wasn't going as planned.

"So you're doing it? You're going to marry him?" I said, finally realizing this was a losing battle.

"We're engaged, Oliver. We're living together. We're

opening a gallery together. That alone is like having a child," she said, her words making me flinch. A child with him.

"This is so hard for me," I whispered, stepping in front of her again.

"What we had . . . it passed," she said, her eyes on the floor beside us.

"Do you really believe that?" I asked, cupping her chin so that she could look at me.

"You need to stop," she whispered, her eyes shining with unshed tears. I hated to be the cause of them. I wondered how many I'd been responsible for throughout the years. That was when it really hit me: I messed up royally. This wasn't an easy fix. This wasn't a *let me come over tomorrow and fix the training wheel I accidently broke.* Or *let me replace the canvas I threw a football in the middle of.* This is life. This is what happens when you stop living in the moment. People grow up. They change, they move on, and you find yourself wishing you had looked up in time to walk with them.

"You're right," I said, stepping back and dropping my hand. "You're right. I'm sorry. If you're happy, I'm happy for you, my beautiful Elle."

I leaned in, gave her a kiss on the cheek, taking one last moment to smell her, and walked away.

Chapter 26

Present

Estelle

MY PHONE RAN out of battery a couple of minutes after I made it through the door last night, and I was actually grateful for the quiet. I'd slept on the couch the realtor insisted I leave in the living room, which was the only room in the house that was somewhat decorated. When I woke up this morning, I went upstairs and sat in the middle of my unfurnished bedroom, thinking about the last time I'd done that. It was when Wyatt had insisted on getting a new bed since I was moving in. He'd bought the house with an ex-girl-friend, way before we met. It didn't bother me until I realized I would sleep in the bed they'd bought together. That was when he threw out the old mattress and told me to go to West Elm to pick out a new bed, which I did. The room is so dull now though—so vacant without the bed sitting in the middle. The bed, I gave to his mother. I couldn't bear to sleep in it anymore. I slept in it for an entire year after he died, and I was done with it. Moving on meant giving up even the smallest sense of comfort I'd shared with him.

Yet here I was, back where I started. It's not that I don't have an identity without Wyatt or our life together, but I liked the simple act of coming home and knowing what I would find here. For some reason, knowing that this place would no longer be mine soon made me feel a little lost. Where do I go now? Sure, I would buy a new place. Sure, I would decorate it to my liking, but would it feel like home to me? I gather myself up and walk downstairs again, peeking into all of the rooms as I go. And when I open the front door to leave, I drop everything in my hands, because Oliver is sitting outside on the steps with his back facing me.

"What are you doing here?" I ask.

He sighs but doesn't turn to face me. His hand runs through his hair. It's getting long again. I'm surprised he doesn't have it up in a small bun already.

"I had this whole speech planned out, and now that you finally came out, I can't even think," he says.

"How long have you been out here?" I ask, sitting beside him on the step.

He shrugs, still not looking at me. "It doesn't matter."

"What was this speech you had planned?"

He dips his head between his legs, resting it in his hands. "That's the problem, Elle. Everything I had planned to say makes me sound like a complete asshole when I repeat it in my head. All my life I've been all about preparing for things and planning things out, and when it comes to you . . . I'm completely lost when it comes to you," he says, tilting his face to look at me.

"I'm not that confusing. I'm simple," I say quietly, tucking my hands behind my knees to resist the urge to touch his hair . . . the scruff on his face . . . his full lips.

"Your simplicity is maddening. Everything about you drives me crazy. The way you smile at me, the way you look at me, the way you talk to those kids at the hospital as if they're adults—as if they matter . . . Not a lot of people do that, you know. Even me sometimes. When I'm working insane hours, I go into their rooms and only address their parents. I saw you teaching them to paint—teaching them to do something with their hands, with their time—and the way you looked at them . . ." he pauses, sighs, and looks at me with those evergreen eyes of his shining like I'm his world. "You know what it made me think? I want to have kids with that girl, because every child deserves to be looked at that way. Everybody deserves to feel that important."

My heart squeezes at his admission. I open my mouth to speak, but words fail me, so instead, I scoot closer and lean my head on his shoulder. He kisses the top of my head and wraps his arm around me.

"Do you think I'm crazy?" he asks after a beat.

"Absolutely," I say, smiling, as I pull back to look at him. "Your complications are completely maddening. Everything about you drives me crazy."

He chuckles, shaking his head. "It sounded better in my head."

I lean into him and brush my nose against his scruffy, cold cheek. "I thought it sounded pretty good."

"You're not mad that I came here?" he asks, running his hand down my side.

"How did you even find me?"

"I called Mia. I mean . . . after a while, I had a feeling you weren't coming back to Vic's house, and then I called Mia. When she said you weren't there, I asked her for this address."

"That girl . . ."

"I owe her a week's worth of coffee."

I laugh. "You're going to be able to afford her addiction on your residency paycheck?"

He smiles. "Maybe she won't notice if I brew it myself."

"Doubtful," I say. We both laugh and look at each other

again, my breath catching in my throat at the emotion in his eyes. He brushes his hand over my cheek softly.

"One date, beautiful Elle," he says in a whisper that makes my stomach coil. I take a deep breath, and I let go of my reservations along with my exhale. I want this. I believe in this.

"One date," I agree, smiling at his wide grin.

I look over my shoulder, at the house I shared with the man I loved, and I sigh. I don't feel as bad as I thought I would, agreeing to this date. Maybe for once the stars will align for us.

Chapter 27

I CHOOSE NOT to tell my brother about my date with Oliver because, well, I don't have the guts to. I know he'd try to stop it before it happens. I don't need him to verbalize that he thinks Oliver is a huge player and isn't worthy of me. Besides, it's just one date. Chances are it'll be a lot less tame than our friends date anyway. In the back of my mind, I'm screaming *don't get attached just yet!* But the thing is, it's Bean. I will forever be attached to him, no matter what happens. I drive to Mia's place and park my car in the visitor's spot, where it'll stay until we get back, then I go upstairs and wait.

"I heard you have a date with Oliver, and from the looks of it, you definitely do. You're sweating like a whore in church!" Rob says as soon as he sees me. I punch him in the shoulder.

"No I'm not! Oh God, am I?" I head toward the bathroom and look at myself, realizing that he was exaggerating. But, damn. I am nervous. "Why am I so nervous about this? And where is Meep?"

"She's in the shower, and you're nervous because this is your first date together. I mean, real date. Shenanigans don't count." He raises a blonde eyebrow and laughs when I glare at him.

"I need a drink," I announce, heading to the kitchen.

"No, you don't. You need to sit and relax and be still. You're going to give me a heart attack!"

"Stop being a pest," I mutter, plopping down on the couch.

"Okay, but on your date, do not sit like that. Nothing is more gross than a careless sitter in a dress."

My eyes widen, and I cross my legs, sitting upright. "Damn you. Maybe I should have worn jeans."

Robert laughs, throwing his head back. He looks so much like Mia when he does that. "I was joking! Geez, you really are nervous."

"Who's nervous?" Mia asks, walking over to us.

"Jitterbug over here is acting like a virgin going to prom," Rob says, earning a laugh from me, and a look from Mia.

"Way to lay it all out there," I say.

"She looks fine," Mia says walking over to me. "It's just Bean."

"Exactly. It's just Bean . . . do I look okay?"

Mia gives me a onceover and nods. "You look beautiful, like you do every other day, when you wear make-up and brush your hair and dress up."

"Meaning not like every other day?"

"Well, you have to save beauty for special occasions, Chicken."

"Bitch," I say, laughing until the knock on the door swallows my smile.

"Ohh here he comes," Rob starts singing like he was singing *Man Eater,* and I want to crawl into a hole and die. Mia swings the door open and whistles loudly.

"Looks like somebody wants to get laid tonight," she announces.

And this time, for real, I want to crawl into a hole and die. I can feel my face burning as I walk to the door and tell Mia and Robert to shut up. Oliver is wearing dark jeans, black shoes, a gray button-down, and a fedora on his head. It's simple and hot, and it matches the gray dress I'm wearing, so I have to laugh.

"It's like they're meant to be!" Rob states loudly. "They match! This is too fucking cute! Mia! Get the camera!"

"I hate you." I say, looking at him. "I hate you." I say, turning to Mia's face, red from laughing. "I don't hate you . . . yet." I say, turning to Oliver, who gives me a slow, cocky half grin that makes me melt a little.

"Please have her home by midnight, and make sure she lays off the vodka," As Mia starts rattling off her list, she stops to look at my blushing face and bursts out laughing. "Awww . . . I'm sorry, Elle, this is so cute though. You haven't been this nervous since you lost your virginity to Hunter Grayson." She stops laughing and turns to Oliver with a serious face. "All jokes aside, if you hurt her again, I will fucking murder you, and I'm not talking about a nice quiet murder, I'm talking dick cut off, internal organs everywhere kind of murder. So please, be mindful of that."

"Okay, time to go," I say, pulling Oliver's arm out the door. "Some people have officially lost their marbles."

Oliver is doubled over in laughter as we walk down the stairs, so he has to stop every so often to catch his breath. I can't even turn to look at him because I'm so embarrassed. And I shouldn't even be embarrassed! We ALL grew up together! This is absolutely ridiculous. When we get to his car, he wipes a tear from his eye as he opens the door for me. I don't even look at him when he gets in. I just stare straight ahead. But then he gets quiet, and his hand reaches for mine on my lap. He squeezes it gently, to get my attention.

"Hey," he says quietly, his eyes smiling.

"I'm glad you enjoyed the show. We'll be here all week," I mumble, making him chuckle. He brings my hand to his lips and brushes against it. I shiver at the feel of his scruff prickling over it.

"They mean well," he says, kissing my hand. "You look beautiful. I'm so happy I finally agreed to go on this date with you."

That makes me laugh. "Really? Were you being hounded relentlessly?"

"Like you wouldn't believe," he says, raising his eyebrows. "It's been exhausting having to dodge your advances."

I finally sigh and get comfortable in my seat. Oliver has a way of making me feel at ease in one moment. His fingers brush my knee and I jolt. *And completely electrified the next.*

"So, where are you taking me?" I ask, turning my face to look at him. He smiles, looking straight ahead.

"If I tell you, it would ruin the surprise aspect of the date."

"We're not going to dinner and a movie, are we?" I say, biting back a laugh when he shoots me a look.

"Do I look that dull to you?"

I shrug. "I don't know. Where do you normally take your dates?"

His gaze cuts to mine again. "To eat."

"And . . . that's it?" I ask, a little unimpressed.

"Well, that's not it, but I don't think you want to talk about that any more than I want to talk about Hunter Grayson."

I look away, smiling. "Fair enough."

"Unless, of course, you want to talk about Hunter Grayson," he says, as he parks the car in the marina.

"I'd rather not," I say, feeling my cheeks flush. Hunter is still a friend of mine, and we each did a pretty good job at burying the memories of the night we had together.

Oliver turns his body to face me and runs the back of his hand down my cheek to my neck, his eyes on mine the entire time. "I'm really glad we're doing this."

I smile softly, suddenly feeling shy under his gaze. "Me too."

He drops his hand, gets out of the car and, while I gather my purse, he comes around to open the door for me. We walk a couple of steps before his hand closes over mine, and he threads our fingers together. It's such a small gesture, but it sets my pulse on fire.

"We're going on a boat?" I ask when we walk past the restaurant there and head toward the vessels.

"Not quite," he says. "Maybe next time." He tilts his head to look down at me, and I feel the warmth of his smile curl through me.

We walk up to the edge of a dock, where there's a table set up. The floor around it is scattered in candles and it's completely desolate, except for the server standing beside it with a champagne bottle in his hands and a smile on his face.

"Mario, good to see you again," Oliver says, dropping my hand and offering it to the server.

"Pleasure is all mine, Dr. Hart," he says with a hint of a Spanish accent, smiling and nodding as he takes the hand he's being offered and shakes it.

"This is Estelle," Oliver says. "Elle, this is Mario."

"Pleased to meet you," I say, offering him my hand as well. Once we're settled in our seats, Mario pours us some champagne, hands us a menu, and tells us he'll be back. My eyes scan everything again—the candles, the table, the boats, the sun that's still setting over the ocean in the distance—and finally, I look up at Oliver's handsome face.

"You know you could have taken me to In-N-Out Burger and I would have been just as happy, right?"

His eyes flick to mine, and he gives me a slow, half-smile. "The night's still young."

I smile and reach for my glass of champagne. "How did you set this up, anyway?" I ask, when I see Mario walking toward us with a tray in his hands. He places it between us, bows and walks away. "Where did you find that guy?" I ask when he's out of earshot. Oliver chuckles, his shoulders shaking. I love that his dimples—although covered by the scruff on his face—are in full sight.

"Are we playing twenty questions?" he asks after a beat, his eyes sparkling with amusement under the brim of his hat.

"We might as well," I retort, smiling back.

"I met him when he brought his kid into the ER. I was on my way out, he and his wife were frantic because David, their son, wiped out and hit his head. So I helped them."

"And you stayed in touch?" I ask, frowning.

"Well, I had to make house calls," he says, looking away.

"You make house calls?"

He sighs and looks at me again. "Not usually." I raise an eyebrow and signal for him to elaborate. Finally, he sighs again, runs a hand through his hair and speaks. "They didn't have medical insurance, so I had to kind of do what I did off the books."

My heart squeezes in my chest and I smile, reaching my hand out and placing it over his on the table. He turns his over and holds it there. We don't say anything. I don't tell him what an amazing man he is for doing that, and he doesn't elaborate further. From experience, I know that Oliver is the kind of guy who would throw himself in front of a bus for you and then deny that he saved your life. He'll chalk it up to *anybody would have done the same.* He doesn't realize that people aren't that nice. People don't push aside their own agenda for the sake of the greater good. He looks into my eyes with this longing—this need—as he draws circles over my hand. For a moment, I can't remember what we were talking about, what we're doing, where we are, or what day it is.

"Shall we eat?" he says, flashing an easy smile that makes my heart stutter. I nod and take my hand back, putting it over my lap and folding it into the other while I wait for him to uncover the plate of oysters between us.

"Did you already work your last day at the hospital?" I ask, slipping a forkful into my mouth.

"Well, I'm done with my residency, so yes, but I've been picking up shifts here and there while I decide what to do next."

"I have to go back on Tuesday for a class. Mae wants me to teach the class how to make sculptures out of shattered glass."

Oliver picks up his gaze from the plate and looks at me, but doesn't say anything, so I continue.

"I wish the *powers that be* would let the kids come to the studio instead. Jen is asking Mr. Frederick about it to see if he'll let me set up a field trip there, just so they can get out. I mean, if it's possible. I'm sure it would be difficult to cover the doctors and nurses and stuff . . . I wish this house would sell already," I say, sighing.

"What are you going to do once it does?"

"Originally I was planning on giving all of the money to Wyatt's parents. Set up an account and be done with it. But then I thought, I mean . . . it was my house too. Maybe I should take some of it and give the rest to them. I don't know. It's confusing. They don't want it, and I don't need it, so I go back and forth on it."

Oliver nods and takes a sip of champagne. "Do you miss your life there?"

My eyes search his. I know what he's asking. I don't know if I want to answer. Finally, I take a breath and look away for a beat. Before I answer, he speaks again.

"Let's do something," he says, his hand reaching out for mine again. "For the remainder of this date, we ask and answer every question imaginable. It doesn't matter how dumb or how hard it is. I want to know everything. Nothing left unsaid, okay?"

"That's a lot for one date," I breathe. He squeezes my hand.

"Sometimes one date is all we have." His response makes me feel like crying, and I guess he sees that, because he brings my hand up to his and kisses it. "I want a lot of dates like this, Elle. A lot. But in the past, we've done things, and we haven't communicated and, well . . . I don't want that to happen again."

I take another breath. "I don't miss it. I mean, I miss the comfort of going there and knowing I was home. I miss Wyatt sometimes," I say, my voice catching. I swallow down the tears I feel coming. "I miss his enthusiasm about art and life and the stories he would tell me about his travels. Is this weird?" I whisper, looking up at him and wiping under my eyes.

He looks like he's being lashed at, but he shakes his head nonetheless. "It's . . . it's fine. I want to hear this. I don't want you to think you have to erase your past because of me, or forget about him or your life together. I just . . . I've never felt like I've had to compete with anybody for someone's affection, and now I feel like I'm competing with a ghost, and sometimes memories are better than realities."

I stare at him for a moment before I stand and walk around the table. Oliver leans back, wordlessly making room for me on his lap. I sit there and wrap my arms around his neck, placing my head on his chest. His arms automatically go around me, holding me there so perfectly, it's as if my body is a puzzle piece snapping in place. So many years I've dreamt of doing this with him and when we finally do, we have the shadow of my past over us. That's how life is—I know that—but it still breaks my heart for him . . . for us.

"Would it help if I told you that the whole time I was with Wyatt he was competing with *your* ghost?" I whisper against his neck, breathing in his calming, clean scent.

His chuckle vibrates through me. "Not really. That would just mean I should have tried harder before. Maybe if I had, you wouldn't have had to experience such a terrible loss."

I inch back from him, to look at his face. "How is it that you haven't found a woman yet? All those women you work with—that you went to school with—all, smart and beautiful. How could perfect Oliver not have found someone?"

He chuckles again, his eyes sparkling as he reaches up and combs the hair out of my face. I do the same for him, but leave my hand on the back of his neck. He closes his eyes for a moment and swallows. "I'm not perfect, Elle. Not even close."

"You are to me," I whisper.

His eyes darken when he looks at me. "Maybe that's your answer."

Chapter 28

"**O**N A SCALE from *happy* to *I can't stop smiling excited,* how thrilled would you be if I told you Mia packed an overnight bag for you?" Oliver asks, placing his fedora on the dashboard.

After dinner, we sat and talked about Wyatt and the house, mostly, and now that we're back in the car driving, I've been kind of anxious. I really, really don't want the date to end. We've been driving for quite a while, listening to music, talking about movies . . . so it isn't until he asks me this question, that I realize that the only thing we haven't talked about are what my plans are for tomorrow.

"Well . . ." I start, pausing to laugh. "I guess you've only given me choices I have to smile about so . . . *really happy?*"

He grins and looks my way. "Good, because it's in the trunk, and I'm kidnapping you for the night. Maybe for the rest of the weekend."

"You realize that you're setting yourself up for failure on any future date, right?"

"Never doubt an overachiever," he says, smiling as he pushes hair out of his eyes.

I laugh and resist the urge to lean in and run my hands

through his hair. "Your hair grows so fast," I say instead.

"Yeah, that's the upside. Too bad I need to cut it short again soon. And shave."

"For job interviews?" I guess.

"Yeah, I let them hire me before I let my hair grow again. Nobody wants to hire a doctor with a man bun."

"It's not even long enough for one yet, but I happen to know somebody who thinks doctors with man buns are hot."

"Do you, now?" he says, flashing a grin my way.

"I'm sure I do."

"Does her name start with an E?"

"Possibly."

"Is she afraid of the dark?"

"No," I grumble, and look away, making him laugh.

"Does she happen to hate my jokes?"

My lips tip up, but I keep looking out the window. "I can't imagine anybody would like your jokes."

"Oh, but they do."

"Oliver," I say, turning to him with a long-suffering sigh. "I'm sorry to break it to you, but they're just pretending."

He scoffs, giving me a bewildered look. "Pretending? Okay, I get it. You just haven't heard my latest."

I groan and laugh at the same time. "Let's hear it."

He waits until we're stopped at a red light to lean in so that his chin is almost on my shoulder. For a moment, I forget how to breathe. Then he starts talking and drops his voice so low that everything inside of me zaps, and I can't help but hold my breath. "If I were an enzyme," he says, his lips, a soft tickle over my ear. "I'd be DNA helicase," he continues, as he trails his lips over my neck. My eyes flutter shut, and I grip on to my knees. "So I could unzip your genes."

I open my eyes as he pulls back, and my heart drops into the pit of my stomach at the hungry look in his eyes. When his gaze moves to my mouth, I can't take any more. I lose all pretenses. I pull him to me and kiss him, frantically at first, then slowly, so that the kiss teases . . . tastes . . . our tongues barely touching. He pulls away and marvels at me for a moment before the sound of honking snaps us of out of the moment and he continues through the intersection.

"Not bad, huh?" he says after a beat. I'm still trying to regain my breath. I lick my lips and close my eyes at the taste of him.

"That wasn't a joke. That was nerdy seduction," I say in a breath. I can't help but smile when he starts laughing.

"Nerdy seduction," he says, still chuckling.

"Next question, are you still dating or hooking up or doing whatever you're doing with Grace . . . or anybody else in the hospital . . . or elsewhere?"

I watch the side of his face as he frowns. When he stops behind a car, he shoots me a look. "I told you I wasn't, Elle. Do you think I would insist on a date if I was seeing someone else?"

"I don't know," I shrug. "I'm not sure how you work in that department."

He raises an eyebrow. "You know exactly how I work in that department."

"So you're not seeing anyone else right now?" I ask, ignoring his comment.

"Are you insinuating that we're seeing each other?" he says.

"No. Why would you . . ."

"You said anyone else, which would mean that we're seeing each other."

"Well that's not what I meant."

He rounds the corner to a nice hotel on the water and pulls up in front of the valet. Oliver's fingers paint over mine. "It's what I want it to mean."

My heart crashes in my chest as the valet guy opens the door for me. I make my feet move and step out of the car, just barely containing my composure. Oliver comes around with two bags in his hands, and I follow him inside. I look around, inhaling the aromas coming from the spa, and read that we're in the Sonoma Coast. I can't believe the car ride seemed so short—not that I'd ever been up here, but I've passed it plenty of times. This is the point where Vic and I usually start bickering, because the road trip is taking so long. I step aside as he goes up to the counter. I watch as he speaks to the lady, making her laugh at something he says, and then meet his eyes as he walks back to me. Oliver has always had this thing about him—this easiness that comes with him. He fits in with any group of people, because he embraces everybody with the way he is.

He carries himself with such confidence that you would think he owns the world. He's the kind of guy who can participate in a conversation amongst important businessmen and doctors alike, and they would never question who he is. They would never suspect he was the guy who arrived in a beat-up car and worked two jobs so he could get it. He has a smile that'll charm the pants off anybody if they're not careful enough, and pairs that with a heart of gold. As he approaches and flashes that very smile at me, I feel myself melt.

"Ready?" he asks. I tuck my arm in his and nod, following him to the elevator. I realize that I haven't asked him why he brought me to a hotel or what his plans are. Something happens to me when I'm around Oliver. It's like the world vanishes around me. Everything can be falling apart, but in his arms, I'm whole.

When we reach the room, he puts our bags down beside the door and waits for me to explore. It's a really big room, with a king-size bed, a bench by the window, and oversized, plush couches and a fireplace off to the side to make a living room. I walk over to the window and sit down on the cushioned bench, touching the cold glass with my hand. Oliver hasn't said anything since we entered the room, and when I turn around, I find him propped up against the wall on the other side of the bed, with his legs crossed and his hands in the front pockets of his jeans. His fedora is slightly tilted down, and his hair is seeping out of it. What I can make out of his green eyes makes my stomach toss uncontrollably.

"Why are you standing all the way over there?" I ask with a nervous laugh.

"I'm kind of worried of what will happen if I step any closer," he says. I inhale sharply.

"Maybe I want you to step closer."

He shakes his head and bites back a smile. "I should have said this sooner, but I didn't bring you here to take this further than, well, sleep." I open my mouth to say something, but stop and wait for him to continue. "This is still part of our date. Tomorrow, the vineyards. We didn't get to do that last time."

I stand and walk over to him, stopping when we're toe-to-toe, and tilt my head to look at him. I reach up, take the hat off his head, and toss it to the floor by the fireplace. "What if I want to take this further than just sleep?"

His face darkens. A slow smile appears over his face as he reaches for me and caresses my cheek softly. "I want to get it right this time, Elle. I don't want to push you. I don't want you to wake up tomorrow and regret something we do tonight."

"I won't," I whisper, leaning into his touch.

"Last time we slept together, I found you crying over a shirt," he says, his voice soft and slightly pained.

"That was different."

"How?" he asks, pushing off the wall and cupping the back of my neck. "Tell me how it was different, because if something happens tonight, it'll be so much more than just touching. You know that, right? And I mean more than just physically. Even if we only touch or kiss, it'll be more, and I don't want you to wake up and feel like you're cheating or being unfair to his memory."

I close my eyes, needing to look away from his understanding gaze, away from the love I see in it. He's right. I know this, and I know he doesn't deserve to be a regret for me, but the thing is, Oliver has never been a regret. Even when it hurt . . . even when he left. Even when he came back and sliced me open again, he wasn't a regret because I loved him. Wyatt may not have been the most understanding man—and maybe his ways of making me move past things weren't perfect—but he did make me understand love for what it was. That's the little tagline I send off my shattered hearts with. Wyatt was the one who opened my eyes to it, but Oliver was the reason for the hearts and the taglines. He was the one I loved first. He was the one who broke my heart first, and here he is again. For how long this time, I wonder? Does it matter? My heart bleeds.

When I open my eyes again, Oliver is looking at me like I might bolt. I wrap my arms around his neck and lean up, kissing his stubbly chin, his strong jaw, and then move up to the shell of his ear.

"What we have isn't aligned with that part of my life. We live in a galaxy of our own," I whisper, kissing his earlobe. I smile when his breath quickens. "Where the storms pass, and the light fades, and everything ceases to exist except for us."

His hands squeeze my waist, and gently push me back. "I planned out this night where I would keep my hands to myself and sleep on the sofa if I had to, and then you say things like that and scatter every part of my brain—like only you can." He dips his face and kisses my neck once, twice, three times . . . soft wet kisses . . . before he leans back and pins his gaze on me again. "You make me get lost in you, Elle. The way you look at me, the way you touch me . . ." He doesn't finish his sentence, but instead, brings his lips down to meet mine in a long, slow kiss. As our hearts beat against each other's chest, and our tongues dance a slow sensual mambo, everything else fades away.

Oliver's hands make their way down my body until they reach the hem of my dress. He pulls it off me without breaking our kiss, while I unbutton his shirt and help him shrug out of it. Even though it hasn't been *that* long since we hooked up that last time, I feel like I haven't seen his body in ages. My eyes drop from his face to his chest. My hands trace every muscle, every contour, and every line etched on the beautiful man in front of me. My fingers reach the top of his jeans, and I begin to unbuckle his belt, and as I bring my gaze back up to his, I watch him as he watches me. A look of ecstasy clouds his face as I dip my hand into his boxers and test the weight of him, my hand squeezing as he sucks in a breath between his teeth.

"Elle," he says, his voice a hoarse whisper, as I kneel down in front of him. He kicks his shoes aside, and I help him step out of his jeans, his boxers, his socks . . . and align my face with his length. I lean forward, placing soft, wet kisses along his abdomen, smiling against him as his muscles spasm. I work my way down, licking each side of the "V" indented on his sides, until I reach what's beckoning me. My tongue slides under his shaft and he groans, his hand threading into my hair. I repeat the motion on either side as my hand holds his balls. He groans again, louder, when I take what I can of him into my mouth.

"Elle," Oliver says again, his voice low and guttural. I look up, meeting his hooded gaze, and a thrill runs through me when his hands brush my hair back, away from my face, as he looks down at me. He grabs my shoulders and pushes me back until he's completely out of my mouth with a pop, then he pulls me up so that we're chest to chest, his nose resting on my forehead.

"What you do to me, Elle," he whispers against me as I breathe into his chest. "It's inexplicable." He drops a kiss on my forehead and walks me backward until I'm forced to sit on the bed. He takes his time undoing the clasp of my bra and then pulls it over my shoulders. He does the same with my panties, sliding them down my thighs until they're off and on the floor with the rest of our clothes. Taking a step back, he looks at me—really looks at me. His gaze leaves a trail of heat with every inch it passes over, then he lets out a laugh. "For maybe the second time in my life, I don't know where to start," he murmurs, kneeling down in front of me and spreading my legs apart. Kissing my knee first, he makes his way up my thigh until he reaches my pelvis, grazing the patch of hair there, then he kisses his way up my stomach. When he reaches my right breast, he pauses and looks at me over the peak of my nipple.

"I can't tell you how many times I've dreamt of doing this again," he says, gliding the slick underside of his tongue over it. I gasp. My hands shoot out to grip his shoulders when he does it again. He blows softly over my little bud, the sensation of hot and cold making me shiver. He drags his face to my other breast and I shiver again, this time, at the feel of his chin scraping against my skin. His mouth closes over my nipple, sucking it into his mouth. As he pulls away and blows softly, his hand tweaks the other. My body feels like it's on fire, at the brink of combustion, and he hasn't even left my breasts yet.

As if hearing my thoughts, Oliver looks at me and flashes a smug smile before continuing to explore south of the border. Reaching the inside of my thighs, he nudges them to the sides and holds them apart with his hands, squeezing, as he dips his face into my center. His tongue peeks out and tastes me—just tastes—and he groans, his mouth vibrating against me. My already shaky hands find his hair, and I pull lightly, pivoting my hips against his face. He stills me with his grip on my knees, and raises his gaze to find mine. The intensity in them is so raw, so pure, that I feel my stomach begin to churn. In his eyes, I find our past and our questionable future. It holds the sadness of lost years, the torturous longing of a million what-ifs, and the possibility of what could be. I try to look away . . . try to close my eyes and shut out the fervor his green eyes spear me with, because I don't want to admit that I'm scared. I don't want to open myself up and admit that he still has the ability to shatter me—to annihilate me completely.

His tongue lashes against me once more and I lose all thought . . . all reason . . . and come undone under his tongue. I finally shut my eyes and moan out his name as my back bows off the bed and an orgasm rocks through me. Oliver's kisses whisper over me as he makes his way back up my body. I open my eyes and he holds himself above me, arms on either side of me, and for the longest time, just looks at me, his eyes searching mine. My hand moves between us. His body shudders when I close my hand around his cock and grasp it, slowly sliding my hand up and down, up and down, until he's breathing heavily.

"We should probably get a condom," he says, his eyes bouncing between mine. I shake my head, bringing my other hand to clasp the back of his neck and pull his face to mine.

"No condom," I whisper against his lips. He stills, and for a moment, I wonder if he would rather use one. Maybe he regrets not doing so all those years ago.

"Elle," he says, letting out a breath. I'm sure he's about to climb off me and reach for a condom, but instead, he wraps an arm around my back and pulls me closer, settling himself between my folds. Slowly, carefully, he pushes in, giving my body time to adjust to his girth. I gasp when I feel him pulsate inside me. He stops to take a breath and chuckles into my neck.

"My beautiful little Elle," he says against my neck. The smile in his voice makes me smile. "You feel so fucking good around me, you have no idea." I arch my back, urging him to continue, because I do have an idea. I have a very good idea. He moves again, not stopping this time, instead, giving me long, deep strokes. "You just . . . swallow me up," he growls, moving faster now, his strokes becoming harder, as if he's staking his claim inside me.

"Do you ever think about this?" he asks, his voice somewhere between a grunt and a growl as he readjusts our position so that my leg is over his shoulder and he can get even deeper inside of me. I cry out, nodding. "Tell me," he says. Oliver pulls back to look first at the spot where we're joined and then to my face, where I'm sure he can see my desire for him.

"I touch myself thinking about you," I admit quietly, my eyes refusing to waver from his. He groans and stops moving, closing his eyes as if he's concentrating. "I picture you taking me like this, on top of me," I continue, pushing onto him. "And sometimes from behind."

Oliver's eyes snap open, and I whimper when he slowly slides out of me, then thrusts in hard and fast. My toes curl, and my eyes start rolling back as I grip on to his ass and encourage him to move faster. It's all I can do to keep myself from crying out at the level of emotion zip-lining through me.

"Please . . ." I'm actually begging. "Please, please, please keep moving faster."

He grins, slow and wide, and does what I say for all of four strokes.

I screw my eyes shut. "Please, please, please. Just . . . faster . . . harder . . ."

But Oliver has other plans. He leans down, stretching my legs further apart and kisses the calf I have resting on his chest. He rubs his face over the soft skin there, as his lips drag up and down, matching his hips in soft, slow, long, hard strokes.

"I want this to last forever," he says, biting the inside of my leg. "I want to make a little house inside your pussy," he says, and if it weren't for his hand tweaking my nipple and his cock pounding harder against me, I would make a joke. But the sensation of an orgasm begins to steamboat inside me, and I can't think anymore. He drops my leg and climbs over me again, his chest just over mine, so that his face is the only thing I can see. I don't know what he wants to find in my eyes, but I feel like he's boring into my soul, as if rummaging through a lost-and-found. Just when I open my mouth to say something, an orgasm slams through me, and I shriek his name instead. As if on cue, he grunts out my name and his eyes close in exhaustion. Oliver lets out a long breath, and when he opens his eyes again, he's wearing the goofy, lopsided smile I've always loved, and it makes me feel like whatever he was searching for has been found.

We lay in bed, naked, facing each other, his hand lazily drawing over my waist and mine over his chest. I've always been a go-with-the-flow kind of girl. I've never wondered where a relationship would take me—I never really bothered to care. But lying here beside Oliver makes me think about the future. It makes me *hope* for the future. And even though I told myself that this was just one date, I can't help the bubble of possibility that pops up in my head.

"What are you thinking about?" I whisper. He pulls my face to his chest, and then kisses the top of my head.

"I'm thinking that this is the best date I've ever been on."

I smile. "Really?"

"Yes, really."

"You realize you completely cheated, right? One date means one date, and you planned this out to be two dates."

He chuckles below me. "I told you I'm not good with rules."

"Thank God for that," I say, yawning against him.

I fall asleep in his arms, and even though I'm looking forward to the rest of our date tomorrow, a part of me is terrified of leaving this room and facing reality.

Chapter 29

I WAKE UP feeling overly warm, as if a heating blanket set on high was covering me. When I open my eyes, I realize that the blanket is Oliver. Our bodies are intertwined around the other's in such a way that I'm sure if there was a painting of this moment, the viewer would have a difficult time deciphering whose limbs were whose. My gaze ascends from his chest to his messy hair, enjoying all the parts in-between, and I sigh contently. Oliver's lids flutter open, and when his sleepy green eyes find mine, I am graced with a breathtaking smile that makes magical creatures ignite deep within my belly.

"Hey," he whispers in a sexy rasp that ratchets up my desire.

I smile, suddenly feeling a little shy. "Hey."

He lifts his hand from my waist and threads his fingers through my hair, pushing long bangs out of my face. He leans in slowly and brushes his soft lips against mine. Tender little bites have my eyelids fluttering shut. A moan resonates from me when his tongue scoops mine, twirling around it gently, and forming the beginning of a seductive dance that makes my breath quicken. Oliver breaks the kiss with the same gentle bites he started it with and drags his mouth down my neck, my chest, my abdomen . . .

My hands fly to his hair, clutching fistfuls, when he reaches my clit and begins to suck lightly. He runs his tongue over it sharply, last night's rendezvous becomes fresh in my mind. My grip tightens and, as my head falls to the side, I gasp simultaneously at the time on the clock, and at the feel of his fingers inside me.

"We're going to be late," I say, gasping again when his hands reach up and cup my breasts, tweaking my nipples.

"I'll make it worth it," he murmurs against me, sucking harder.

My eyes roll back.

"Oliver," I say, his name a guttural moan.

"Estelle," he answers, blowing over the wetness on my nipples as his fingers continue to move inside me.

"Oh God."

"Mmmm," he groans as he quickens the lash of his tongue.

My back arches at the wave of heat that courses through me. He makes his way back up my body with open, wet kisses, and positions the head of his cock at my entrance. I open my eyes to find him staring down at me, his eyes hooded with desire. He licks his bottom lip slowly and bites down on it as he begins to push inside me with a measured thrust.

"This is how all of our mornings should start," he grunts when he's all the way inside me. My eyes roll back at the way he fills me up. And then he begins to move, and I feel myself fall with every thrust, with every moment his green eyes stay on mine, and with every crease that forms between his eyebrows as he makes me feel like the most beautiful woman in the world. Yes, this is how all of our mornings should start, I think to myself. This is how they could have been before, but I don't think I could have survived them when he left.

"How did he propose?" Oliver asks later, after we've shared enough samples of wine to fill two bottles. We've been asking each other questions all day. It started as a game—so that the person who didn't want to answer would have to down a glass—but then we kept on hounding until we answered anyway, so we dropped the game and kept the questions.

I take a large gulp of wine. He doesn't laugh this time, because this particular question is as uncomfortable for him to hear as it is for me to answer. "It was the day we got the space for the gallery. We were home celebrating with a couple of our friends. Dallas and Micah were there," I say, pausing. When he nods in recognition of the names, I continue. "So we were home, drinking . . . the guys telling jokes, the girls laughing along . . . and suddenly, he gets down on one knee in front of me and just proposes." I shrug, recalling the memory and smiling sadly. I remember feeling so excited over it. I didn't cry of happiness. I wasn't overwhelmed, but I was so, so happy.

Oliver takes my empty glass and deposits it beside his, picking up our small tray of grapes and cheese as we continue walking along the vineyard. "Was it everything you hoped it would be?" he asks. I glance up to search his face. He doesn't seem angry or jealous, just curious.

"I had never really thought about it before that night," I say with a shrug. "Our relationship was kind of . . . I don't know. I just never really thought we would get engaged or married. We were living together and everything, so you would think it would be the next step, but I never really . . ." I never expected it. I never needed it. I never wanted it until the day he asked, and then suddenly I wanted it all. I don't say that because I don't want to go there.

"Are you happy you did? That you got engaged and moved in together?"

This time we stop walking. I tilt my head so I can see him, even as he keeps his eyes out into the distance. Every time I look at him, even now, it feels like my heart is getting tazed.

I have to remind myself that this man—the one I've always wanted—is really here with me.

"I am," I say, because it's true. I loved him and don't regret a single moment I spent with Wyatt.

Oliver nods and throws a grape into his mouth. When he doesn't look at me, I reach out for him, tucking my hand under his bicep, needing to touch him and make sure we're still okay. His gaze cuts to mine, and the side of his mouth turns up in a somewhat regretful smile.

"I'm sorry. I don't want to be a mood killer. That was just a little harder to take in than I thought it would be."

I reach up and run a hand through his thick hair. He closes his eyes and leans into my touch, his nostrils flaring slightly as he takes a deep breath.

"Why didn't you get married? It was a long engagement," he says, keeping his eyes shut. My hand freezes in his hair. I drop it and step back. He opens his eyes when I do, and we look at each other for what seems like forever, before I answer.

"We never talked about it," I say, my voice a whisper. I look away from his intent gaze. I have to. The only other person I've spoken to about this is Mia, and although she held my hand and kissed my head, I could see the judgment and the sympathy she held in her eyes. I know she was thinking the same thing I was, but we were both afraid to voice it. The thing is, we were happy, Wyatt and I. We argued like any other couple, but we were happy for the most part. Things were comfortable with him, and I never really wanted to question the bigger things, out of fear that it would mean the end of our relationship. I figured that when we really got to those points in our life together, we would face any issues in real time.

"Ever?" Oliver asks, and I can hear the frown in his voice. I shake my head.

"Tell me something else," he says, and the way he says it makes me want to tell him everything, because his voice holds understanding and a sadness that can only be formed through true comprehension.

"He didn't want kids," I say, still whispering, as if it's a great big secret I'm keeping from the universe, and I guess I was, for a while. "Or at least he didn't want kids with me. I can't really be sure."

Oliver's hand finds mine, and I finally turn to meet his gaze. As soon as I do, I regret it, because the look on his face makes me want to cry. "Not wanting kids with you is insane. He probably just didn't want any. Some people don't." When I stay silent, he squeezes my hand. "You're going to make an incredible mother one day, Elle." He leans down and kisses my lips softly. It's not a long, lingering kiss, but it's enough to warm me all over.

"Anyway," I say in a breath, as I reach into the little tub of cheese and pop a square into my mouth. "Your turn . . . How long are you usually with a woman before you go your separate ways?"

His mouth twitches, and I can tell he's trying not to laugh. "It depends."

"On the woman?"

"Yeah, and the situation."

"What's the longest you've stayed? I'm not sure if I should say *what's the longest relationship you've had* because I know you don't call them that," I say, looking away when I feel myself blush. This is more awkward than when he asked me about Wyatt.

Oliver chuckles. "The longest I've stayed . . ." My eyes cut to his when he sighs loudly. "Probably two months, give or take."

"That's it?"

He smiles, running his thumb over my eyebrows to clear my frown. "I had a romantic affair with my school work. You know that's always been my top priority."

I sigh and wrap my arms around his torso, burying my face in his hard chest. "Thank you. This date has been everything.

I mean it." Against my face, I feel his abdomen constrict and hear him take a deep breath.

"Thank you for letting me kidnap you."

I smile, tilting my head back to prop my chin on his chest as he looks down at me. "You're welcome to kidnap me any time you want."

His entire face lights up as he smiles at me, his dimples wink, and his eyes twinkle. It feels like my birthday and Christmas all wrapped up in one beautiful face.

"I just might," he says, with promise in his deep voice.

Chapter 30

I WIPE MY hands on a kitchen towel and pick up my phone to read the incoming text message from Oliver.

`Come outside.`

I frown and glance over my shoulder at the open back door where my brother stands. I can't tell what he's doing, but I'm pretty sure his surfboard is involved. I walk to the front of the house, and look through the peephole, smiling at the sight of Oliver on the other side with his hands tucked into the front pockets of his jeans. He's wearing a gray-checkered button-down and a matching beanie pulled down so low, that his sandy hair brushes against the collar of his shirt. I open the door and lean against it, holding the knob as he gives me a slow once-over. As always, his eyes leave a trail of heat behind as they travel the length of my body.

"You look cute," I say, and laugh when he raises an eyebrow.

"Cute?"

"Cute is a compliment."

"For a four-year-old, maybe," he says, stepping in to share the space of the threshold with me.

I smile. "Nope. The word holds weight for life. You can be cute even if you're eighty."

The side of his mouth turns up slowly as he leans into me, stretching his arms above me so that he's clutching the top of the doorframe and his chest is flush against mine. I catch a glimpse of tanned stomach peeking out from under his shirt and reach out to touch it. He tucks his face into my neck, kissing me there and hissing when I grip tighter.

"I'll show you cute," he says, his voice low and husky. I smile, and throw my head back. "Where's your brother?" he asks, as his lips move from my throat to my shoulder.

"Out back," I whisper, closing my eyes as I push myself up against him.

"Let's go somewhere."

I bite down on my lip to stifle a moan, as his tongue runs over my clavicle. "Where?"

"Anywhere. The beach, pier, sushi . . . wherever you want." He kisses his way along my jaw and up my cheek.

"You hate sushi," I say, opening my eyes to meet his. He drops his hands from the door and straightens, brushing my face with the back of his hand.

"I can get tempura."

"Okay. Let me tell Vic I'm leaving."

Oliver steps away and signals for me to lead the way.

"What's he doing anyway?" he asks as we reach the back door.

"I'm not sure. I think cleaning his surfboards."

"Waxing," Victor corrects, startling me. "Why are you so jumpy lately?"

"I'm not jumpy," I say, swallowing to contain my rapid heartbeat.

"You are." He raises an eyebrow and runs a hand through his hair. "What's up, man?" he says to Oliver.

"Not much. Day off."

"I'm surprised you're not sleeping," Victor says, going

back to his surfboard.

"Nah. I wanted to take advantage of the day. Estelle and I are going to go get sushi. Want to come?"

Victor's hands come to a stop on the board, and he looks up, his eyes narrowing as they look from me to Oliver and back again. "No, thanks," he says, looking at the board once more and then back at us. I'm pretty sure he can hear the hammering in my chest from where he's sitting. I brace myself for the inevitable question when he opens his mouth. "You're never going to get back on the dating bandwagon if you keep hanging out with Oliver. You realize that, right?"

"How many times are you going to wax over the same spot?" I ask, turning my back to him and walking back into the house to hide my irritation.

"This is a different board," he calls out.

"No, it's not. I've never seen anybody wax the same board as many times as you do," I call back.

I hear Oliver say his goodbyes before he walks back inside, and I feel him behind me shortly after. "Some people just don't know how to wax boards," he murmurs, his breath tickling the back of my neck.

"Do you?" I ask, flashing a smile over my shoulder.

He leans in and kisses me—a quick, hard peck on my lips. "How 'bout I show you?" he says in my ear.

"What do you have in mind?" I ask, as we step out and walk toward his car.

"Let's pick up the sushi and have a beach picnic."

"I like that plan."

"I love that plan," he says, depositing a kiss on my cheek before he drops his arms and opens the door for me.

He orders food for us, stopping and glancing my way for approval every time he names a roll he thinks I might like. Once he hangs up the phone, we're silent for a long moment until he speaks up again.

"I think we should tell him," he says, threading his fingers through mine. My heart threatens to leap out of my chest at his suggestion.

"What would we tell him?" I ask quietly, facing forward.

"That we're together."

"We're together?" I ask quietly, smiling at the thought.

Oliver chuckles and drops my hand, bringing it up to cup my chin. "Aren't we?"

My smile grows wider. "I don't know, Doctor. Are we?"

His hand makes its way to the nape of my neck. He pulls my face closer to his until the tips of our noses touch. "I think it's safe to say we are."

"What do you think he'll say if we tell him?" I ask in a breath against his lips.

"He'll be pissed." He pauses to search my eyes. "At me, not you."

"Aren't you worried it'll ruin your friendship?" I whisper.

The breath he releases blows over my lips. It smells like peppermint, the residue of the mints he constantly pops in his mouth. "Why do you think it's taken me so long to come around, Elle?" he says in a low voice, dropping a kiss on one side of my mouth and then the other.

I close my eyes, relishing the feel of his soft lips on me. "I think we should just wait a little longer," I say finally.

Oliver backs away and looks at me, waiting for an explanation. After a couple of beats, I finally open my mouth to voice my opinion, but shut it again when his phone vibrates. He answers, telling the restaurant he'll be right in for the food.

"Hold that thought," he says, tapping the tip of my nose before getting out.

I sag against the seat behind me, and let out a deep breath. How do I explain everything I'm feeling? I'm not sure I can put it into words. I can only remember what everybody said when Wyatt and I started dating. Their whispered disapproval becomes a shout in my head as I sit there, wondering if Oliver and I hold the same fate. Wyatt was just some random to everybody. Oliver is family to us. I have no doubt in my mind that Victor would see our relationship as incestuous, even though we have no ties aside from him. I watch Oliver walk back to the car with a bag in one hand and his phone in the other. He has a worried look on his face that instantly puts me on edge.

"Everything okay?" I ask when he gets in and closes the door.

"Yeah, I had to call the hospital and check on a patient," he responds, his lips pursed.

"Anyone I know?" I ask, waiting on bated breath when he doesn't respond right away. I don't know what I would do if something happens to one of the kids I've grown to love so much.

"No. It's one of my toddlers."

"I don't know how you do it," I whisper.

"Sometimes I don't either," he says quietly, letting out a sigh. He claps his hands together loudly, making me jump in my seat and look at him. He chuckles at the look on my face. "You really are easily startled lately."

I try to hide my smile by looking away as he starts driving.

"You never answered why you want to wait," he says once we're back on PCH.

I sigh. "I just want to keep this to myself for a while."

"You want me to be your dirty little secret," he says with a wolfish grin.

"I didn't say that."

He shrugs. "I'm not against it. I like being a dirty little secret."

Every time he says *dirty little secret,* something inside me stirs. Somehow, Oliver manages to make everything sound sexy.

"I'm not saying I don't want anybody knowing because I'm ashamed or anything," I say, feeling the need to make that clear.

He pulls into the parking lot of the 1,000 Steps Beach and

smiles as he gets out of the car to open the door for me. Once I'm out, he pops the trunk and grabs a couple of beach towels.

"Do you have impromptu picnics often?" I ask, raising an eyebrow as I hold out my hand to take the towels.

Oliver laughs, shakes his head, and pulls me into an embrace. "Only with women named Estelle."

"I can think of a couple of Estelle's," I say, pushing him away from me lightly, as I feign anger.

He cocks his head, still smiling. "So can I, but I can only think of one I would resort to eating Japanese food with and take to the beach without demanding she dress down to a bikini."

I purse my lips and walk toward the stairs. "Does that mean you don't like to see me in a bikini?"

We step to the side so that some people leaving the beach can walk by us, and Oliver leans down to whisper in my ear. "You look great in a bikini, but you look better naked, on my bed, with your legs spread open for me."

I stop suddenly, holding on to the rocks of the wall beside me. Oliver's arm goes around my waist to keep us from toppling down the nine hundred steps we have left to navigate. I turn around in his arm and crane my head to look at him.

"You need to keep those comments to yourself when we're in public," I say.

He bites down on his bottom lip, trying, and failing, to hold back a smile. "Why? Because it gets you all hot and bothered?" he asks, dipping his face to meet mine when I nod. He runs the tip of his nose from my jaw to my ear in a slow caress, breathing me in as he does so. "What if I told you I want you that way?"

"Why would you want to do that to me when we're about to eat on a public beach?" I ask in a whisper against his neck.

He chuckles. "Maybe I like knowing that I get to you."

"You know you get to me," I say, leaning away so that I can take a good look at his face.

His green eyes twinkle. "Maybe I want you begging me to

take you back to my place," he says, his voice low as he runs his hand under the filmy shirt I'm wearing. I suck in a breath, my eyes widening as I look around at the people walking past us, up and down the stairs.

"Oliver," I say in warning.

"Estelle," he says, mimicking my voice as his hand moves up to the side of my rib cage and stops there, right below my left breast.

"Do you want to just go back to your place?" I ask breathily.

His lips slightly part as he shakes his head slowly. When he looks at me the way he's looking at me now, like it's the first time he's seeing me—like I'm the most fascinating woman he's ever laid eyes on—I'll melt in his arms.

"I want to do what I promised and take my girl on a picnic," he says quietly, before leaning in closer and letting his lips fall over mine. His mouth molds against mine, moving slowly, as he takes his time to feel me. His tongue dances with mine in a slow seduction—the complete opposite of the rapid fire coursing inside of me. At the sound of a catcall by one of the bystanders, we break away and look into each other's eyes with a short laugh. He runs the tips of his fingers over my bottom lip and smiles.

"Let's go eat before this sushi goes bad and we end up in the ER," he says, turning me around to keep walking.

After we eat, we sit on the beach with our legs outstretched and braided around the other's. We people-watch, as the beach is full of runners, surfers, sunbathers and tourists.

"I think I've only been here a handful of times," he says after a while.

"Yeah?"

"My parents used to bring us here when we were kids. Every time we came, Sophie would bury me in the sand, until one day she put so much sand on me I almost drowned in it," he says, chuckling at the memory. "My dad was so mad at her at first because he had to unbury me in a hurry, but then I was fine, and we all laughed until we had tears in our eyes." He pauses and flashes me a sad smile. "I think that was the only time my parents cried out of happiness. That I saw, anyway."

I scoot closer to him and lean my head on his shoulder. He puts his head against mine and reaches out to hold my hand.

"It's a good memory," I comment.

"This one's better," he responds, squeezing my hand.

For the next week, Oliver and I meet up like that. Not at the beach, but in quick segments that turn into long installments. We talk, we laugh, we kiss, we make love, and we joke around. I don't want to say that I feel complete when I'm with him—because I'm complete without him—but when I'm with him I feel like a better version of myself. And I think that's what has always drawn me to Oliver. He makes me feel good about who I am, and I don't feel like I need to change or pretend when I'm around him. I'm just me, and being me has never felt better.

Chapter 31

THE FOLLOWING SUNDAY night, I opt out of dinner at Wyatt's parents' house. I don't even bother hiding the reason from Felicia.

"I went on a date last week," I tell her, to which she gasps. I don't mention that a date turned into a weeklong event of nonstop dates. Even when we don't see each other, we talk on the phone or text message back and forth.

"And? How did it go?"

"It went well," I say, holding a breath. "I . . . it went really well."

"Good. I'm glad. We're happy for you, Elle. You know that, right? We're happy if you move on. You're young, you're beautiful . . . you deserve it. Wyatt would want that."

I don't tell her that I kind of doubt that, because I can't imagine him wanting me to move on, but obviously I'm doing it anyway. The worst part is, that I don't even feel guilty about it when I'm in the moment. It isn't until late at night when I'm alone and think about how happy Oliver makes me, that it kind of seeps in. It's like my heart has already decided what to do with itself, but my mind keeps tripping over the box of guilt. When I hang up with her, I head downstairs to make myself a sandwich because I'm starving. It seems that unless I set the Crock-pot before I leave for the day, nobody eats around here.

"Elle, can you order pizza?" Victor yells from the living room, followed by a slew of curse words aimed at the television. My best guess is that the Forty-Niners are losing.

"Yes!" I shout back. I order it, make my sandwich, and take a bite as I walk over to where he is. "What the hell did you do when I wasn't living here?" I ask, opening my mouth to take another bite and stop when I see he's not alone. Oliver holds his beer up to me, as does Jenson, who shoots a weird look between Oliver and me. I know it has everything to do with what he saw—or thought he saw—outside of the club a couple of weeks ago. Victor just watches the game and waves his hand.

"Obviously I survived," he says.

Normally Oliver would pat the seat beside him, but he doesn't today. I take a seat beside Victor and prop my foot on his coffee table, as I take another bite of my sandwich.

"What does that have in it?" Jenson asks, looking at my sandwich like he's going to bite it out of my hand.

"Turkey and Swiss," I respond, and hold it out for him to take, because it's either that, make him his own, or tell him to go fuck himself—which will result in an argument I don't want to start—especially with his big mouth.

"Thanks," he says, taking it from me with a wide grin. He winks at me and makes a satisfied sound as he bites into it. I roll my eyes and lean back into the couch. I sort of watch the game until the pizza gets there, and then end up falling asleep leaning against Jenson's muscled arm. I only wake up because I hear Vic screaming again, and it startles me. That's when I realize I am completely wrapped in Jenson's arm. He hugs me closer when I jolt and try to pull away. My eyes flicker to Oliver, who's relaxed and watching the game, but I keep staring until his gaze finds mine. I catch the discomfort in his eyes as they jump from me to Jenson. He grumbles, exhales and looks away. I don't know what I expect him to do, but the fact that he does nothing at all makes me want to scream. It's not like I want him to be jealous over this—it would be ridiculous for him to be threatened over Jenson—but still. I berate myself, since I was the one who insisted we keep whatever is going on between us a secret. *Give me time,* I said, but I kind of wish he would just tell Victor despite what I said. I wish he wouldn't listen to me for once. I sigh and pinch the inside of Jenson's arm hard. He yelps and lets go of me.

"You had that coming," Victor says with a chuckle.

"Are you regretting moving to the big apple?" I ask Jenson, as I fold my legs underneath me.

"Nope. Most of the time I like it, but I miss home . . . and I have stuff I need to take care of here."

I sink back into the couch and think about this scenario, wondering if this is what it would be like if Oliver and I were really dating. Would we hang out with my brother and their friends? Would it be awkward? Would we sit across the room from each other because he's too scared of his best friend and what he would have to say about our relationship? My shoulders slump at the thought. I look up when I feel Oliver's eyes on me, and smile when he taps the spot beside him on the couch. Finally, against my better judgment, or maybe because of it, I stand and sit beside him, snatching the huge Forty-Niners throw draped over the couch to bring with me.

"I missed you today," he whispers as soon as my ass touches the couch. I try to hide my smile with the throw I'm adjusting, but fail when he speaks up again, louder this time. "Are we sharing that? It's cold as hell in here."

"Sure."

"It's not cold," Jenson says, raising his eyebrows at us.

"We're sitting right under the air vent," Oliver says, nodding up. I bring my knees up so that they're touching the side of his leg, and he scoots closer to me, pulling my knees so they're completely on his lap. He leaves his hand there, running his palm over my thighs, making me visibly shiver with the movement. Our eyes meet at the same time and my stomach dips because I know that look. I know in an instant that his gaze will drop from my eyes to my lips, and then he'll lick his slowly, while my heart begins to thunder in my ears. The moment drowns out the game, and Victor and Jenson's shouts at whatever play Frank Gore made or missed. It doesn't matter to me either way, because the only game I want to play involves the long fingers that are inching up my thigh, and the lips that part as I near them.

A loud cough snaps us into reality, and we practically jump away from each other to look at Jenson, who's shooting us a *what the fuck are you doing* look.

"You all right?" Victor asks, tearing his eyes from the TV to look at him.

"Yeah, sure. Beer went down the wrong pipe."

Vic shakes his head and pops open another can. "Hey, Bean, you heard anything from those practices?"

"I go for an interview at the end of the week," he replies.

"San Fran?" Jenson asks.

"Yeah."

"Damn. Won't you miss being home again?"

I really try not to look at him when he answers. I try not to focus my peripheral vision on the way he shrugs his shoulders, or the way his hands move in a motion that says he's fine either way. I try not to let that pierce a hole in my heart, but it happens anyway. All of it does. We've talked about his job and the fact that there aren't too many openings here in his field right now. It doesn't lessen the blow that he's been looking at places that are far away from here when our relationship is finally on the right foot for once. That is, until his job is mentioned and his natural ambition takes over, squashing it all. As usual.

"Home is where you make it," he says.

I close my eyes and stand up, dropping the throw and going around the couch to leave the room. "I'm going to . . ." My voice trails off, and I just keep walking when I can't think of an excuse. I stop by the kitchen to grab a bottle of water, and as I'm closing the refrigerator, Oliver steps in.

"You're mad," he whispers.

I sigh. "Yes, I'm mad, genius!"

He's looking at me as if the answer may be written somewhere on my face, and that's when I realize that he really doesn't get it. He really doesn't understand how the possibility of a job in San Francisco would affect me.

"Why didn't you tell me about the interviews?" I whisper-shout. When he doesn't respond, I shake my head. "I can't do this right now. I promised my mom I would go help her with some things. I have to go."

"You can't leave in the middle of this," he says, turning me to face him and ducking his head to look me in the eyes. "I haven't even interviewed yet, Elle. It's not like I got a job over there."

"But you will."

"I may not, babe," he says, his voice a rasp against my ear.

"You will," I say, feeling tears prick my eyes. "You will, because you're smart and you're a hard worker, and you graduated with a damn near perfect GPA, and any practice would be lucky to have you. You told me you couldn't compete with a ghost. Well, I can't compete with your job." I pull away from him.

"You're not," Oliver says, just as Victor walks into the kitchen and bumps into me.

"What's wrong?" he asks. "What's going on?"

"Nothing," I say.

"Just talking about life," Oliver chimes in.

"I'm going out. I won't be back tonight," I respond, as I head toward the door.

Victor whistles. "Damn, three nights in a row? Do I get to meet the bastard any time soon? Did you tell him your brother is a lawyer, has a gun, and knows a lot of people in law enforcement?"

"I'm going to Mom's house, doofus," I say, shaking my head. I look behind him when he moves toward the refrigerator, and catch Oliver's eyes.

"We need to talk," he mouths. I nod in agreement and signal him to call me before I turn to leave.

An hour and 100 holiday cards folded and put in envelopes later, I go upstairs to check my phone. Seeing a missed call from Oliver, I call him back.

"Where are you?" he asks after the phone rings once.

"My parents'."

"I'm on my way."

"What? No," I say, looking around at the mess I managed to make in less than ten minutes of being in my old room.

"Leave your window unlocked."

"Oliver! We're not teenagers. How are you going to climb a tree?"

"Are you calling me old?" he asks, and I can hear the smile in his voice.

"If the shoe fits."

"It doesn't," he says in a little growl that makes me laugh, despite myself.

"Are you saying you have small feet?"

"Are you telling me you need me to remind you that I don't?"

Somehow, I manage a laugh over my stuttering heart. "Fine. I'll leave the window unlocked."

What feels like hours later, Oliver climbs into my window and settles in beside me in bed, pulling me so that my back is to his chest.

"You took forever," I whisper.

"I took ten minutes."

"It seemed like forever."

"It always does when I'm not with you," he murmurs, pulling me into him.

"You said you couldn't compete against my job," he says

against my neck. "And I agree. Is that the only part you can't do?"

I breathe out loudly. "That and the part where we have an amazing weekend together, and then you leave me. I don't have it in me to let you in completely and then lose you. But I did, Oliver. I let you in completely this time, despite my reservations," I respond, closing my eyes.

It seems like we've done this song and dance a million times before. Yet, here we are, and I realize that I'd rather let history repeat itself because the other option—the one where I live life without the way he makes me feel when I'm with him—seems like it's missing everything I need. If this is love . . . real love . . . like I've always thought, it's nothing more than a vicious game of Russian roulette. The gun clicks when it comes to you, and you cringe in anticipation that this may just be the last breath you take, but then it continues on, until the next round . . . and the next. Then there's that one time when it clicks and hits you, and you just can't walk away.

"And I'm thankful for that, Estelle. I really am." He exhales. "I wish I had all the answers. I wish I knew what tomorrow would bring, so that this wouldn't be so difficult."

"I don't care what it will bring, Oliver."

"You do, Elle. You can lie to yourself and say you don't, and that you just want to have fun and take what you can when you can, but you do care."

I pause. "You date women and never get involved in anything serious. All my brother talks about is how easy it is for you to walk away, and how little you care when they do, so why do you care when it comes to me?"

He drops a kiss on my shoulder and settles his face into my neck. "If I get offered a job I want, I'll tell you, and we can figure out what to do together, okay? I don't climb into windows, Elle. I don't do chasing. I don't go out of my way to explain my decisions to women I date. If they don't like something about me, they're free to go, as am I. I think the fact that I'm here right now says a lot."

"I know it does," I whisper.

"So you believe me when I tell you that I care?" he murmurs against the back of my shoulder.

"I do believe you, and I don't want you worried about me when you go up there next week." I doubt he would be worried about me. When he gets his game face on, he does a good job at tuning everything else out, but I figure I should say the words out loud anyway. I feel myself begin to pull back, gathering the scattered notions of hope I've been putting into this thing between us.

He lets out a heavy sigh and wraps his legs over mine, his face in my neck, and his arms around my middle . . . and that's how we spend the night. But even though I'm wrapped up in my favorite little nook, I get little sleep. The only thing I can think about is how I'm in too deep, as usual, and I know I won't make it out unscathed.

Days later, when I walk into the hospital, I spot Oliver from afar talking to one of the doctors—a man I've seen, but don't know. I don't catch his eye before I slip into the art room, and I prefer it that way. I told myself I wouldn't lose my head over this man, even if I never got it back from him to begin with. Still, with the talk of his interviews, I need to keep taking this one day at a time. The last time we were together, when he left my parents' house at the break of dawn, I told him we needed to slow down. I've dodged the calls he's made my way, although there haven't been many of them. I heard through the grapevine (or really, Mae), that he's been working non-stop these past couple of days, so I know he hasn't had much down time.

In the art room, I lay newspaper over the long table and place transparent, empty boxes by each setting. In the boxes,

I place different glass pieces, all colorful and pretty, and then put a mallet beside each box. When the kids come in with their nurse for the day (today it's Tara), I welcome each of them and signal to the seats. Oliver walks in shortly after, shooting a lingering smile and a wink my way. He approaches Danny and checks the chart that hangs from his oxygen pump.

"Don't tell me we're going to break these things," Mae says.

"Holy shit, we're going to break things!" Mike shouts, doing a fist pump in the air.

Tara, Oliver and I laugh and shake our heads at his excitement.

"You may want to put the mallet down for now, Thor," I say, raising an eyebrow at Mike, who smiles widely.

"Thor, huh?" he says. I roll my eyes.

"Remember the rules."

"I don't really like rules," he says, and I laugh, looking at Oliver. I expect to find him laughing, but instead, he is glaring at Mike, which makes the entire thing even more comical.

"Anyway, to answer your question, yes, we are going to break things today."

"But . . . a dolphin?" Mae says, bringing up the glass dolphin in her box. "And a surfboard?"

I smile and nod. "They're just things."

"Pretty things."

"Well, we're going to make something even prettier with them. Besides, if you notice, they're all a little broken," I say, pointing at the dolphin missing a tail and the chip in the surfboard.

I don't notice when Oliver steps out of the room, but when I glance up at the sound of the door closing behind him, we're already well underway with the project. We're able to make very small versions of the heart, although all of them look more like a ball, but the kids are excited about them nonetheless.

"Now I have to take them home to bake them," I say.

"Bake them?" Danny asks.

"Yeah, they have to bake, then dry, and then they'll be done. Do you want to make them into key chains or just leave them as is?"

"Key chains!" Mae says.

Mike furrows his eyebrows at her. "We don't even drive."

She smiles. "Speak for yourself. I'll be driving soon."

"Fine. I'll take a key chain," Mike mumbles.

They start heading out, and while I'm cleaning up, the door re-opens and Jen walks in with a guy in a suit.

"Hey! I'm so glad I caught you," she says, smiling. "This is Chris. He's the head of my department, and the reason your project got the green light."

I step back, a little stunned, because Chris looks like he's about my age, so I'm surprised he's in a position above Jen's.

"It's so nice to meet you," I say, wiping my hands over the now dirty apron I have on. "Sorry, I'm kind of . . . dirty right now." I let out a small, nervous laugh.

Jen smiles. "Hey, at least nobody can say you weren't working . . ." She looks around and gasps when she sees what we were making. "You guys made these today? They're beautiful."

"They're not set yet, so I have to take them home," I say, hoping she catches the caution in my voice and doesn't try to pick them up. Thankfully, she just looks at them in amazement, which makes me smile brighter.

"I love what you've done with the place, Estelle. Everybody does, actually. The rooms, the hallways . . . it doesn't feel like a hospital anymore," Chris says, turning his attention to me.

Jen looks down at her watch. "I'm so sorry to step out, but I have a meeting with a vendor." She looks at Chris, who smiles and nods her away. When she leaves and the door closes, I start feeling a little awkward just standing there with this guy in a suit, and I don't know what else to say. He's looking around though, so I don't feel weird for too long. I wash my hands and take off my apron, kind of bouncing from one foot to the other, before heading toward the door. He opens it for me, and we walk out together.

"How long were you thinking of continuing the program?" he asks.

"Honestly? I hadn't thought about it. I figured Jen would tell me to stop when I wasn't wanted anymore," I say with a smile.

"Well, that's why I wanted to meet you, actually," he says, stopping when we get to the nurses' station, which has been moved back over since this part of the hospital is open again.

"Because you want me to stop coming?" I ask slowly. I wouldn't take it personally if he said no, because I knew this was temporary to begin with, but I definitely need to see this project through. I gear myself up to tell him that while I wait for his response.

Chris frowns and looks behind him at nurses chattering and turns to me again. "Do you think we can go somewhere and talk?"

"Sure. Your office?"

"Actually," he says, cringing a little and looking sheepish. "Would you mind if we go down to the food court? I kind of missed lunch . . . again."

I laugh. "Not at all."

On our way down, Chris tells me that although he started working in the hospital while he was in college, he moved up to a higher position when he graduated, and even higher once he got his Masters.

"What do you do when you're not here?" he asks, when he gets a tray of food and meets me at the table.

"Make art," I say, and smile when he nods, as if making art is a hobby. "I also have an after school program for kids who have no place to go."

"Wow. You must really like kids," he says, wiping his

mouth.

"I guess I do."

"Do you have a lot of siblings?"

"Just one. Older brother, but we had a house full of boys growing up, so I guess I might as well say that I'm the youngest of four," I say with a laugh. I look away as he eats and spot Oliver sitting in a table on the opposite side of the room. He's with the same doctor guy I saw him talking to earlier. I don't know how I hadn't spotted him, but from the way he's looking at me, it seems as if he saw me a while ago. I tuck my hands into my purse to fish out my phone, and notice I have one missed call and two text messages.

"I know what that's like, sort of. I have two younger brothers," Chris says. I make a sound letting him know I heard him as I sort through my messages.

Did you leave?

Never mind. Just saw you.

I frown.

"Everything okay?" Chris asks.

I bring my eyes to him. "Yeah, sure. So what did you want to tell me about the program?" I ask, as I type a message.

Just saw you too.

"I was wondering if you could keep coming. The program was kind of dull when the last lady was running it. I think maybe the kids couldn't relate with her since she was older and more strict, and quite frankly, her art wasn't as nice," he says, smiling.

"Was she responsible for the fish on the wall?" I ask.

"You have no idea how bad I wanted to cover those walls up myself."

I laugh at the horrified look on his face. "And here I thought nobody in the hospital had good taste."

"My taste is perfect. Anyway, so maybe once a week?

Would that work for you? We'd love to keep you here twice a week, but I'm not sure the board would be willing to pay for that."

The mention of pay surprises me. "I didn't really sign up for this to get compensated."

"I know, but everybody needs something," he says with a shrug, checking his own phone.

"Not me." I match his shrug, and look down at mine.

`I miss you.`

My stomach flutters. I look up and see that he's still sitting at the same table, by himself now, still looking at me.

`Is that why you're staring at me like you're mad at the world?`

"Those hearts that you had the kids make," Chris says suddenly. "Is that what you do?"

I nod.

"You sell them?"

I nod again. "Yeah."

"How much are they?"

"Well, it depends on the size, I guess."

"Do you custom-make them, or do you have some already made?"

I frown slightly as I smile. "I have some made, but I also accept custom jobs."

Chris breathes out harshly and rubs his forehead. "I kind of have to get my fiancée a gift for our anniversary, and I have no clue what to get her. You would think after eight years of being together I'd know, right?" He laughs. "She would love one of those hearts, though."

"Well, I can bring some by on Thursday when I come back with the ones for the kids."

He smiles. "That would be awesome. Do you know where my office is? It's on the opposite side of Jen's, same wing as you."

"I'm sure I'll find it."

We get up at the same time and awkwardly looking at one another, back to our phones, and then to the other. Finally, he holds out his hand, and I shake it. "I'll see you Thursday."

I say goodbye and walk over to Oliver's table, but he stands before I get there, and signals me to the hallway. I follow him into a room beside the food court. He closes the door behind us and pins me to the wall, kissing me before I can get a word out. I tug on his hair, he pulls on mine, and our hands hold the other's face as our tongues collide. I pull apart on a breath.

"You really did miss me," I pant. "Do you normally accost women in random hospital rooms?"

Oliver puts his forehead against mine and breathes out heavily. "Definitely not. I'm usually never this desperate."

He groans when I drag my nails down his chest. "Tell me more about this desperation, Dr. Hart," I murmur, leaning in and licking the seam of his lips. He pushes his hips against me, and I moan at how hard he feels.

"I need another date," he whispers against my lips, his hands going under my shirt.

"Are you trying to take advantage of me in the middle of the workday?" I ask, arching my back when he tucks his hands under my bra.

"I clocked out over an hour ago," he says, brushing my nipples with his thumb.

"And you stayed?"

"I wanted to wait for you."

"Really?" I ask, gasping when his mouth dips and he takes in my nipple.

"Hmmm," he responds against my skin.

"And then you sat there staring at me from across the room?"

"He's not your type," he says, licking my other nipple.

"What?" I grab his head to stop his movements, and he looks up at me.

"That guy you had your little lunch with. He's not your type."

I can't help but smile. "You think I was on a date with a guy in the lunch room of the hospital you work at?"

He lets out a long breath, still cupping my breasts. "What would you call it?"

I laugh, shaking my head and cup his chin so that he looks at me again. "Calling it a date would be ridiculous. Would it bother you if it was?"

It takes everything in me not to laugh at the way he shrugs and looks away.

"Are you telling me you brought me in here because you got jealous?"

His eyes flicker to mine. "I'm not jealous."

"So if I tell you that the guy you saw me with asked me out on a date—a real one—outside of the hospital, you wouldn't mind?"

"Did he?" he growls.

"Would it matter?"

"Yes."

"Because?" I ask, running both of my hands through his hair. He closes his eyes at the motion.

"Because." He leans into my touch. "Because . . ."

"Uh-huh?"

His eyes pop open. "Because I want it to be me. I want to be that guy who takes you out all the time."

"So be that guy," I respond.

"I will be," he says, leaning in to kiss me. "I will be."

"Okay," I respond, folding into his arms, wishing I could stay in them forever.

The reality that this may not be something I can do every day makes me ache.

As if uneasiness is seeping from me, he pulls away and touches my cheek with the back of his hands.

"It's just an interview, Elle," he whispers, looking at me.

I take a long, deep breath and close my eyes. It's not really just an interview, though. It's a life-changer. Life is short, I remind myself. Look at what happened to Wyatt. I'm not going to make Oliver feel bad for doing something he loves. I can't be that girl—the one who demands someone give up their dreams in exchange for my happiness. When I feel calm again, I reopen my eyes. "I know. Go kick ass on your interview, Bean. Do what you need to do."

I reach up and kiss him on the cheek. He grabs for me again, but I stop him.

"Call me when you get back."

Somehow, I turn away from his big green eyes, from those large, warm hands, and from the sense of comfort he brings me. I walk out of the room and the hospital without looking back.

Chapter 32

SITTING OUTSIDE on one of my parent's lawn chairs, I reach over for a bigger piece of glass and prick myself with it. I start swearing and alternating between flicking my wrist and sucking the tiny cut on the tip of my finger. That hasn't happened to me in . . . a while.

"Today is supposed to be a celebration," my mom says, coming up behind me with two glasses of lemonade in her hands.

"It is," I say, reaching out for the one she hands me.

"Are you happy you finally sold the house?"

I sigh, moving the box on my lap aside and propping my legs up on the chair. "Happy, relieved, a tiny bit excited."

"Not sad," she says in a statement. I look over to her and catch her smiling at me.

"Not sad," I reply, and am relieved that it's true. Maybe it has to do with the fact that I've been living with Victor for what now feels like forever. Maybe I've come to accept that, while a part of me will always be sad when I think of losing Wyatt the way I did, I survived it and have found a way to move on.

"And you sold that painting of Wyatt's you love so much. You're taking a lot of big steps. I'm proud of you," she says with a smile.

"Thanks. I am too," I respond with a small laugh.

"But you will keep the gallery?" my mom asks, again in what's more of a statement than a question.

I frown at her words. "Of course."

"You know if you need help opening up a new one and getting a fresh start, we'll gladly do that for you, right?"

I stay silent for a moment. The gallery has as many memories as the house does, but somehow I've managed to compartmentalize them differently. When we were in there together, I was off in my studio, and Wyatt was off in his. We didn't share the space the way we shared our bedroom.

"Thanks, but I'm fine for now. I'll reconsider when my lease is up."

"When is that?"

"End of the month," I snort. My mother shakes her head.

"You embody procrastination so well," she responds with a small laugh. "That's a lot of glass. How many hearts have been broken this time?"

My parents have a running joke about my hearts. They don't even know how they came to be, but they think they're pretty and are in support of me making them. The first people who bought the hearts were a group of pissed off older women with no Valentine dates. They made them the center of their "Who needs a man anyway? Party." The next year, all three of them were married. That last part is usually ignored in the broken hearts conversation though, because everybody prefers to recount the sadder part, which was that they were divorcées who were sick of going on bad dates.

I smile. "I am pleased to report that these hearts are for a bridal party."

"Really?"

"Really. The guy that runs the department in charge of the art program at the hospital bought one for his fiancée, and she decided she wanted one for each of her maids."

"That's nice. She must have a lot of money to dish out," she comments. We both turn around at the sound of my father shouting that people are starting to arrive for the barbeque.

"I'm going to put this away," I say, standing and stretching.

"I'm here," Mia calls out, stepping into the yard. For the first time in a couple of days, I feel something other than stress.

"Help me with this, please," I call out as I pick up one of the boxes. She saunters over to me and picks up the other box.

"They're so pretty," she says, as we walk toward the house. We set them aside in the sitting area by the front door and end up staying there as her mom arrives. Conversation continues about the hearts, Mia's pictures, and boys. It's the same thing every time my parents have a barbeque. Same conversations . . . same people . . . yet it never gets old. I skipped out on a ton of these when I was with Wyatt because, well, he didn't really like coming. He said everybody made him feel like an outsider, and it hurt me that he thought that, so I didn't come either. I don't regret it, even though I did miss it at the time. My family understood it. They knew that if they were in my shoes, they would have done the same.

Victor gets there shortly after, with some girl I've never seen before, in tow, followed by a friend of hers.

"This is Madelyn and her friend Emma," he says by way of introduction. "Madelyn is Bobby's sister."

Mia and I share a look, and then share it with Victor before we greet Madelyn and Emma, who look like they could be *my* little sisters. My first thought is—I wonder what Oliver thinks about this whole thing. We haven't spoken much since he left for his interview last week. There have been a couple of text messages and a phone call one night when he called "wanting to hear my voice," but nothing about where we stand has been established. Thankfully, I've been busy enough that I'm only left to wonder about those things at night or in times like these, when the reality of everything closes in on me.

"Jenson's on his way," Vic says after the girls walk off. He likes to give Mia a heads-up on his friend's status. At least he's not clueless enough to let him trample in here and catch her off guard.

"I thought he was away on a job," Mia says, her voice quieter than it was just moments earlier.

"Got rescheduled." Vic says, as he turns away.

"How did you end up bringing Bobby's sister anyway?" I ask, nodding at the women who are now talking to my mom and Bettina.

"She stayed the night."

I gape at him. "You hooked up with your friend's sister? How old is she?"

"Relax," he says, laughing at the look on my face. "She's old enough, and we're consenting adults. Staying over just seemed like the gentleman thing to do since they were over so late, and Emma was sick from drinking all day."

I feel my ears get hot at his easy confession, but I try not to let my bubbling anger seep through enough to show. He's right about the consenting adults part, but he's such a hypocrite for hooking up with his friend's little sister, when all he's ever done is warn his friends away from me.

"Where was her brother?"

"Working on a case."

"I can't believe you hooked up with her," I say, glaring at him.

"It's not like she's seventeen," he says back, as if he's offended or something.

From my peripheral vision, I see Mia cross her arms. I do the same and glare at him harder, mentally shooting daggers through his brain. Vic laughs under his breath, then looks down at the floor.

"I like her, okay?" he says, walking away. I turn to Mia and wordlessly tell her I hate him, to which she nods sharply in agreement. After our mutual hate for my brother is established, we head back outside and pour ourselves extra large glasses of her mom's Sangria.

"You okay?" I ask Mia, who looks like she's swallowed a frog.

When she nods without saying a word, my gaze follows her to Jenson and Oliver who are laughing and talking as they walk in, looking like they just got out of a goddamn Abercrombie photo shoot. As if they're not responsible for our discomfort and restlessness. The sight of them makes my insides churn.

"You want to leave? We can just skip out," I suggest, hoping she agrees, but she doesn't. She puts a smile on her face and turns to me with suddenly clear eyes.

"Nope. Your parents are really happy you're here this year," she says, placing her hand in mine. "I'll survive."

"We always do, don't we?" I say, smiling sadly, as I watch Oliver and Jenson walk over to Vic and the girls. They both greet the guys with overly excited hugs that make my stomach dip. I squeeze Mia's hand tighter as I watch Emma practically drape herself over Oliver, who's smiling down at her.

"I'm calling Nathan," she says suddenly, which makes my mouth drop open.

"You're not," I say, smiling despite myself. Neither of us normally plays head games or tries to make anybody jealous. I guess I never needed to make Wyatt jealous because he was born with an overly jealous bone, but Mia has never been like that either. My brother's friends are all similar in one thing: They're sure of themselves. So confident, that they believe every woman is a sure thing when it comes to them. Jenson always treated Mia like she would never go anywhere—not that he was mean, but he clearly took her for granted. As outlandish as Mia is now, she was the opposite with Jenson—always serving him, always quiet when he was around, because he was the boisterous one. When things went wrong, she climbed out of her shell like a mummy ready for rebirth. I know she uses her loud comments as a shield more than anything, because she's never been the same after Jenson. Not out in public anyway. The only time I get the real Mia is in times like these, where she's quietly vulnerable. I look over at them, talking and laughing with those girls. I decide that . . . fuck it . . . we can have fun too.

"Tell him to bring some friends," I say, glaring at the back of Oliver's now short hair. He must have cut it before his interview. Of course, it's still gorgeous, brushed back so that it curls over the collar of his polo. He shaved down his beard too, so it looks lighter, barely there.

"Let's go," Mia says, typing furiously into her phone. "We'll be back." I follow her out the side door and laugh when she lets out a grumbled "motherfuckers" under her breath. I love her.

We go upstairs to my room, and she helps me sort out the hearts I was working on, until Nathan calls to let us know they're outside. We practically trot downstairs and bolt outside to meet Nathan, Hunter (yes, my "first" Hunter), and Steven. They're guys we hung out with through high school and college. They're just downright fun, nice people.

"I haven't seen you in ages," Hunter says to me after he gives us each a huge hug.

"I know. Whatever happened to that girl you were dating? Emily?"

"We're kind of on a break. Long distance relationships are tough," he says with a shrug. "I do think we have something though."

I smile at that. We talk for a while, and I completely forget about the party in the backyard and the guys we were going to try to make jealous. I'm pretty sure Mia does too. It feels like high school all over again, and sometimes acting juvenile is all you need. We're laughing and joking about Nathan's wrestling days, and after a stupid demonstration of one of the moves—where I was used as a sparring partner—I land knee-first on the ground. Even though I laugh, it hurts.

"You okay?" Nathan asks, inspecting it like the concerned EMT he is.

"I'm fine. Obviously too old to be playing this crap, but I'll live," I say, making us all laugh.

"Come on, I'll piggyback you inside for old time's sake," Hunter says with a wink.

Hunter, for some weird reason, runs into the yard shouting something about a zombie apocalypse. I'm pretty sure he's trying to imitate somebody from The Walking Dead, but the voice he's using is way off. I hang on for dear life, laughing hysterically, my hair swinging back and forth, as Mia, Nathan, and Steven follow behind. We are all laughing so hard, the crowd in the backyard turns as a unit to face us.

"Great, there goes the neighborhood," Vic says, smiling when Hunter stops to greet him, still holding me over his shoulder. Vic and his friends have always been fond of these guys. They used to surf together, and I'm pretty sure they still play football together on Thanksgiving.

"Long time no see, man," Hunter says, walking around and greeting everyone with me still hanging on his back. I complain about my knee and am about to hop off, when he swings me and catches me in a cradle like we're on the cheerleading squad, my head hanging upside down, and hair dragging on the grass.

"Are you going to put her down? You know it's not safe for her circulation to be in that position for too long," says Oliver the doctor, as if anybody asked him.

Everybody snorts at that.

"Dude, please, leave work in the workplace," Jenson says.

"Will you put me down?" I say, laughing as I push the hair out of my face.

Hunter laughs, looking down at me and shakes his head. When he leans into me, my eyes widen. I don't think he's going to kiss me or anything, but still, I inwardly freak out. He leans into my ear and whispers, loudly, so that everyone can hear him. "The zombies are still out there, but sure, if your knee feels fine, I can put you down."

I laugh when he pulls back and slap him on the chest,

then shimmy so he drops me on my feet. I hold on to his arms, steadying myself.

"If you wanted to cop a feel, all you had to do was ask," he says, flirting.

"I told you we were too old for that stuff. Now I'm dizzy," I say.

"*You're* too old for that stuff. I feel fine. If you want another go at it later, you know where to find me."

"Elle, can I talk to you for a second?" Oliver says suddenly. Both Hunter and I dart our eyes to him, as does Vic and Jenson.

"I guess?" I squeak. When my eyes meet his glaring green eyes, my heart plummets to somewhere between my liver and my gallbladder. I look at Hunter and smile. "I'll be right back."

He smiles and shrugs. "We'll be here. Come here, Meep, you're next," he says, lunging at Mia, who laughs and backs away.

"This just got interesting," Jenson mumbles under his breath.

"You can't afford another black eye," Vic says, as I follow Oliver out of earshot.

He leads me under the huge tree on the other side of the yard. I walk until I'm standing directly in front of him, where the trunk of the tree mostly blocks us from my brother and the rest of the people.

"What's up," I say, keeping my gaze on the grass between our feet.

"What's up?" he says. "What's up? That's what you're going to say?"

I sigh and look up at him tiredly. I hate that his face makes my heart pound the way it does. I hate that his eyes and the way he looks at me makes everything else seem so . . . small.

"How'd your interview go?" I ask.

He closes his eyes for a moment and runs his hand over his hair.

"I like your hair like that," I offer. "And your trimmed

beard."

Oliver opens his eyes again and smiles—a small one—but I'll take it. "Thank you, and the interview went great. The interviews . . . there were two . . ." He looks away, over my shoulder when he says that, so I wait. When he doesn't make further comment, I smile uneasily.

"Good. I knew they would."

We look at each other for a long, silent moment, and I wish so much he would put his soft lips on mine and kiss this hesitation away.

"So . . . Hunter . . ." he says, finally.

I let out a short laugh. "We're not dating or anything, if that's where you're going with this," I say, recalling our hospital run in.

"I wasn't . . ." He stops talking, sighs, and presses his back against the tree trunk, tilting his head up so that his throat is exposed. I want nothing more but to lean in and kiss the knot of his Adam's apple.

"This is so hard for me, Elle. I don't think you understand how hard."

"What is?" I ask, my heart lurching into my throat as I wait for him to drop the bomb that he's leaving on me.

He looks at me again. "I really thought I was going to hit him earlier. Hunter, I mean."

My heart lurches at his admission, and I feel sick for his jealousy having that impact on me. I hated Wyatt's jealousy; it annoyed me, and it made me angry, but Oliver saying these things makes my body feel like it's going to break out in song.

"Why?" I ask, stepping closer.

"He came in here carrying you without a care in the world. It's so easy for him. Vic didn't even bat an eyelash when he saw you guys."

"Because we're friends," I whisper, moving a little closer to him.

"I know that, but still. I pictured what would happen if I

did the same thing, and the outcome didn't turn out so nice in my head."

"Are you saying we should put a stop to this?" I ask, looking between our feet.

"No. I would never say that." The sternness in his voices brings my eyes back to his.

"Why?"

"We already went over this," he says quietly, his hand reaching out to take mine. "I want you."

"So take me," I respond, and his face darkens. He threads his fingers through mine and pulls me a little closer. "We're going to get caught," I whisper.

"I want you so bad right now," he says, his voice a growl against my cheek.

I pull away from him and drop his hand, looking up at him through my lashes. "Maybe you should go to the bathroom on the side of the house in a couple of minutes," I whisper in a conspiracy. I want this . . . whatever this is. For as long as I can have it, I want it.

He bites his bottom lip. "Five minutes."

"Five minutes," I say, smiling as I walk away from him and head over to Mia.

"What did he want?" she whispers.

"He said he wanted to kill Hunter when he saw us walk in."

She laughs. "That was quite a show. Jenson has been glaring at me since we got here, too."

"Well, we knew that would happen."

"He's such an asshole. Such a good-looking, too responsible, asshole," she says in a breath, referring to Jenson as she shakes her head. "Did Bean say if he took the job?"

I purse my lips. "He had interviews. I doubt they offered anything on the spot." The idea of him taking a job so far away any time soon, makes my heart hurt. I decided to use these final weeks, or month together to be just that—together. I'll worry about the rest later. I'll deal with the pain when it comes, and I admit that I'm secretly hoping it doesn't.

"Guys! The steaks are ready!" my mom calls out. The crowd seems to shift her way as a group.

"You're not coming?" Mia asks when she notices I stay behind.

"I'll be right there. I have to go get something inside," I say, walking the opposite way when she darts ahead to catch up to Steven, Nathan, and the rest of the crew.

Once I'm in the bathroom, I blow out a breath in anticipation. At the sound of footsteps, my heart skips a beat, and then stops beating altogether when Oliver steps inside the bathroom with me, his presence commanding every bit of my attention. My eyes travel the length of a body I don't think I'll ever tire of seeing. It feels like he's been getting this reaction out of me for as long as I can remember. His arm reaches back to turn the lock on the door and he smiles that slow, sensual smile that always makes me turn into a softer version of myself. In another breath, his hands are around my waist, pulling me forward, as his lips capture mine in a slow kiss. It's a sweet, tender kiss that wraps my insides in knots.

My hands reach for his face, frantic to touch everything at once—his neck, his arms, his shirt . . . and even though we're in a bathroom, and this is supposed to be quick, the look he gives me says otherwise. He unzips his jeans and pulls them down along with his boxers. His eyes tear down every bit of resolve I had built up, as he watches me do the same. I slip out of my flip-flops, my jeans, my thong, and turn around, bracing myself on the sink, and my eyes meet his in the mirror. When I lean over, his gaze leaves mine momentarily to look at what I'm baring for him. When his eyes return to mine, the hunger in them makes me hold on tighter. My eyes linger on the length of him, and I lick my lips in anticipation of feeling him inside of me again.

Oliver moves between my legs, and for a long moment, simply palms my ass in both of his hands, eyes closed, his chest expanding heavily. I step back and urge him to push inside me, but he continues to feel my cheeks and run his fingers up and down my wet folds.

"I'm ready for you," I whisper, shivering at his touch.

"I know." He leans in and drops a kiss between my shoulder blades. "You've always been ready for me." He sinks into me slowly, fully, and I bite down on my lip to keep from crying out. "You are so ready for me," he says, groaning as he picks up the pace. One of his arms goes to my shoulder, and the other moves to my waist as his thrusts get harder. I try not to make a sound, but I can't help it. I feel so full, so good.

"Shhh," he murmurs under my ear, licking there. "You're so perfect, Elle. So perfect for me."

His words, and the look of adoration I see in the mirror, make my heart quicken further. I push into him as his teeth clamp down on my shoulder.

"Oliver," I moan, biting my lip, when his hand moves to rub my clit. His strokes quicken, the wet sound of his pelvis slapping over my ass becoming louder and faster.

"Elle," he groans against me, followed by a slew of *come, please come, baby. I can't take it when you clench around me like that.* A spark blazes through me, starting from the tips of my toes to the top of my head, and spreads like rapid fire as my core tightens and my insides coil. An orgasm rocks through me as he unloads inside of me, his cock jerking in spurts.

Oliver tucks his face into my neck and breathes hard as my head falls forward, and I try to catch my breath. Footsteps ring out outside and our heads snap up to look at each other in alarm. I flinch when he pulls out of me quickly, handing me tissues, and I start redressing as he buttons himself up. We're not even close to being presentable—my hair is a mess, our faces are glistening with the aftermath of our quick sexcapade—but I signal for him to go outside anyway. He closes the door behind him, but I hear loud voices as soon as he steps out, followed by the doorknob turning.

"Who the fuck is in there?"

My breath catches in my throat in a panicked gasp, when I realize it's my brother's accusing voice outside the door.

"I swear to God, Oliver, I love you. You're my brother, but if who I think is in there is . . ." he says, letting that thought hang and marinate a while. He slams his hand against the door. "Open the door!" he shouts, making me jump back a step.

But I can't, because I am completely frozen. Completely and utterly frozen, just staring at the door, as a new wave of anticipation rocks through me—a very different one than the one I had coming into this bathroom. Finally, feeling tears prick my eyes, I go to unlock the door, but stop when I hear him speak again.

"Estelle is missing from the table . . . Estelle and you are the only ones missing. She's not in her room; Mia has no idea where she is . . . Hunter doesn't know where she is . . . and I am really trying to assume she wasn't in there with you," Victor says, his voice low and menacing.

"I'm in love with her, okay?" Oliver says suddenly. My knees go weak, and tears brim in my eyes. I turn the lock on the door and open it. My brother's mouth goes completely slack, and as soon as he composes himself, his glare turns murderous.

"My sister?" he says. "You're fucking my sister?" he shouts as if he needs confirmation beyond seeing me right there.

Oliver shoots me a look that makes my chest squeeze tighter. "I'm in love with her."

"In love?" Victor screams, pushing him back. I scurry toward them and grip on to Victor's arm.

"Vic, stop!"

"You're in love with her? How can you be in love with her if you're leaving? You just accepted a job four hours north of here, you fuck," he yells.

"They offered you a job there, and you took it?" I ask quietly, my voice shaky as I drop my hand from Victor's arm. He uses the moment to tread forward and swing at Oliver, clocking him in the face.

Oliver flinches and grabs his face, but his eyes stay on mine. "I was going to talk to you about that."

"You didn't even tell her?" Victor yells, punching him again. "You're fucking my sister, and you didn't even have the decency to tell her you're leaving? How long has this been going on?"

"That's between me and her," Oliver says, spitting out blood, his hands bunched at his sides as if it's taking everything in him not to hit back.

"You and her? There is no you and her!" Victor yells, panting a breath and turning to me. "Elle, there is no you and Oliver."

He says the words, and I don't know what my face must look like, but if it's as crumbled as my insides, I guess he sees it. It ignites another round of anger within him.

"You motherfucker," he says, stepping toward Oliver again, and that's when I snap and react, grabbing on to Victor's arm for dear life and dragging him back. As much as I'm hurting, I don't want him to keep throwing unsheltered punches at Oliver, who's just taking the beating as if he deserves it.

"Stop, Victor. Just stop," I cry.

"Do you know how much she's been through? Do you fucking know how much she's been through in the past year? She doesn't need a guy like you to tear her up all over again!" Victor continues, yelling.

Finally, a crowd runs to us, everybody appearing out of nowhere all at once. Jenson drops his plate on the floor and runs full speed at us, pushing Victor back.

"This bastard is . . ." he takes a ragged breath. "Screwing around with Estelle!"

"I'm not screwing around with her!" Oliver growls. Victor rears forward again, but Jenson holds him back.

"I trusted you. When did this start? I fucking trusted you! You're like my brother! How could you fucking do that?" Victor shouts.

It isn't until Mia runs over to me and wraps her arms around me that I realize how bad I'm shaking. She walks me backwards, away from the commotion, but I don't budge until my dad stomps over to us.

"Victor, my office. Now," he says in a tone that doesn't leave room for discussion. "Oliver. My office. Now."

Victor shoots him a look. "Can you believe—"

"Shut up and go to my office, and don't touch him again."

Silence falls over us, and Oliver tries to walk past them and over to me, but I shake my head slowly, not wanting things to get worse. Either way, I need to think. I need to get away from these people and think. I swallow my broken emotions and walk to Mia's car in silence. My mom and hers stop us to hug me and say how sorry they are, amidst a million different questions. *When did this happen? Are you in love with him? Why did you keep it from us?* But I don't respond. I don't say that it happened so long ago, I can't remember a time when it wasn't happening. I don't yell that I kept it from them because I wanted to avoid exactly what happened, or that I didn't know what there was to report in the first place. And lastly, I definitely don't talk about the way my heart feels like it's been split open so completely that it didn't even shatter, it exploded in a big, bloody mess.

I get in the car, and the guys, Nathan, Steven and Hunter come with us. Steven and Nathan find a way to squeeze in the back, as I'm forced to sit on Hunter's lap in the front. As soon as my face touches his chest, I lose it and sob into him. He just holds me, wordlessly, until we get to Nathan's house, and they get out of the car.

"I'm so sorry, Elle," the three of them say, giving me a quick hug. They know what I've been through. They were present at the funeral, and after. They've held my hand through the years when my heart was only a bit chipped, and later, only a bit broken, so it's only right they'd be present to see the complete demise of it all.

When I get back in the car, we drive quietly to the beach, where we usually go when we're having extra good days and pitifully bad ones. We walk to the black rocks that have become our third wheel—our extra best friend—a stepping stool for our successes, and a mule to our problems. Once we take a seat beside the other, she offers me her hand . . . her shoulder . . . her ear . . . and I cry until my tears compete with the waves in a sad, broken symphony.

Chapter 33

I CONSIDER MYSELF lucky to have been in love twice. Some people don't have the luxury of finding one person they connect with on a deeper level. I found two. I loved both the same, yet differently. One was my mentor, my friend, my lover. He opened my eyes to the greatness I was capable of. He believed in me when others thought I would fail. When I lost him, I cried every day for weeks, grieved for months. I grieved for the loss of a young life, a loved artist, a beacon of light in our community and my life. I still miss his smile and the smell of his hands, even after he'd smoked ten cigarettes. I miss listening to him tell me about the villages he saw and the people he met in them. I even miss his temper tantrums and the way he would throw paint everywhere when the outside light was fading into the moonlight. The day Wyatt taught me to channel my pain in my art was the day I fell in love with him. Shatter it all, he said, helping me break plates and glasses. Hate the world, he shouted, taking a mallet to wooden serving spoons. He watched me break down, and when I was finished, he scooped me up along with the shattered pieces of glass around me. One by one, we glued it all together, and when we were finished, we'd made the most beautiful broken heart I'd ever seen.

The first boy I fell in love with used to regale me with stories about kings and queens and war and peace, and how he hoped to one day be somebody's knight in shining armor. I lived vicariously through his late night adventures, watching the way he swung his hands animatedly as he told his stories and loving the way his green eyes twinkled when I laughed at his jokes.

He taught me what it feels like to be touched and thoroughly kissed. Later, he taught me the level of pain one feels at the loss of someone you've grown attached to. The one thing he forgot to teach me was how to deal with the pain that squeezed my chest after he broke the ghost of what heart I had left. I'd always wondered if it had been a missed lesson. Now, I wonder if maybe he'd been trying to figure it out for himself, or if he just never felt anything at all. I'd wondered, when he left that night, if he would come back. When things got serious with Wyatt, I found myself lying awake at night thinking, *what if Oliver came through that door right now and asked me to be with him? Would I leave?* I never found my answer, because he never came. I like to think I didn't base my engagement on anything but my love for Wyatt, but still, that "what if" always remained.

Unlike Wyatt's loss, I never stopped mourning Oliver. I never stopped, because my heart didn't have time to mend before he came back in and surged through it again. Oliver taught me heartache and longing. He taught me to greet pain with a smile, because as beautiful as life is, sometimes it comes to us in forms we don't recognize. He taught me to understand that the thing about love—real, over the top, makes you feel crazy, overpowering, strips you bare kind of love—is that when you're soaring, you're higher than you dreamed possible. But when you fall, you land inside the deepest darkest crevices, and are left alone to pull yourself out.

The hearts I make are shattered, but whole. They're kaleidoscopes that beam under the sun. They signify hope in love when you've lost it because, like love, you can look at a kalei-doscope a thousand different ways and find something new every time. Shattered or not, if you look carefully enough, you'll find something beautiful in them, and all beautiful things are a little broken.

Chapter 34

WHY COULDN'T I just ship the painting? I sigh for what seems like the millionth time, and Mia finally switches off the music.

"Okay, talk. I know you're miserable, and I know how annoying you get when you mope internally, so let it out. What are you thinking?"

I sigh again.

"And stop fucking sighing!" she says in a tone that makes me laugh.

"Sorry. I'm just . . . I feel like an idiot. I knew," I stop to take a breath and hold back fresh tears. I am so sick of crying over this guy. "I know him . . ."

"You know what bothers me about him?" Mia says suddenly, reaching for my hand to squeeze. "How can someone so smart be so fucking stupid?"

I wipe my face with a laugh. "I wonder that all the time."

"Just goes to show you. Men. No matter how strong, how smart, how successful . . . they're just missing that chip that separates them from the better gender."

When our laughter dies down, I turn and face her. "You know what bothers me about him? That I truly believe that he

263

loves me. I see it when he looks at me. I feel it when he touches me. For the longest time, I wondered what this was to him and the fact that I still can't get him to actually stay, is pretty telling, isn't it?"

I lean back in my seat and shake my head, a short laugh escaping me. "Funny thing, all of you think I'm in love with a ghost, and I do love Wyatt, but I've been in love with Oliver for as long as I can remember. And everything I love about him is a memory. Good memories, bad memories . . . and it hurts more since Oliver is a ghost I can touch, and feel, and one that beckons to me and brings me under his spell every time he's around." I sigh. "Life's a bitch."

I check in the painting and board the plane just in time and, as I'm about to switch the phone off, it vibrates with a call from Oliver. I stare at it until it goes to voicemail before I put it in airplane mode. During the flight, I watch a movie that makes me cry, because I'm an idiot and chose to watch one that was nominated for a ton of Golden Globes. By the time I get to New York, I'm ready for a shower and my bed and, after a lengthy conversation with my realtor on the cab ride, I feel like I need a drink to add to all of that. After a long shower, I settle in bed and listen to my voice message from Oliver. My phone is about to die, so I just want to get through this one before I call it a night. As soon as I hear his voice, I close my eyes and wrap my arms around . . . *myself.*

"I'm so sorry, Elle," he says, his voice a low rasp. "I know you're in New York, but we need to talk. Call me, please. I understand if you're busy, but I'll be here, so please . . ."

My battery dies before he finishes his sentence. I put it down with a trembling hand and close my eyes. I have other things I need to focus on right now, and even though it may not seem like a huge deal to everybody else, it is to me. Selling Wyatt's painting was one thing, but physically letting go of it will be a different task.

The next morning, after pushing the snooze button a million times, I rush to make it to the buyer's apartment on time. Just as I'm reaching her floor, my phone buzzes again. I tear my eyes away from the painting, sitting on the bellman's cart, to rummage through my purse. When I find it, I see the picture I took of Oliver one night at the hospital. His flirty grin, the twinkle in his green eyes, his dimples, they all beam at me as I hold my ringing phone. When I can't bear to look at him anymore, I answer the call.

"Elle, I'm sorry," he says instantly, as if I'm going to hang up the phone before he gets the words out. His words do nothing to alleviate the pain I feel inside.

If anything, it feels like his voice is breaking me open once again. I take a breath once the elevator doors open, and I'm standing in a foyer. Priscilla Woods, the buyer, owns the penthouse.

"Hey," I respond.

"How was your flight?" he asks, and when I don't respond, continues, "Elle? Are you there?"

"Yeah, yeah, I'm here," I reply, staring at the dark, paneled door as if it's going to give me the strength I need to get through this conversation and the meeting inside.

"You busy?"

I clear my throat when the door opens for us, and the bellman greets the coiffed socialite inside. "Yeah. I'll call you when I get back home."

He pauses for a long time, and I can hear the argument going on in his head. *Do I force the issue, or do I give her space?* When he finally speaks again, he sounds defeated. "Please do. We need to talk."

I press the end button without saying goodbye, and glance up as Priscilla ushers the bellman inside.

"Estelle," she says, smiling as she turns her attention to me. "Great to see you again."

"Likewise, Mrs. Woods." I walk over and extend my hand to her, which she takes.

"Please, call me Priscilla."

I trail behind her, our heels clicking against the marble floor of her lavish apartment.

"Connor, just settle it down there, please," she says to the bellman. He does as she asks and bows upon leaving. "I'm thrilled to finally have my painting," she says, looking at me again. "I was surprised to hear from you as soon as I did. What made you decide to let go of it?"

I stare at the canvas, still covered in layers of wrapping, and shrug. "I realized that sometimes in order to move forward you have to let go of the past, even if it hurts. Especially if it hurts," I correct, smiling sadly.

Priscilla nods. Her pristine hands reach for two glasses of champagne waiting on the table. I hadn't noticed them there. She hands one to me and takes a sip of her own. "I lost my first husband when we were pretty young. We were so in love." Her gaze wanders to the side as she smiles at the memory. "He got killed in a car accident. Drunk driver. We had only been together for a couple of months. We got married after a week of knowing each other. It was a whirlwind romance," she says, laughing lightly before taking another sip. "When I lost him, I thought I would die, but I didn't . . . and I found love again in Matthew. We've been together for twenty years now. It's been twenty-three since I lost Eric, and still there's not a day that goes by when I don't think of him."

I take a gulp of champagne hoping to push down the knot in my throat, and realize that the knot is not there because of Wyatt. "You've made a beautiful life with him," I say, pointing at the photo frames on the mantle that hold pictures of her with a smiling man. Others hold photos of graduates and small children.

"We do have a beautiful life," she says, smiling as her eyes follow mine. When our eyes meet again, hers are full of compassion. "Okay, let's see my new painting."

Her painting. I take a breath and realize that I'm okay with that this time. I unwrap the canvas, and as I tear the layers off, the image becomes visible. My fingertips graze the outer part of the eye and the memory of watching him paint it resurfaces. This is my goodbye, I say to myself.

Priscilla clutches the pearls of her necklace as she admires it. "It's even more beautiful than I remember," she whispers.

"It is," I agree, twisting the paper in my hands, as I stare at the eye that's been watching over me for the past couple of years—the one I felt more potently after Wyatt's death.

We talk a little longer and when my kaleidoscope hearts catch her attention, she promises to give me a call soon so that she can look at the rest of my catalog. When we say our goodbyes, I look over my shoulder one last time, and I burn the image of the way it looks on her wall into my memory bank. I go back to the hotel and let myself cry a little for my losses, and when I'm finished crying, I put a smile on my face. I'm okay despite these things, and maybe even better than I was before them. When twilight rolls around, and I realize I have one more night in the city with nothing to do, I decide to take a page out of the book of Wyatt and go explore on my own.

Chapter 35

Oliver

Present

I CAN COUNT on one hand the amount of times I've felt anxious in my life, and I'm not proud to say that this is one of them, and furthermore, that I have nobody to blame but myself. I don't allow myself to entertain the idea that maybe this time I lost her, because I refuse to accept that possibility. I pick up my phone and dial the number I've been calling every day since she left.

"What's up?" Victor says after two rings.

"Has she called yet?" I ask.

"Dude, you need to chill. Maybe you should take an extra shift or something," he offers.

I laugh. "I just worked fourteen hours. The last thing I need is an extra shift."

"I don't know what else to tell you, man."

I sigh. *Tell me I still have a chance. Tell me she's mentioned me, that she's thinking about me, and that she hasn't given up on us.* I don't say any of those things, only because I know I'll never hear the end of it.

"Have you talked to her?" I ask finally. She's been back for two days, and I haven't heard a word from her.

"For like two seconds. Other than the fact that she's pissed off at me, she's been busy. She's . . ." he pauses, letting out a breath. "She's moving her stuff out of my house. Apparently her realtor got her a place on the beach that she's in love with," he adds in a lower voice.

That she's in love with. His words simmer in my head for a beat. I want to be the object of that love. I'm not worthy of it, but I want it.

"When is she moving?" I ask.

"I'm supposed to help her this weekend. She's been busy with the gallery too, though, I don't think she's purposely avoiding you, I just think it's bad timing."

"Fuck bad timing," I say, hitting my steering wheel. I let out a long breath.

"I'll . . ." he pauses. "Bean, you're my brother, you know that. You've been there for me more times than I can count, but she's my little sister."

"I love her more than you can ever imagine," I say, not caring whether that makes me sound like a pussy, because it's true.

"I know. That's why I'm going to talk to her, but I really think she'll come around and call you."

"Just tell her, please. If you talk to her before I do, make sure you tell her."

"I will," he promises. "All right, I gotta go. My client just got here."

Chapter 36

Estelle

A WHIRLWIND OF emotions runs through me as I leave my realtor's office with the keys to my new place. When I left, she promised she would call me soon with some possible gallery locations. The lease is up where I am now, and after discussing it with Wyatt's mom, I decided I want to move the gallery closer to me. It's currently positioned conveniently close to our old house and his parents', which is far from my new place and my parents'. Felicia, once again, gave me her blessing and told me to do whatever I needed to do with it. She did ask for one of Wyatt's paintings, but that was it.

I park outside the gallery, where Dallas has been a permanent fixture for a couple of weeks now, and I'm grateful for it. He's standing right by the front door, giving me a grand smile when I walk in, and he greets me like a game show host.

"Oh God, I hope this isn't how you greet people, because at this rate, my three customers will turn into none," I say, and laugh when he waggles his eyebrows.

"This right here," he says signaling at himself. "Sold a

painting today!"

My mouth drops in surprise for a moment before I beam at him. "What? You're serious? Which one?"

"One of Wyatt's," he says with a shrug, walking toward the one with a sold sticker on the sign beside it. It's one he drew of a naked woman . . . well, her silhouette. He never told me who she was, but I assumed it was his ex.

"My God," I breathe. "You really should keep working here."

Dallas laughs. "I do what I can. I put the paperwork in your studio. By the way, Oliver has come by a couple of times."

I stop walking and turn around. "And?"

"Just letting you know. He has a busted lip. He still looks good though," he says with a wink. I roll my eyes and smile. I step into my studio, picking up the paperwork as I sit in my chair. I leaf through it, making sure Dallas filled it out properly, and look up when I notice something in front of me. There's a large white canvas sitting on the easel that faces my desk. Oliver's handwriting covers it. *This is our canvas. Let's paint it how we want it. I love you, always, Oliver.*

Happiness blooms inside of me as I stare at it. It's so simple . . . so him . . . and I love it. I know I have to call him, but every time I think about it, my heart sinks at the thought of him leaving. I finish signing the papers and leave them in the same spot. When I step out of the room and start making my way back to the door, I see Dallas on his phone.

"When did he do that?" I ask, nodding toward my studio.

"Last night."

"Does he know I haven't been in since I got back?"

"I told him you hadn't," he says.

"If he comes back, tell him I saw it. I left the contract on the table. Thank you so much, Dal," I say, kissing him on the cheek.

"Anything for you, dahling," he responds. "I'm taking lunch in two minutes, wanna grab something?"

"Not today. I have to go have an actual conversation with my brother and convince him to help me move this weekend."

"You let me know if you need anything," Dallas calls out as I shut the door behind me.

On my way to Victor's, I call Mia and tell her about the canvas.

"That's so sweet," she says. "Are you going to call him before or after you move?"

I groan as I park my car outside of Victor's law firm. "I haven't had time, and I don't think what needs to be said can be said over the phone."

"I don't think he's left to San Fran yet," she says.

"I don't know what I'm more scared of—calling him and him being over there or calling him and him being here. If he's over there, I know he left for good. If he's here, I'll get my hopes up that maybe he's staying . . . but it's Oliver. He's not going to back out of a job once he got it," I say with a sigh as I turn off my car and walk toward the building.

"He might surprise you, Elle," she says reassuringly.

"I don't know if I want him to. I don't want him not to take the job and hate me for it."

"You'll figure it out."

Upon hanging up with Mia, I greet Victor's secretary and sit and wait until he's done with his meeting. She calls to tell him somebody outside of his schedule is there to see him. He growls for her to let whomever it is in, and I can already picture him rubbing his forehead as if he has a ton of bricks on it.

"I would never hire you if I was a new client," I say, walking in. His head snaps up from his hands, and his eyes widen. He stands quickly, but stays behind his desk.

"I wasn't expecting you."

"I noticed." I take a seat in one of the chairs across from him. "Don't worry, I'll only be ten minutes."

"I can cancel my next meeting."

I put my hand up. "Not necessary."

His lips twitch into a smile. "You ready to talk to me without chopping my head off?"

"I can't promise that last part, but yeah," I say with a smile.

"Sit," he says, taking a seat across from me.

I take a breath and let it out, trying to figure out where to begin. "You tried to kill Oliver," I say, pausing when he rolls his eyes and shakes his head. "The guy who beat up those guys who were making fun of you and kicking you into the ground in sixth grade. The one who was there for you when you didn't make the varsity baseball team in school and decided to quit, even though he would have been starting pitcher. The guy who left his house, numerous times, in the middle of the night to pick you up at parties because you were too drunk to drive. The one who would take you home and make sure you made it all the way into your room."

"How did you know about that?" he asks quietly.

"Because he told me. Because every time he did those things for you, he would come up to the roof to talk to me, because I was up."

Victor looks away, his eyes settling somewhere between the big globe bar in the corner of his office and the bookshelf beside it. "I was pissed off. We already hashed it out, Elle. It was just a tough thing to come to terms with like that . . . and it's Bean, you know? I freaked out."

"He's a good guy," I say quietly.

"He's a great guy, but you're my baby sister. Nobody's good enough for you," he says, flashing a smile my way. I return it and lean forward, resting my elbows on his desk.

"I don't know if it'll work out," I whisper, dropping my eyes to the stack of papers on his desk.

"Why not? Because of the job?"

I nod, looking at him again. "Yeah. He lied to me. Or omitted the truth, I guess."

Victor shrugs. "That doesn't hold up in court, you know?"

I frown. "What?"

"Omitting the truth . . . it's not really the same as lying. If you were getting a divorce . . ."

I put my hands up before he can finish his sentence. "Victor. For five minutes can you please not talk about work or divorce or court?"

He makes an apologetic face. "Sorry. Anyway, I think you should just talk to him, Elle. Hear him out."

I nod slowly, tearing my eyes away from his.

"How did you know?" he asks. "That you were in love with him, I mean."

I shrug, smiling. "One night, he dropped you off after a party, and I was crying over my blown knee. It was the day I found out I wouldn't be able to dance. He came up and talked to me. I asked him to come back, and he did. It was innocent. We were just talking, but you know how Oliver is when he tells a story. He gets all animated, and his eyes light up, and well . . . I fell in love with him. I fell in love with the way he was, with his caring heart and his loyalty to you guys. I guess I've been in love with him since," I end in a whisper.

"You were engaged to another man. Obviously it was puppy love, and you grew out of it," he points out. "Just playing Devil's Advocate," he adds with a shrug.

"Sometimes I wish it had been. You don't know the amount of times I've wished so badly that what we had was just a stupid fling. I tried to lie to myself and say it was about the hook ups. I tried to bury any remnants of my feelings for him countless times. Nothing works, Vic. The heart wants what it wants, and mine is clearly a sucker for pain."

He rubs his temple. "I was so mad at him. At first, because he went behind my back, and then the more I thought about it, the angrier I became. He's a serial dater, you know? If you can even call it that. He likes women. He likes older women. I think in all these years, he's only dated one girl our age, and that was in middle school, so when I found out about you I was just . . . at a loss, I guess."

"I know. I get it. You see Bean, the player . . . the guy who has a different girl every month . . . so I get it. I grew up with him too, but I truly believe he loves me. Despite the fact that I'm younger than his usual," I add with a laugh.

There's a slight smile on his face as he shakes his head. "I think he loves you too."

"But it doesn't matter," I add. "His profession comes first, and honestly, I don't blame him. I get that, too."

He closes his eyes for a moment and takes a deep breath. "He's always been the planner . . . the perfectionist . . . the one who needs to have all his ducks in a row before he attacks. I don't know anybody else who sets up a spreadsheet for a fantasy football draft." He raises his eyebrows. "And I know a lot of nerdy guys."

His secretary buzzing in the next client interrupts our laughter, so I stand. Victor goes around his desk and wraps his arms around me.

"I love you, and I'm with you, okay? If you want to be with him, I'm okay with it. I'm sorry I freaked out like that, because you're right—if it weren't for Bean, none of us would be where we are today. I wish you weren't moving though."

I kiss his chest and rear back to look at his face. "You just want me to stick around so I can cook for you."

He laughs against my face. "Yeah, that's part of it, but I like having you around."

"I'm not moving far, Vic."

"I know, I know. So this weekend?" he asks.

"This weekend," I respond with a smile as I back away. "And for the record, I am really pissed off that it happened the day you admitted to hooking up with your friend's little sister."

Victor lets out a loud laugh. "Bean said the same thing."

"I'm sure he did," I reply, shaking my head as I leave. I bump into an older man in a suit and excuse myself.

"Did hell freeze over, or did I just hear you laughing?" the man says as I walk.

Vic's secretary thanks me for putting him in a good mood, and I make a mental note to send these people a box of donuts or something for putting up with my jerk of a brother every day. Then I smile, because I know how lucky I am to have him.

Chapter 37

I DON'T GO on the lunch date my mother sends me on because I want to. I go because she proposes it as a business opportunity. Really, it's more of a delivery than a date, but Derek said we may as well eat while we're there, so I accept. When I get to the place, I feel terribly underdressed, even if it is a Friday afternoon, and we are eating in a restaurant inside the mall. Everybody else seems to be wearing nicer clothes, and I'm in ripped jeans, boots, and an off-the-shoulder sweater. I set down the box with the heart his mother bought from me, take a seat, and look at the menu, while keeping an eye out for Derek. When my phone buzzes in my purse, I start flipping through the million items I have in it while my guest finally arrives and sits across from me.

"For a moment I didn't think you were coming," I say, without looking up.

"For a moment I didn't think you would bite," a voice says, and my heart just stops. I look up to find Oliver sitting in the chair reserved for Derek, and for a multitude of reasons, I'm confused by his presence. I don't gasp because he's there, though, I gasp because his mouth is still swollen, and he has a couple of stitches on his jaw. His green eyes scan my face, and his lips slightly part with the longing I see on his face.

"What are you doing here?"

"Picking up a heart," he says, folding his hands on the table. I let out a sarcastic laugh. "I'm serious," he adds.

"Okay. Well, it's in the box," I say, nodding toward it.

He leans down and lifts the box beside my feet, bringing it up to the table. When the waiter finally comes back, we both ask for more time and send him on his way. Oliver opens the lid and looks inside it, taking out the heart and the tag it comes with before he puts the box back under the table. I watch as he looks at the heart, turning it over and over, the light from outside bouncing off it with each twist of his hand.

"I took that job because I was thinking like my old self— like Oliver, the guy who tries to set up everything in his life because he needs it to be perfect," he says, his eyes shifting from the heart to meet mine. "I'm sorry that I didn't think to ask what you thought about all of it."

"I wasn't angry because you took the job, I was angry because you didn't tell me that you did."

He opens his mouth to say something, but closes it quickly before turning his gaze back to the heart in his hands.

"Is this your definition of love?" he asks, reading the little tag.

I swallow and nod.

"Love is beautiful, shattering, moving, haunting. Love is everything," he reads. His eyes flicker to mine. "Who defines love?"

"People who have it. People who had it and lost it."

"Which are you?"

"Both." I pause and look around. "Is Derek really not coming?"

He picks up the heart and puts it back in the box, sliding the tag in and closing it. He looks at me again, folding his hands on the table, and smiles slowly. "He's really not."

"But I spoke to him."

"And he lied, like he was asked to."

I shake my head. "The people in my life know no bounds."

"Go out with me tonight."

My gaze cuts to his. "Why would I do that?"

"Because I'm asking you to," he says quietly, reaching for my hands, which I quickly hide under the table. If he touches me, I'll agree. I'll probably agree anyway, but if he touches me, I'll agree too soon.

The waiter comes by and asks us if we'd like to order something, and we both look at each other like, *are we staying? Are we leaving? Can you really eat in a time like this?"* We each ask for water to buy time.

"So I go out with you and then . . . ?"

He sighs. "Give me one date, Elle."

I mimic his sigh and look away. "I feel like we've been here before."

Oliver gets up suddenly and comes around the table, moving his chair with him until he's sitting next to me. He turns my chair so that our knees our touching, and when he takes both of my hands in his, my heart starts to sledgehammer inside my chest.

"What are you doing?" I whisper loudly, looking around at the occupied tables with curious patrons who are now interested in this beautiful, crazy man playing musical chairs inside the quiet restaurant.

One side of his lip turns up, and for a split second, I get lost in the little dimple I see, finally not hidden by facial hair. "Relax. I'm not asking you to marry me . . . yet," he says. All of my thoughts go haywire for a second . . . *Yet?*

"What are you doing then?"

Oliver leans into me, his face inching closer to mine, and I hold my breath. My eyes flutter closed as his breath whispers over my face, slowly moving over my cheeks, my nose . . . my mouth. His air is everywhere. His lips touch the tip of my nose, my cheek, then the corners of my mouth, and when I no longer feel his breath on me, I open my eyes and seek him out.

"I know you've been patient enough with me in the past, and I'm asking you to be patient with me one more time." I don't move away when his hands close over mine.

"I can't keep doing this, Oliver. I can deal with being second place to your job sometimes, because I know how demanding it is and how much worse it will probably get, but I can't be continually thrown for a loop every time you decide to do something to better your career," I say, searching his face for a sign of understanding.

He opens his mouth, then closes it, pausing for a moment as he lets his eyes wash over every single one of my features as if he'd forgotten them in the weeks we've been apart. "Taking the job was a knee-jerk reaction. I was thinking like the single, ambitious Oliver, and I screwed up. I do that a lot. I didn't tell you about it, because when I saw you at that barbeque, I knew I wouldn't go through with the job. I don't want to move four hours away from you." He pauses to search my face.

"You will never come in second place in any aspect of my life, Estelle. Yes, sometimes things will be difficult. Yes, some days I may have more work than others, but you will never come in second. I promise you that. What we have is so special. It's so real. I don't want to lose this ever again." His fingers thread through mine as he speaks. "This is what people spend their lives dreaming about. I'm asking you to go out with me tonight," he says, bringing my hands to his mouth and setting them there. "I'm *begging* you to go out with me tonight."

He has a look I've seen on his face a million times before, when he's changing a flat tire or when he's reading a patient's chart at the hospital. I realize it's his determined look. His *I'm not going to stop until you say yes to me* look. And then he smiles, this sweet, charming, boy next door, *let's pretend I'm not a wolf in sheep's clothing* kind of smile, and I know I'm not going to turn him down.

"This is the last time I'm agreeing to this," I say after a

long pause.

"This is the last time I'm asking," he replies, winking as he stands and brings me up with him. We gather our things and leave after I give him the address of my new place. Later, when I'm home, I wonder if part of his grand plan is to ask me to move to San Francisco with him. I honestly don't know if I would do it, but I also don't know how I wouldn't. I feel like I've waited for this for . . . ever.

I shower and dress casually, as he asked me to. I wear jeans and boots and throw a scarf over my simple t-shirt. After I close the windows around the house, I sit outside on the porch to enjoy the view while I wait. The cottage is small, and the front door is really the back door, since the porch faces the beach, and where you park your car faces PCH. I'm not surprised when I hear the sound of his footsteps on the pavement on the side of the house, though. Oliver has never been one to use the front door.

He appears at the foot of the porch steps, but he hasn't spotted me, and if he has, he gives nothing away. I see his eyes close as he faces the water, and I smile. His hands are tucked into the pockets of his jeans, his face is tilted back slightly, and the look on it is the embodiment of relaxation. He runs a hand through his light brown hair when a gust of wind flitters through it. After a moment of standing like that, he straightens and turns to face me, his green eyes flashing in surprise when he sees me sitting there.

"I got a little distracted," he says with a chuckle.

"It's hard not to," I respond, standing up. Victor helped me bring the most important things over here, because once I got the keys, I didn't want to wait until the weekend to move.

Oliver takes the two steps it takes to get to me and sighs when he looks down at me. "Ready?"

"You look like you're regretting the date," I say with a laugh.

He looks over his shoulder, and my eyes follow. The waves

are slowly tumbling into the sand, dying down as the sun begins to dwindle. His gaze finds mine again, and he smiles.

"If I would have seen this place before, I would have moved the date here."

I smile and take his hand, stopping when he starts to lead me down the steps. "Car's that way," I say, laughing when he gives the beach a final, forlorn look. "We can come back," I whisper loudly, as if it were some kind of big secret.

His face is serious when he turns to face me again, walking me back a step until my back hits the closed door. Suddenly, as if he's warring with himself, he rears back with a breath.

"Let's go. Lead the way."

I'm a little stunned. A part of me wishes he'd just kissed me and gotten it over with. Another part is glad he hasn't, but that part is so tiny I can barely hear it. Turning, I open the door, lock it behind us, and walk through the cottage slowly so that he can look around as we pass through.

"You like it?" I ask.

"I think love is a better word," he says, eyes on me. My stomach dips a little, and I smile.

We drive a very familiar route, and he ignores the questioning glances I shoot his way, but the ghost of the smile on his face lets me know he feels them. Although I want to ask, I am quiet, waiting for him to speak first. He doesn't though; he stays silent until we get to a house on the hills. The car stops in front of a gate, and he clicks a button that opens it gracefully. He drives in slowly and parks the car in the circular driveway.

"I have to drop something off for Sander," he says. "We'll only be a minute."

"Okay." I'm not sure whether to get out of the car. I haven't seen his sister in years. The last time I saw her, she was carrying baby Sander in a sling over her stomach, and from what Oliver has told me, he's almost four now.

He pushes the button to switch off the ignition and shoots me a smile. "One minute."

I smile and get out of the car, walking toward the trunk when he does.

"You have to be the neatest person I know," I comment, looking at his nearly empty trunk. What he does have in there—a white doctor's coat and a pair of sneakers—are neatly stacked to one side. He smiles, putting the bag in his hands on the ground, as he pulls the black knit sweater he's wearing over his head. It tugs the gray V-neck t-shirt he's wearing beneath it up his stomach, and my eyes stay glued there until he chuckles and pulls it back down. My eyes snap up to his, and his hand taps my chin up as he ducks his face to mine.

"You, my little Elle, are trouble," he says, his green eyes twinkling. He drops his hand, picks up the bag, and starts walking toward the house. I follow closely behind him and watch the door as we wait for somebody to answer.

A little flash of curly brown hair runs to the door, and Sander's little face appears on the other side of the glass. His big green eyes widen into saucers when he sees Oliver.

"It's Uncle Bean!" he shouts. "Mommy, Uncle Bean is here!"

"I heard you. I'm coming," she shouts, walking down the hall and smiling widely when she sees me. Oliver crouches down, and as soon as she unlocks and opens the door, Sander throws himself on top of him, wrapping his arms around his neck and squealing as Oliver makes raspberries on his neck. The sight of him with this adorable little boy is almost too much for me to handle.

"Long time no see, Elle," Sophie says, reaching out for a hug.

"It seems like every time I see you, you have exciting news to share," I say, smiling as my hands rub over her very pregnant belly.

She makes a face, smiling and shaking her head. "This news was not planned." She gestures for us to go inside, and we follow her to the kitchen.

"Sander, this is Estelle. I think you met her once, but you were a baby, so you probably don't remember her," Oliver says, flipping him so that he's looking at me upside down.

"Hi, Estelle. You have pretty hair," he says, making me laugh.

"Hi, Sander, you have pretty eyes."

Oliver grins at me, and I feel like he's reaching into my ovaries and squeezing to make sure I'm paying attention.

"Your house is beautiful," I comment, looking around.

"Thank you. Dan will be happy to hear that," Sophie says, smiling. "How's the art business?"

"It's going pretty well." I smile and think about the painting Dallas sold, and the amount of kaleidoscope hearts I've been selling lately.

"I'm in love with the hearts you make," she says.

"On that note," Oliver says, as he deposits Sander on the countertop and reaches into the bag for the box I gave him this morning. He hands it to his sister and reaches back into the bag again, lifting out a superhero toy for Sander.

"Whoa! Cool! Thanks, Uncle Bean," Sander says, trying to rip the toy out of the package.

"This is so beautiful," Sophie says, holding the heart in her hands. "Thank you."

I smile, blushing a little and look at my feet. Oliver's chuckle makes my face heat further. I love what I make. I'm proud of my art, but it makes me feel weird when someone like Sophie, who I guess I kind of seek approval from, examines it.

"Stop being so fucking cute," Oliver growls into my ear. I smile and nudge him away with my shoulder.

"Have you been making a lot of these?" Sophie asks.

"Yes, actually, but I'm going to stop for a while."

"Really?" she asks, looking surprised. I can feel Oliver's eyes on me as well. I haven't really told anybody yet.

"I feel like if I make too many, they lose their uniqueness. Not that they're so special, but you know what I mean." I blush again. I can't remember the last time I felt like I was under a microscope.

"I know exactly what you mean," Sophie says, nodding. "That's how I feel about my stories. I love writing and illustrating them, but sometimes I feel like if I put too many out there at once, it'll be 'just another Sophie Hart story.' I get it."

"Yeah, so I'll probably take a little break. I mean, I'll still be painting and making them—it's not like I can switch myself off—but I probably won't sell them for a while."

"All right, guys, we need to get going. I just wanted to bring this by before I get busy," Oliver says, kissing Sander on the forehead and helping him hop off the counter. He rounds the counter and gives his sister a hug, laughing at whatever she whispers in his ear.

I say goodbye to Sander and Sophie. "Do you know what you're having?" I ask after I give her a quick hug.

"We want it to be a surprise. At this point, it doesn't matter, it's coming anyway," she says with a laugh that makes me smile.

"That's kind of cool."

"It's completely nuts is what it is," Oliver says, shaking his head.

"Don't start, Oliver."

"I'm just saying." He shrugs.

Sophie rolls her eyes and looks at me, pointing at him. "That is why it's taken him so long to get you, you know that, right?"

"Sophie," Oliver groans.

"I'm just saying," she responds, mimicking him.

He wraps his arms around my shoulders from behind as we walk to the car, tucking his face into my neck. "You think that's funny?"

"The fact that everybody says you have the ultimate anal retentive personality? Yes."

He nips my earlobe and opens the door for me. "Speaking

of anal . . ."

"Ohmygod," I say, groaning and laughing as I sink into the seat.

"I'm just saying," he says, grinning as he starts the car.

After a couple of minutes of arguing about whose music we're going to play—his hip hop or my folk—we end up playing none, because his phone rings and my brother's voice seeps through the speakers of the car.

"You're with my sister?" he asks from the get-go.

"Yeah, and you're on Bluetooth," Oliver responds.

"Hey, Elle," Victor says.

"Hey, Vic," I respond.

"What are you guys up to? Jenson's in town again and wants to meet up for drinks at the usual bar, want to come?" he asks.

Oliver glances at me from the corner of his eye.

"Is this code for 'bring her to the bar for a group date so she'll know you're not serious about her?'" I ask, raising an eyebrow at Oliver. His mouth drops, a surprised laugh leaving his lips. Victor stays silent for a beat before he joins in on Oliver's laughter.

"Hell no," Victor says.

Oliver finds my hand and squeezes it. "Just so we're clear, this is going to be the complete opposite of that. This will be me saying, 'I am so serious about this girl. I want to take her everywhere with me, any chance I get,'" he says, looking at me when we reach a red light.

"This is going to be interesting," Victor mutters. "I'll save you two seats."

We laugh once the line is disconnected.

"I want it to be like this, Elle. Always," he says as he parks in front of the bar. When we get out, he wraps his arm around me and pulls me into his side. "I want to bring you here, and if you decide you don't want to come, I want to get texts from you that say you miss me."

I turn to face him when we reach the door. "I want that too," I respond with a smile.

We walk in with our fingers intertwined, and are greeted with a catcall from Jenson and claps from Victor. We sit down beside each other, talking and laughing the way we always have, but this time freely, and everything feels like it's finally falling into place.

Chapter 38

"**Y**OU'RE SO GOOD with kids. Do you want any?" I ask, as Oliver winds down the road after we leave a charity event at the hospital.

His hand finds mine on my lap, and I sneak a look at his serious face. "Are we starting twenty-one questions?"

"Maybe," I say, a smile tugging my lips.

"Can we start in about . . . three minutes?" he says. "How many dates do you think we've been on now?"

I frown, trying to figure it out in my head. "I don't know . . . wow, I really don't know," I say quietly. "Definitely more than I bargained for."

Oliver chuckles. "Nice, Elle. Real nice," he says, as he turns onto my parents' street.

"What in the world?" I say in a breath, more to myself than to him. He squeezes my hand and doesn't respond, only winks as he parks the car in my parents' driveway. "You know they're out of town this weekend, right?"

Oliver doesn't say anything, just gets out of the car and rounds it quickly to open my door. He grabs my hand and looks at me before sighing and placing a kiss on the top of my head. I follow him as he opens the side gate and walks to the back of the house, passing the bathroom where we were last together. He stops when he reaches the back door.

"Go to the kitchen. I left something there," he says.

I stare at him. "Are you going to climb the tree?"

He chuckles. "Would you stop asking questions until it's time?"

"Okay," I say, sounding unconvinced. I unlock the door and open it, heading to the kitchen. I pick up a note card that reads:

I frown at it until I notice a piece of broken, black glass under it. I fight the overwhelming emotions that start building in my chest as I pick it up. I leave the kitchen, and make for the stairs. I lift my foot to take a step, but stop with a gasp when I notice there's a note card on every step, all beside a piece of broken, black glass.

For dance.

For that time I locked you in a dark room.

For the time I broke your canvas.

For the time I called you a Chicken (and meant it).

For every time I pretended not to see you.

For every kiss I didn't give you.

For every laugh I missed.

For every accomplishment we didn't get to share.

For every time I left.

For every tear I made you shed.

By the time I reach my room, I'm holding eleven broken pieces of black glass with as many note cards, and the tears are falling freely down my face. I push the door open with my foot and find Oliver sitting on the roof outside my window, holding a little white box in his hands. I walk over, placing the glass pieces on my desk and duck my head as I make my way to him. He frames my face with his hands and wipes my tears with his thumbs, but the motion makes me cry harder, until I'm laughing and crying at the same time.

"I'm sorry. I think the tears are stopping now," I say, wiping my nose with my hand as I kneel in front of him the way he's facing me. He opens the box as he looks in my eyes, and mine leave his only to see what's in the box. It contains more broken glass pieces, but these are colorful and vibrant.

"For every smile," he says, taking out the first piece and putting it beside us.

"For every happy tear," he sets down another.

"For every laugh."

"For every time your eyes light up."

"For every piece of good news."

"For every piece of bad news."

"For every fight."

"For every kiss."

"For every hug."

"For every morning."

"For every night."

"For every wrong I'll try to make right."

When he's finished setting down every piece, he looks at me. "I want an October 21st," he says, and continues when I just stare. "I want to travel back in time and go back to the beginning. I want to tell my father he was wrong about life. I want to tell him that it doesn't wait for anybody, and that you can't put love on hold for trivial things like money. I want to climb back on this roof and shout on the day I fell in love with you. Because I do love you, Elle. And despite my stupidities and my running away, I never stopped being in love with you. I want to go back to that party and make myself stay in bed with you so I could have dealt with this." He points at his chin. "And we could have figured out the consequences together. But most of all, I want to go back to all the times I dodged your questions about love and tell you that I did find the one. I found her crying on this roof one night. I found her in a coffee shop when I needed her. I found her dancing with another guy and planting edible trees. I found her caring for strangers and kids who needed someone to listen to them."

"And how do you know she's the one?" I whisper, wiping the tears spilling down my face.

He brings a hand up to my cheek and caresses over it with his thumb. "I know because, when she's not with me, I feel like I lack oxygen, and even when I am with her, I feel like I can't breathe enough. You asked me if I want kids, and the answer is, that I want anything—everything—you want to give me. I want your mornings and your nights. I want your bickering and your eye rolls. I want your nudges when I'm hugging you too tight at night. I want your groans when I tell you a joke, and your moans when I'm making you feel good."

"And what do I get?" I ask, my voice a hoarse whisper.

"You get everything," he says, looking at me like I'm insane for even asking. "My career is just starting, and I have a million student loans. I don't have a million dollars, and I can't buy you a gallery yet." He pauses to flash me a smile. "Or take you on a hundred trips. And it might take me some time to find a job here with more stable hours than the hospital has to offer, but if you're with me, Elle, I don't care. My body is yours." He puts my hands on his chest. "My mind is yours. My hands are yours. My heart is yours. Everything I have is yours. Everything I am is yours."

I lean up on my knees and take my hands from his, wrapping them around his neck. "For every time you made me feel smart," I say, dropping a kiss on his temple. "For looking at me like I'm the only girl in the world." I kiss the edge of his eye.

"You're my favorite girl in the world," he murmurs, closing his eyes and breathing deeply as if he's claiming my scent as his.

"For treating me like I'm important." I kiss his cheek.

"You're the most important person in my life," he says, opening his eyes to meet my gaze.

"For giving me space so I could grow." I kiss the side of his mouth. "For loving me." I kiss his jaw, over his stitches. He watches me in awe when I back away and smile.

"Marry me," he says with a determination in his voice that makes my heart shake uncontrollably. "I don't mean get engaged for a year and just live together. I don't want to put a ring on your finger to claim you so the world can know you're mine. *I* want to know you're mine. I want you to know I'm yours, and that this isn't some relationship we can easily get out of. I want your forever, and I want it to start now." He takes a breath, his eyes flickering between mine to make sure I'm still with him. "Let's go get married tomorrow. If you want the big wedding, we can do that after."

When I pause for too long, because I'm in complete shock, he chuckles. "Or not. If you just want to move in together, let's do that instead, but I don't want to do this thing where we go our separate ways after our dates. I don't want the one drawer in each house. I want the whole closet full of both of our clothes," he says, grabbing both sides of my face. "I want the bumping into each other when we're trying to get dressed in the morning. I want it all, Elle. I don't—"

I lean in and kiss him, swallowing his pending words and hopefully whatever thoughts are running through his head. The picture he paints is too beautiful for me not to want it. I want all of his mornings and his nights. I feel like I've been waiting to hear those words from him for ten years, and even though I had the engagement and the living with somebody else for a while, I never got the *what if it had been Oliver* out of my head. We kiss for a long moment, our tongues intertwined, my fingers buried into his hair, his hands on my face, and our heart beating against each other. When we break the kiss, I nod furiously, and he sighs the longest, relieved breath, and looks like he just won some kind of silent auction.

"I want that too. I want everything," I whisper, earning a huge grin from him. "I can move, you know . . . my lease on the gallery is almost up." I pause to take a deep breath. "I can move with you, anywhere," I say, smiling up at him when we climb back into my room.

"Move? Are you kidding? I'm thinking about putting down whatever I have in my savings account to buy that cottage you've been living in."

I laugh. "I'm just saying that—if you want to go—you have my full support."

"This is home, Elle. I want to stay." He stops when he reaches the bottom step and brings his hand to my face, brushing over my lips. "Besides, I'm simple. I just need you."

And that's the promise we made to each other. No matter how crazy life gets, we'll always stick by the other. We'll share our dreams, our failures, our smiles and our frowns. Day after day, we'll drive each other a little crazy and remind the other how head over heels in love we are. Because that's the kind of love we have—the kind that doesn't come in a bottle, but can fill thousands of them, because we have that much of it to spare.

Epilogue

Oliver

WHEN WE WERE kids, my sister always wished upon stars. She swore that all of her wishes came true because she did that. Being that she was older and wiser, I believed her, and I too started doing the same. When I was five, I wished for toy dinosaurs. When I was seven, I wished my dad would come back home. When I was eight, I wished my mom would work fewer hours. When I was nine, I realized wishing upon stars was a waste of time because none of my wishes came true.

Still, when I was nineteen, I sat on the roof of a pretty girl's house and wished for things to be different. When I was twenty-one, I realized that circumstances were everything, and I wished we met under different ones. At twenty-six, I wished things had turned out differently, and that I hadn't lost her. At twenty-eight, when life brought us together again, I stopped wishing and started doing.

And here I am, at twenty-nine, watching as she walks over to me in a long white dress, in front of a crowd of our loved ones, wishing I could freeze frame this moment in time. I want to remember the one where her expressive, hazel eyes find mine, and she's visibly taken aback by the emotion she sees on my face. I know, without a shadow of a doubt, that I will never tire of watching her walk toward me. I hear the clicking of the camera beside me, and smile as a gust of wind hits us. It awakens the waves behind us, and makes Estelle's long, dark hair splash across her face. She takes a moment to gather it in one hand and push it aside, as I give her father a huge hug.

"I don't need to welcome you to the family that you've been a part of all along, but I'm proud to call you my son. Officially. Again," Thomas says with a hearty chuckle and a squeeze.

I don't respond, opting to smile instead. I'm not a crier, but his words make a surge of emotions rise inside of me. I turn to the woman who has been my wife for the past four months and grin, feeling like the luckiest motherfucker in the world, because I am. We married the day after I proposed, just as I told her we would. As soon as her parents' flight landed, we picked them up from the airport, called Vic and Mia and had them drive to the courthouse. Even Dallas showed up to help us celebrate, which was an added bonus, since I associate him with her Wyatt-era, or used to.

I moved my stuff into her cottage on the beach and worked in the hospital while I found a permanent job, which took a couple of months, but it happened. The best part about my job, aside from the fact that I work with a great team of doctors in a good environment, is that we stayed in Santa Barbara. When Estelle's lease was up, we bought a space together, close to our little beach cottage. It's still a work in progress, and although I help her as much as I can with it, ultimately it's her space. It's her dream that she brings to life every time she walks in there. I'm just happy she lets me be a part of it all.

At the feel of Estelle's hand sliding into mine, I smile and lead her to the officiate to be married again, in front of all of our friends and family.

"You're supposed to look at him," she whispers.

"I'm here to marry you, not him."

She laughs, her eyes flittering up to mine. "I promise you can stare at me for the rest of your life. But not all the time, because that would be totally creepy."

I lean down and kiss the tip of her nose. "Kind of how you were staring—"

"Okay, you guys need to seriously shut up," Victor interrupts from beside me with a groan.

"Yeah, nobody wants to know where that conversation was going," Mia adds.

"Keep it PG," Jenson chimes in.

"I'm about to kick everybody out of here," I say in response to the officiate clearing his throat and raising his eyebrows with impatience.

The ceremony continues without interruptions. We say our vows, which are short and generic, and we both smile at the memory of our longer vows, the ones we recited to each other in bed the night after we got our marriage license. We slide the rings on each other's fingers and hold hands again, and, as soon as we're pronounced Mr. and Mrs. Hart, we turn to one another. It's as if everybody around us disappears. Our eyes lock, my hands comb into her hair, hers cup my jaw, and we move almost as if in slow motion, our eyes scanning every inch of the other's face, completely immersed in this moment.

At the sound of the waves crashing in the distance, Estelle's eyes start to brim with tears, but she's smiling, the elation in her eyes matching what I feel inside. Suddenly, the moment right before our lips touch, droplets of rain start to fall over us. We pull back slightly and turn our heads up to the sky. Our guests start chanting for us to kiss. A slew of "Hurry up already! What are you waiting for?" surround us, but Elle and I remain unmoved. We smile, we laugh, and finally I pull her face to mine and my lips close over hers, taking, giving, offering, asking, pleading, promising. I kiss her with all that I am, imperfect but willing, hopeful and full of potential. Take me, I say with my tongue. Let me prove myself to you. I'll be worthy, I promise. And she kisses me back with the same ardor, sealing our vow.

Thank you for reading!

To get exclusives and information on new releases, sign up for
Claire's Mailing List- http://bit.ly/CLaireContreras

More books by this author-

Catch Me

The Darkness Series- Book 1- There is No Light in Darkness

The Contracts & Deception Series
Book 1 – The Devil's Contract
Book 2 – The Sinner's Bargain

Acknowledgements

Corinne Michaels & CD Reiss (for giving me great and useful feedback!), Christine Estevez, and my Crazies.

MIA ASHER (if it weren't for you, this would not have gotten written), BARBIE MESSNER (for your expertise LOL). RACHEL KEENAN (for EVERYTHING, as usual), BRIDGET PEOPLES, CALIA READ, JENNIFER WOLFEL, MILASY, HAPPY DRIGGS, TRISH MINT, JESSICA SOTELO, ROXIE MADAR, TARYN CELLUCCI, SANDRA CORTEZ, YAYA CITRON, CRYSTI PERRY, TRISHA RAI, LISA CHAMBERLIN, MJ ABRAHAM, STEPHANIE SSB BROWN, AMY COSSE

My agent, Rebecca, for being a badass.

My editor, Tracey, who worked tirelessly on this during the holidays!

My cover designer, Sarah (Okay Creations), for creating something beyond what I had envisioned.

Stacey at Champagne Formats for always taking the time to fit me into your schedule!

My PR girls, Melissa and Sharon at Sassy and Savvy . . . I would be lost without you. Literally.

Perrywinkle Photography, for taking the most amazing photos ever.

Jenn Watson for your incredible graphics.

Rockstars of Romance- for handling my promo and dealing with my crazy freakouts.

Made in the USA
Lexington, KY
22 November 2015